BOOK ONE

GOMADA ACADEMY

CYNTHIA BRUBAKER

Early Praise for Gomada Academy

"Gomada Academy is a fast-paced read that hits a pace set to draw you into the story of the magical students. Cynthia Brubaker establishes a well-developed world and magic system sure to please all fantasy fans of enchanted academies."

— ALISON WILLIAMS, AUTHOR OF *THE WITCH'S FOUNDLING SERIES*

Gomada Academy
Copyright © 2023 Cynthia Brubaker

Published by Midnight Tide Publishing
www.midnighttidepublishing.com

Cover design by Covers by Jules
www.coversbyjules.crd.co

Interior Formatting by Book Savvy Services

Edited by
R. Walden

Content Warnings

This book contains instances of or references to the following material. Trigger warnings include but are not limited to: bullying, physical violence, sexual content, drug use, smoking, drinking, anxiety, swearing, racism/discrimination, blood, abductions, death, and fantasy violence.

To Nathan.
Our first encounter wasn't combustible. We weren't mythical beings with secrets to hide. Even so, seeing you for the first time was magical. After a few short minutes standing next to you in line waiting for ice cream, I knew in my heart that I wanted to be with you.

You are my fated mate and my HEA.

One

ARYA'S MENTOR

My entire body trembles as I approach the front gates of Gomada Academy. Everywhere I look, students of different ages walk around the paved cobblestone pathways leading in and out of the wooded area. I'm sure this forest has a name, but I'm so new to Gomada that I have no idea about its culture, geography, or anything like that. I barely know anything about Earth's geography (or, um, the Overworld) – and now, I'm expected to know the ins and outs of four other realms?

I try not to look so overwhelmed as I pass through the wrought-iron gates. There are other students here that look just as nervous as I am. And then, some look well-seasoned as they pass through the open gates and walk ahead of me. I bet they're Juniors or older.

Apparently Gomada Academy has five different classes of students: Freshman, Sophomore, Junior, Senior, and Master. Every Freshman who enters through the academy's gates is assigned a Mentor – someone to show you around; get you acquainted with Gomadian life; escorting you to your classes and dorm.

Glancing about my surroundings feels useless as I don't recognize anything, but I do it anyway. I pull my phone out of my leggings' side pocket, trying to locate the email from the academy telling me about the first day's itinerary and my Mentor assignment.

What a horrible way to start the school year! I am in a new realm, a new place, with no friends – I also have to be assigned an older stranger to show me around campus. I think I'd rather stick a fork in a toaster than make an 'ice-breaker' conversation with someone who probably doesn't even want to be a Mentor in the first place.

I jump when someone bumps into me from behind – maybe because I stopped dead in my tracks – and I turn quickly to apologize, but the girl is already walking away from me. She eyes me angrily as she goes, making me want to cry.

I find a secluded spot along the wrought-iron fenceline and my personal welcome letter – an attachment in the email from Gomada Academy. I know I'll find the name of my Mentor there. I keep on forgetting his name – though at least I know he's a boy. On the other hand, it's not like that narrows it down.

Cole Hudson, I read and then whisper under my breath, hoping that if I repeat the name enough times, I'll be able to remember it. I don't know how the academy expects Freshmen to find their Mentors in the first place because all we have going for us is a name. I don't even know if this 'Cole' is a Nymph, a Shifter, or an Enchanter.

With my luck, he won't be a Nymph.

I try to remember what Mom and Dad told me as I head back onto the cobblestone path and try and locate the campus map that was also an attachment in the email.

Treat everyone with kindness – even if they're a different race than you.

Everyone will be nervous on their first day – even if they don't look like it.

Don't put any pressure on yourself. Just get through the day. It'll get easier.

Even my little sister, Macey, had advice for me – and though I'd never tell her, it was actually pretty bang-on regarding how I act around people...

Don't cry on your first day of school. It'll set a bad precedent.

Even though my parents were supportive and loving when I left San Francisco using Grandma's topaz ring, I'm sure they're worried about me. Not only am I going to a new realm – which has connections to three other realms, as well – they're also sending me to this school, knowing that if others discover our family secret, I'll be ostracized.

I just hope that doesn't happen.

It's cold as I tug my tight jean jacket around my chest. Maybe it's cold because I'm terrified, not necessarily due to the weather. It's a sunny Fall day, and apparently Gomada has similar seasons and climate to many countries on Earth.

I see dozens upon dozens of students congregating around the large campus. I know the castle-like structure – the academy – is where all our classes will take place. There are supposedly three different dormitory areas that house the three different races, but there are so many students here that I don't see any other buildings besides the school.

Finally, I gather my already-dwindling reserves of courage and approach the nearest cluster of boys. I choose them because they look older, and if my Mentor is at least one year older than me, perhaps they may know of him. It's a long shot, but I'm tired of walking aimlessly. I already want to go home. Thankfully, I have Grandpa's pocket watch in my duffel bag, so

I can take advantage of that opportunity if I ever need to experience the comforts of home.

Reaching out, I hesitantly tap the back of a tall boy with long brown hair. When he turns and looks down at me – which interrupts the conversation between him and his two friends – I stammer out a quick,

"Excuse me. Do you know Cole Hudson?"

The boy blinks briefly – and suddenly bursts out laughing. The other two boys laugh with him as if they're all in on the joke.

Just as I open my mouth to ask if they at least know what race he is, they walk away from me, continuing their conversation.

As they walk away, I'm suddenly hit with a painful realization.

If they're laughing at my question, maybe they're laughing at my fate – not necessarily because I don't know anything about this place, or its students.

"You're looking for Cole Hudson?"

I whirl around, astonished to be spoken to – and spoken to by someone who knows Cole. My dark brown eyes register a petite redhead – a bit shorter than me – with freckles and green eyes. She's wearing a trendy red leather jacket with a black backpack slung over her shoulder. Her long hair is pulled into a fast ponytail – but she still looks effortlessly beautiful.

"Yeah," I agree, tucking my hair behind my ears when an unsavoury gust of wind blows my hair in my face.

The girl frowns slightly. "He's a Sophomore. Shifter. Usually hangs out in the Shifter's Field. Behind the school," she adds when my face must betray my curious and desperate innermost thoughts.

Come to think of it, this girl seems just as put off by Cole as the three boys from before – just in a different way. But that's nothing compared to the big news.

Cole's a Shifter.

Mom and Dad have usually only let me spend time with other Nymphs – not necessarily because they're anti-Shifter or anti-Enchanter, but mostly because they wanted to protect me. Now that I'm 'older', they want me to 'expand my horizons'. I guess this is Step One in that area.

"Thank you," I try to smile at the redhead. She must be older, too, because she seems to know a lot about Sophomores. Maybe Cole travels in her circle, so she just knows a specific set of people.

She smiles back at me. "Don't thank me." She holds her hand out. "I'm Taylor. Taylor Hayden. I'm a Shifter, too."

Oh. So that's how she knows of Cole. They may not travel in the same circle, but they're in the same race.

I shake her hand. "Nice to meet you," I tell her.

It's true. I may be intimidated by her beauty and her confidence – and because she's a Shifter, different from me – but she's been the only helpful person here thus far.

"I'm Arya Willow," I add, just so she doesn't think I'm trying to be unfriendly.

She nods at me. "Cool to meet you. Anyway, I gotta find my own Mentor. See you later."

If Taylor's looking for her own Mentor, she must be a Freshman, too. That makes me feel a little bit better. Maybe we can be friends – or, at least, acquaintances. I've never had a Shifter as an acquaintance before – and definitely not a friend – but maybe it's possible.

"Bye. Thanks again," I bade her, just as Taylor walks away from me, her black high-heeled boots clicking against the cobblestone as she walks.

Well, at least I have a general idea of how to find this Cole

Hudson – though part of me doesn't really want to find him anymore. But I don't want to get into trouble with the Head-mistress – I can't remember her name, either – so I begin to make my way closer to Gomada Academy, preparing myself to walk around the large building so I can find the Shifter's Field. I caught sight of the Shifter's Field general location after looking at the campus map.

It's a long walk to the school, and another long walk around the side of the large structure. I feel in the way – maybe because students are everywhere, or because I'm dragging my feet. I'm afraid of what I'll find behind the school – but when I finally cross behind the academy, I'm met with a tall and ominous-looking building that I assume is one of the dorms. Could it be the Shifter dorm, since the Shifter's Field should be behind the school?

Willing my feet to walk in the general direction of the building – a large sign around its fence telling me that it's called 'Feara' – I notice a few clusters of students. Some are leaning against the wall of the building, chatting. Others seem to be sightseeing – perhaps they're already paired up with their Mentors.

Getting closer to the building, I'm attacked by this creepy feeling that I shouldn't be back here. It's like every nerve in my body is begging me to turn around and go back. I know I need to find my Mentor – even if I'm terrified to be back here – so I quicken my pace. The sooner I do this, the sooner I can–

"Check you later, Hudson."

I turn my head to the left, surprised at my luck – or lack of it, depending on what happens next. I see a really tall boy with long black hair tied into a ponytail slap the back of another boy, who's almost as tall as his friend. I assume this boy is Cole, though I can't decipher anything about him from behind. He's wearing a black hoodie with the hood yanked over his head. He slaps the shoulder of the taller boy and starts to walk away from him.

I try not to make it look like I am watching them – the last thing I want is one or both of them to figure that out and target me – so I put my head down and try to follow Cole covertly.

I'm not good at following people, or doing anything secret – which is evident, because Cole turns his head left and right a few times, but never turns around fully. It bothers me that I still don't know what he looks like.

I know I need to get to him before he goes inside Feara – which must be the dorm for Shifters – so I hasten my pace, and soon, I'm inches behind him. We're almost at the brick wall of the dorm now.

Just as I'm about to tap his shoulder – or, in reality, the nearest thing on his body that I can reach, because he towers over me, even from behind – he turns around gruffly. I'm stared down by a pair of green eyes.

I would throw up, but I don't think that would help my case. He clearly heard me following him for the last minute or so.

"What do you want?" he snaps.

When he talks, a strange billow of smoke escapes his mouth. At least, I think it's smoke. And then I zero in on the item in his hand – a cigarette, I think. Disgusting!

I clear my throat and begin, "Um, sorry. I've been looking for you."

It's hard to glean much from Cole based on how he's

dressed. A black hoodie covers most of him, with a beanie underneath. I see some dark hair sticking out, and dark jeans and a black backpack.

Everything about this boy scares me.

Cole frowns down at me. "Who's been looking for me?" he asks firmly.

It takes me a minute to realize he's asking for my name.

"Arya. Arya Willow," I try, holding out my hand.

Cole stares at it, and puts his cigarette to his lips. He sucks in a drag.

"The academy – um, we're – you're – my Mentor," I stammer. With each mistake I make, Cole's green eyes get increasingly impatient.

He suddenly rolls his eyes and exhales, a cloud of gross smoke flying in my face. I cough and step back from him, aghast.

Oh, my God! No wonder those three boys and Taylor were so wary about pointing Cole out to me! He's obnoxious!

Cole looks amused that I didn't like smoke being blown in my face – though he doesn't smile or laugh. It's just a creepy feeling I get.

Speaking of 'creepy', that feeling I had before? It's tripled now.

Cole looks annoyed now. He's cycling through negative emotions so quickly that it's making me even more nervous.

"What are you? A Nymph?" he asks off-hand. The way he's asking tells me he's making an insult.

I look up at him, wary. "Um–"

Cole laughs. "Good God. Stay away from me, Pixie."

He moves away from me. Despite the cigarette smoke that makes me want to hurl, I also feel anger, shock, and pain that he'd use such a derogatory name against my race, without even knowing me.

"Don't call me that."

Cole turns and looks down at me, clearly surprised at my retort. Come to think of it, I'm surprised, too. I usually don't confront people. But for some reason – maybe it was the callousness, the cigarette smoke, or the 'Pixie' comment – I forget about my usual passive nature.

Now, Cole looks amused again, but like before, there's no smile or laughter.

"Why not?" he asks. "What are you going to do about it?"

When I don't have anything to say to that, Cole grins at me – but it's a triumphant, victorious one that a bully would give to his victim.

Cole takes one step toward me, but a sudden rumble from above makes us both look up.

Oh, my God! A dark, angry cloud is hovering over both of us now. We're suddenly shrouded in darkness.

Could this be what will trigger my Air Affinity – or its electrical component? I should've known that being threatened would have tripped it. I've been trying for months to try and activate this part of my Affinity before classes start, but–

When nothing else happens, Cole raises an eyebrow. "Is that it?" he asks, sounding unimpressed.

Bright sun and puffy white clouds now dance about the sky, just as before. Cole laughs for the first time. The sound is like nails on a chalkboard.

"That was pointless – just like you. Now back off, *pipsqueak*."

Something horrifying happens when Cole finishes his sentence – no, when he's saying the last word. His green eyes suddenly shift in shape, becoming more oval. When he says 'pipsqueak', his voice dips down two or maybe even three octaves.

As soon as I realize what he's doing, I jump back as far as I can, terrified all over again.

Cole just channelled some of his Shifter's powers. The creature he Shifts into must have green eyes and a frightening voice.

I don't know much about Shifters. I know they don't need celestial events like full moons to Shift. I know they have to work at it. I also know they can be very aggressive and very mean. And Cole Hudson seems to be no different.

I move away from him as quickly as possible, ready to just forget about this whole 'Mentorship Program' business. I hear Cole laughing at me as I run away – but the frightening thing is that half of his laugh is still lower-pitched like his voice.

I shouldn't have come back here! Why didn't I listen to the gut feeling I'd been experiencing all this time?

Two

COLE'S JUDGEMENT

I'm laughing as I walk toward the double-door entrance to Feara. I'm just about to head inside when something weird and furry presses into my foot.

Without even looking, I know exactly what's doing this to me. I move my sneaker away from the damned white fox, and my eyes look up to see one of the most annoying Enchantresses here, Lucy Chapin. Granted, her cousin is much worse – but it's not like it's much of a horse race.

Still, I find it weird that Lucy's here, in Shifter territory.

"Are you lost, Chapin?" I ask, knowing Lucy hates it when people 'address her improperly'. Diego and I had a lot of fun messing with her last year.

Her blue eyes narrow at me. "No. Whitney just smelled refuse and came to investigate."

I'm pissed off now, but I decide not to show her that she got to me. That's a step in the wrong direction when tangling with an Enchantress.

"Hilarious," I comment dryly instead, taking another drag of my cigarette.

"I thought so." Lucy folds her arms and looks at me in a way that Diego would call 'scrutinizing'.

She's sizing up the competition, resuming the fight from last year. I'm sure her cousin will be along any minute to do that, too.

"Looks like Summer Break at Houssan did nothing to mature or educate you," she comments. She looks at me disdainfully, her eyes going to my cigarette. All this causes me to see red.

Crushing Nymphs like that little girl – whatever her name was – is one thing. But going after Enchantresses, who are stronger than Nymphs, even if they could have the same Affinity – is another ballgame.

"Maybe I'll just eat your dog instead of talking to you," I state off-hand as if the life of her stupid fluffy stuffed animal means nothing to me. And it doesn't.

Lucy looks riled up at my threat. Not only does she hate anyone coming near her precious Whitney, but she also hates it when anyone addresses her Familiar as anything other than a fox.

Her lips form into a thin line. I love how angry she is now. About fucking time!

"If you so much as harm a hair on her head–" Lucy begins, her voice trembling – not from fear, but anger.

"You'll what?" I interrupt. "You're gonna hurt me? I'm terrified," I add dryly.

I don't know why these girls think they're all so invincible and tough. The last one ran off crying. Lucy will get mad but will do nothing about it so her nails don't get ruined. They're all the same.

"Causing a ruckus already?"

Lucy turns halfway but I don't bother, because I recognize the voice; and I smelled him coming.

My best friend (even though those titles are lame), Diego Jasper, is now in the small semicircle Lucy and I are using. I guess he's already found his Mentee and sent them on their merry way. Unlike me, Diego seems more 'whatever' about his role. I'm surprised I was eligible enough to even become a Mentor in the first place.

Lucy narrows her eyes at Diego, too – it's her trademark.

"You'll get wrinkles if you keep doing that, you know," Diego points out, causing Whitney to snarl at him. I wonder if the stupid animal understands words or tone – but I doubt it understands both.

I laugh at the counter, but I still have my suspicions about Diego. He seemed way too eager to make fun of Lucy all of last year. Sure, I joined in, and it was great – but after a while, I wondered if there was more to it than the typical 'Shifter versus Enchantress' thing.

Even the way Diego is talking to Lucy now has me worried. His body language is relaxed. His hazel eyes are looking at her calmly and without any kind of animosity. A true Shifter wouldn't be this comfy around an Enchantress. They're scum.

This leads me to my theory.

Diego has a thing for Lucy, which is about as close to Hell as you can get without dying. Having a thing for another class or race is like shooting yourself in the foot. It'll never end well. He's playing with fire here – especially since Lucy's Affinity (that she knows of) is Darkness. She could probably send him straight to Hell if her dark little soul wished it.

Lucy huffs and stomps away from us without another word. Figures. As soon as you insult their looks, girls are quick to fold and run.

Whitney gives us one last evil eye before she saunters off with her annoying-as-fuck owner. Enchanters, Enchantresses, and their damned Familiars. I hope Diego and I get one up on Lucy and her messed-up cousin this year.

This brings me to my question.

"Jasper," I protest when I see Diego watching Lucy walk away.

He turns to look at me, acting as if he wasn't doing anything sketchy. He forgets that we've been friends since the age of ten. I've got years of experience to draw back on, here.

"You dig her, bro," I accuse, folding my arms and staring up at him now. He's barely got anything on me height-wise, but I'm not going to let this go until he gives me an answer, one way or another.

I didn't think he'd do this, but Diego throws his head back and laughs. "What?" he breathes, in between his laughing. "Come on, Hudson! You're drunk already, huh?"

I frown at him. "Jasper, you're flirting with Hellfire if you're even thinking about–"

"*Flirting with Hellfire?*" Diego guffaws, causing me to frown at him now. "Where did you hear *that* from, Hudson? You're not exactly a wordsmith."

I roll my eyes at that. It's true. Diego's definitely the smarter one out of the two of us. I suck at writing and expressing myself. But when I'm a Tedla, I don't have to worry about any of that shit.

"Relax, Hudson. I'm not into her," Diego assures me, clamping my shoulder with one hand and yanking my cigarette out of my right hand with the other. "You know Frow will beat your ass if she catches you with this on-campus," he reminds me.

I shrug. "Get to go home early, then," I respond as Diego squishes my cigarette under his boot heel.

If anyone else took away my smokes and crushed them under their foot like that, I'd rip them apart. Diego is different.

Besides, I have more packs in my bag. I'm sure Diego knows this because he's eyeing me suspiciously now.

How interesting it is that we're both suspicious of the other's intentions.

"Just watch yourself, Jasper," I warn him. "The last thing I want is for you to be fucked with."

Diego shrugs. "You worry too much, Hudson. I'll be just fine."

I frown at him. I worry too much? Not even close. I don't have a care in the world most days. But I see what he's saying. Maybe when it comes to some things, even I can get paranoid. I just don't trust Enchanters – and Enchantresses, most of all. Especially anyone related to that *other* Chapin bitch.

Diego gives me a small smile as we head through the double-door entrance to Feara.

"You're being a judgmental douche today, by the way," he accuses, slapping me upside the head as we walk. My head shoots down in response, and I rub it immediately.

"Fuck off," I growl, yanking my hood down to rub my head a bit better.

But I guess Diego's right about that, too. Everyone's always telling me I'm a douche – or a 'judgmental douche', to quote Diego. I'm used to it. The thing is, there are reasons why I'm this way. Experience has taught me that being on the safe side – or, as others would say, 'judgemental' – is how you protect yourself from assholes.

We make our way through Feara. There aren't usually a ton of Shifters hanging around on the main floor and in the hallways

– but the first day of school is always different. Come tomorrow; it'll be a lot easier to breathe in here.

As we walk past a small cluster of girls – probably a mixture of Freshmen and Sophomores because I recognize a few – they stare as Diego passes by. Even though Diego and I do our own thing and don't bother with shit like groups and girls, I'm sure there are ones around here who wish he'd notice them. To be honest, I wish he'd give these girls attention instead of an entitled, spoiled Enchantress who's only out for herself.

We both know where we're going. We're heading to the third floor, where our room assignment is located. Last year, we both roomed with duds. My roommate – what was his name again? Chad? – was annoying and stupid. Diego's roommate wasn't anything too pathetic, but he still didn't get along well with him. I can't remember his name, either. Anyway, this year, we requested to be roommates. When you're past that wet-behind-the-ears Freshman stage, you get more respect around here.

Usually.

I tack on 'usually' because, standing at what I can only assume is our room – 301 – is Blake Qadir, one of our professors. He's an okay guy – like I'd ever tell him that – but the crappy thing here is that he knows *me*. Or, he knows my family.

He folds his arms as we approach. "Gentlemen," he greets us. "Welcome back to Gomada Academy."

"Hey, Professor Qadir," Diego greets him. Diego's always been the better one with adults and teachers. I do whatever I can to make those conversations last as short as possible.

I nod at Professor Qadir, too numb to say anything to him. I don't get intimidated very often by people – least of all by professors – but because Professor Qadir knows my grandfather, well–

Sure enough, Professor Qadir looks at Diego with a knowing look in his brown eyes, leaning his right side against the wall. Great. He's going to be here for a while

"Mister Jasper, would you excuse Mr. Hudson and I for a quick minute?" he asks.

Diego nods right away. "Sure," he responds, digging the key to our room out of his pocket and jamming it into the keyhole of the closed door. He probably wants to get away from the two of us as soon as possible because Diego knows what this is about, too.

As soon as Diego edges himself inside and closes the door – leaving it unlocked for me, from the sounds of things – Professor Qadir fixes his stance against the wall.

"How was your Summer, Mr. Hudson?" he asks, instead of launching right into whatever 'talk' he's going to spew on me this year. I'd rather have the talk than the pointless small talk. Get it over and done with. But Professor Qadir isn't like that.

I shrug. "Fine," I finally respond.

Professor Qadir leans slightly closer to me, his brown eyes ablaze now. I straighten immediately.

"Sophomore Year is an entirely different arena than Freshman Year, Mr. Hudson," he tells me firmly. "You have much potential and a legacy to draw upon, and yet you use neither."

I swallow nervously. Here it comes.

"Your grandfather wanted more for you than this," he adds.

And there it is. 'Your grandfather would be disappointed in you', 'you're squandering the family legacy', blah-blah-blah. As if I haven't gotten the same lecture from Dad. I fold my arms and put my head down. I should be used to this by now, but for some reason, it still stings.

"Not everyone in the Germain family gets chosen by the

Tedla," Professor Qadir tells me – or reminds me. Dad has told me this, too. "You are squandering–" there it is! "–your heritage by treating the Tedla so disrespectfully."

I guess he's referring to me bullying people by poking out the Tedla every now and then. But even I don't push the envelope. It's been a year, and no Shifter at this school knows my alter ego. It's too dangerous. When I Shift, I'm too powerful. I've read accounts of Germain Tedlas ripping apart entire villages because they couldn't control their Shifter form – and they were veterans. I only Shift at home – or when I know I'm by myself at the Shifter's Field. There's no telling what can happen when Tedla comes out to play.

"Your attitude, academic performance, and training better be much improved this year," Professor Qadir seems to finish – thank God.

I put my head down and finally just nod. I highly doubt I'll change, but I don't think a 'hell, no' will work in this situation.

"Getting back to current affairs," Professor Qadir pushes, causing me to look up at him. "Have you taken the Mentorship Program seriously?"

He asks this as if I haven't been taking it seriously. Professor Qadir knows me all too well. It's annoying.

Saying nothing is answer enough, because Professor Qadir narrows his eyes at me knowingly.

"I've taken the liberty to look through the pairings," he begins. "It seems your Mentee is a Nymph named Arya Willow. Have you been of any assistance to her as of yet?"

If making her cry is 'being of assistance', then absolutely.

When I say nothing to that, Professor Qadir sighs, looking drained from talking to me. That happens a lot. I'm a soul-sucker, apparently.

"I suggest you find this Miss Willow, and do as you're told – or perhaps I'll come to your dorm at five o'clock tomorrow morning and make you run laps around the Field before class-es," Professor Qadir threatens. Even the way he threatens people sounds tame and calm – which is fucking creepy if you ask me. His smooth accent makes it even more terrifying.

Five AM? Laps?

No fucking way!

"Alright," I give in, causing Professor Qadir's facial expression to, well, not go away.

"I'll be waiting to hear from you," he tells me. "And I'll be sure to check in with Miss Willow, as well," he adds as if he has a sneaking suspicion that I'm going to shrug this off and not do it. I hate how well he knows me.

It takes me a while to get to the Meera dorm – not because I don't know where it is, but because I don't want to be there. As soon as I approach the steps and open one of the double doors, I feel the eyes of Nymphs everywhere on me. Even the Freshmen who don't know me can sense that I'm different. The three classes have this sixth sense, I guess. It's probably why some girls and guys I don't even know make way for me in the halls. I also wonder if the Tedla living inside me causes people to be wary of me. I don't really care – people are point-less – but sometimes, when I'm feeling particularly low, like today, it feels kind of shitty.

Professor Qadir really knows how to ruin what was turning out to be a fun day. Cutting down a Nymph and an Enchantress – but then he cut me down, ruining all that fun. But I know he means business. If I don't take school, Shifting and training more seriously this year, I'm sure

Professor Qadir will Shift on me himself. And I don't want to see that.

I don't know where this girl lives – and I've already forgotten her name – so I wander through the halls, feeling more frustrated by the second. I'm sure if I read the names on the doors, I'll eventually recognize hers.

When I get to the fourth floor, I'm getting really annoyed. I want to throw myself out that window at the end of the hall. I could've passed her door already. I can't for the life of me remember her fucking name!

Suddenly, I stop at a door. There are two names here.

Nora Leith.

Nope. Not her.

Arya Willow.

That's her.

I suck in an aggravated breath and knock three times on the door. I know I can't avoid this job. If Professor Qadir looked up the pairing and then told me he'd seek out the Nymph to make sure I didn't screw up, I needed to do this. Maybe if I just do this one small thing, it'll get him off my back – for now.

The door opens quickly, surprising me. I'm sure the two Nymphs in there know a Shifter is at their door – or, at least, someone different from them.

I frown at the girl standing in front of me, her hand on the door. Long black hair and blue eyes. A big-ass necklace with a blue stone is around her neck. Probably a Trinket.

Is this her? I can't even remember what she looks like.

"Can I help you?" she asks.

Well, this can't be her. Even her voice doesn't remind me of – Arya? Man, she's so forgettable that I come up with jack shit when I'm trying to place her.

"I'm looking for Arya," I finally respond.

The name does something to the girl – whose name must

be Nora, I guess – because she turns halfway and calls into the room,

"Arya! Someone's here to see you."

She turns to look at me. "Shifter?" she guesses.

Hmm. For a Freshman, she's got a good sixth sense. Most Freshmen would just know I'm different. But this Nora picked up on my class, race, immediately.

"Yeah," I agree.

She doesn't look intimidated by me. It annoys me a little bit. Nymphs are usually so spineless – probably because they know they're not as strong as Enchanters and can only wield one Affinity. Enchanters think they're badass because they can wield two.

Shuffling sounds occur near the door and then behind Nora. I can smell her. Right. Fear and shyness, with a hint of vanilla. I can recognize her scent but not her face. That's fairly typical. Even as a human, Shifters inherit some traits of their alter egos.

Nora steps aside, revealing Arya. She looks shocked, then horrified, that I'm in the hallway. That's much better.

As Nora walks away, Arya looks like a deer caught in head-lights. Well, at least this will be more fun than I originally thought.

I'm not going to tell her *why* I'm here – I don't like people, especially Nymphs, knowing that I have weaknesses for people that intimidate me – so I keep it short and sweet.

"Do you want that tour, or not?" I question.

It's hard for me to sense what's going through her mind. Tedlas are very intuitive. I think she's scared that I remembered I'm her Mentor. It's hard to figure her out. Luckily I won't have to be at this for very long, because from what I remember about my Mentor from last year, it wasn't a very long gig.

"Yeah," she agrees, after a very long time.

It doesn't sound like she particularly wants to do this. That makes two of us. But like I said, it won't be forever.

As soon as we're out of Meera, I find it easier to breathe. I'm already jonesing for another cigarette, but it looks like more professors are out here now, so I hold off. There are no-smoking rules this close to buildings.

"There's the school," I tell her, after we walk silently for a few minutes. I point to it, because I bet she's clueless enough that she needs confirmation.

"I know where the school is," she states, sounding a bit frustrated – or embarrassed – now. I'm not sure which, and I really don't care.

"So I guess that look is just how your face is all the time," I shoot back, but she doesn't say anything.

"Prof dorms are between Feara and Meera," I explain, as we continue to walk. "Curfew is ten PM. Don't let 'em catch you sneaking out." I look over at her for the first time. She's still looking at the school. "Not like you'd ever sneak out, though," I add.

She looks up at me. "What's wrong with following the rules?" she counters. Just like before, it sounds like she doesn't mean to bite back, but she is, anyway.

It's fun when they try and fight back.

I laugh. "Everything," is all I respond.

She looks unconvinced.

We walk a little farther. "Don't go off-campus without permission. But like I said, I'm sure that won't be a problem for you," I can't help but tack on.

She steps in front of me. "Are you just going to berate me the entire time?" she asks.

I fold my arms. "Maybe. Gotta pass the time somehow."

She doesn't look happy about that. "Well, if that's the case, I don't need the tour." She begins to walk around me.

This would have been a dream come true for me, but with my luck, profs will notice this and report to Professor Qadir that I messed up. Again. But at the same time, I'm not going to go after a Nymph. If he asks, I'll tell him that I tried. There's no way I'm begging her to spend more time with me. That would be a fate worse than death.

Three

ARYA MEETS DÉSIRÉE CHAPIN

I can't get away from him fast enough.

He's so mean! I can't believe I was somehow paired up with someone like him!

It's hard to believe that someone as obnoxious and cruel as Cole could exist. He reminds me of one of my bullies from Freshman Year back when I attended human high school. Transferring to Gomada Academy as soon as I turned sixteen was like a breath of fresh air – but now, it looks like I've just traded one bully for another.

I hate bullies. I don't understand how, why, someone could be so mean to someone else – especially for no reason. But unlike before, this bully is way more powerful. I don't know what kind of creature Cole Shifts into, but whatever it is, it's terrifying and powerful. I can sense it somehow – just that it's evil – but that's about it. One wrong move from me, and I could quite literally be killed. I need to stay as far away from Cole as possible.

Maybe I should have expected friction from members of different races. But I don't want to start out the school year making enemies. At the same time, I don't think I can do anything about Cole.

So far, the only nice people I've met here are Taylor and Nora. As I try to make my way back to Meera, I suddenly take sight of the girl I inconvenienced earlier. I'd recognize her sharp green eyes anywhere.

She has long, wavy brown hair and is dressed to kill. A white cashmere trenchcoat, black high-heeled boots, and a black dress that leaves little to the imagination. At her heels is a black cat with green eyes as sharp as its master's. I'm sure now that this girl is an Enchantress and that this black cat must be her Familiar. I usually like cats, but this one looks like it could claw my eyes out if I get too close.

Just as we're about to pass one another, this girl makes eye contact with me. Recognition lights up her face. Just my luck!

I try to give her a small smile in greeting – or in surrender – but it doesn't work, because she looks me up and down pitifully, as if she's readying herself to make fun of me.

"I hope you've been bothering less people in the last hour," she states off-hand as if she's a parent disciplining a naughty child who doesn't know any better.

"I'm sorry about before," I try to tell her, holding out my hand. "I'm Arya–"

"I don't care who you are, Nymph," the girl snaps at me, causing me to retrieve my hand. The way she says the name of my race sounds like an insult.

I don't know what to do or say. Part of me wants to run, but it looks like this unnamed Enchantress isn't finished with me.

Suddenly, the black cat launches itself up on the tips of its paws. Its back arches, hair stands up, and the cat lets out an aggravated hiss.

The Enchantress and I look in the direction the cat

Familiar is currently glaring. Cole is walking by us, several feet away. He must have good hearing, because he turns as soon as the cat hisses.

He stares at the cat and gives it a disgusted expression as if it's annoying and not a threat. "Keep your cat on a leash, Chapin!" he calls.

"Surround, Ebony," the girl whose last name must be Chapin commands quietly. She looks angry that Cole decided to address her by her surname.

To my surprise, the cat propels itself toward Cole. In a second, it's mid-air and Cole yells.

"Fuck my life!" he hollers as the cat slashes at his face.

Maybe I should be satisfied by this attack. At the same time, I'm appalled that another bully is walking the grounds of Gomada Academy—and is using her Familiar as a weapon.

The cat is suddenly on the ground, and a bloodied Cole gets into a crouched position. I can see his eyes change from all the way over here, and I take a step back.

"Beat it, furball!" he snarls at the cat in the same darker voice he used earlier.

The cat arches its back and growls at Cole but is slowly inching itself backward.

"Come, Ebony!" the girl calls, causing the cat to immediately lap back to her. "Don't waste precious energy on that beast."

Wiping the slash marks across his cheek that are clearly bleeding, Cole points at the cat.

"I'll eat that fucking puffball for lunch next time you do that!" he snaps.

The girl's eyes abruptly turn red. A strange *hissing* envelopes her and her cat, who's now at her side. It almost looks like this student could burn someone if they get too close.

Cole scoffs and stomps away from her. Who is this Enchantress that even a big bully with a powerful Shifter ability leaves her alone?

The red leaves her eyes; they're green again when the girl looks down at me.

"What's your Affinity, Nymph?" she asks me. The way she asks, I'm assuming she's just making sure she has no 'competition' if we share the same Affinity.

Based on the red in her eyes and the hot-to-the-touch look she manipulated earlier, I bet her Affinity – or one of them – is Fire.

"Air," I respond, wondering if this will cost me later.

She gives me a smug smile. "Interesting. For me," she tells me, bending down to pick up her cat, who is putty in her arms.

She gives me one last chilling look before walking away, a black purse slung over her shoulder. I never got her first name – but part of me doesn't want to find out. I don't know how it happened, but I've suddenly made not just one, but two, enemies here – and it's only my first day.

Just my luck.

I'd cry, but I don't want to do that a second time today. I'm sure bullies like Cole and this Enchantress get power and superior smugness from things like that.

Thankfully, I had the thought to stash my key to my new dorm room in the left side pocket of my leggings because I was afraid I was locked out for a minute. As soon as I open the door, Nora turns from her position at the foot of her bed, giving me a small smile.

"How was your – oh," she corrects, probably seeing my expression.

I close the door and lock it – just in case. "I'm just glad it's over," I sigh.

For such a quiet Freshman, Norsa seems to be very

comfortable here. She's quick to smile and to share. I forgot to pack toothpaste, and she gave me her second tube so I wouldn't have to ask to leave campus to buy some.

"Well, it won't be forever," Nora tells me, pulling a pink blouse out of her suitcase. She must be unpacking her clothes now. When I left earlier, she was working on toiletries in our shared bathroom.

"How long does the Mentorship Program last?" I ask her, surprised that she knows this information.

Nora walks over to the large closet that's to the left of our bathroom, hanging up her blouse on her side of the closet. We decided to use the shelving cubby in the middle of the closet as a divider for our things.

"From what I was told, a month or so," she responds.

A *month?*

That's torture!

"Who's your Mentor?" I ask, sitting on my bed that I'd just finished making before Cole showed up. Mom and Dad bought me a pink twin sheet set and a pink duvet before I left for school. Pink is my favourite colour.

"An Enchanter named Ryker Johnson," Nora tells me, turning around to face me now. She folds her arms and leans against the small patch of wall that separates the closet from the bathroom. "He's actually pretty nice. His Familiar is a black panther. I'm surprised it fits in his dorm room."

I wonder who's more dangerous – Ryker's black panther Familiar or Ebony, the unnamed-to-me Enchantress' Familiar.

Speaking of which...

"I'm glad he's nice," I breathe. Nora's a kind person. I'm glad she's not dealing with a bully – at least, not that I know of. "Um, do you know the brunette Enchantress who has a black cat Familiar – Ebony?" I fumble.

Nora snorts a laugh at that. "Oh, you mean Désirée

Chapin?" she asks around her laugh, but it's incredulous. "I sure do know her. Or, *of her*, I guess. Most people here do." She frowns at me suddenly. "Why? Did you rumble with her?"

"Yeah, but it was an accident," I agree.

Nora laughs, playing with a lock of her black hair. "Well, I'd stay away from her, that's for sure. And her cousin, uh – I think her name is Lucille."

No problem there, I think – but I think I accidentally voiced that thought out loud because Nora throws her head back and laughs at my candid and honest response.

"Well, the assembly's starting in an hour," she reminds me. It's eleven o'clock now and the 'welcome assembly' starts at noon. I remember that much from my welcome package email. "We should get unpacking and head down to the academy."

I stand up from the bed, feeling like I could nap all day. The stress of coming to a new place – a new *realm* – and the plaguing of my being by two different bullies definitely drains on my soul.

I hate assemblies, group projects, public speaking – anything that puts me around people without my consent. At least at the assembly, I can hide in the back and blend into the crowd. And maybe I can sit with Nora, so I'm not alone.

At least this assembly just seems to be an orientation, and going over the rules of campus. After that, I'm hoping that I can go get lunch somewhere. Maybe if my Mentor was a human being (or something resembling one), I would have been able to ask where I could get things like meals and school supplies – but I got the feeling before that Cole isn't one for questions.

An hour of unpacking goes by pretty quickly. I'm finally finished with my clothes, toiletries, and organizing my book-bag. I definitely need more school supplies. I want to get more pens and maybe some page protectors for handouts. Hopefully, after lunch, I'll be able to find a stationery store on campus and will be able to check that off my ever-growing to-do list.

A little before noon, Nora and I leave our dorm and lock the door. The one good thing about today is that my roommate and I are getting along well. I'd rather have an Enchantress and a Shifter as bullies instead of my roommate, that's for sure.

It feels chillier as we walk to Gomada Academy from Meera, but maybe that's because we were in a warm space for so long. The academy resembles a castle, with high, overarching towers and a vibe that screams 'significant'. I'm kind of scared to go inside – and one look at Nora tells me she may feel similar.

Lots of students are congregating around the school's entrance – maybe because we have about five minutes until the assembly starts. I like being early for things, so I hope Nora is okay with us going in now. Much to my relief, she and I approach the double doors together and head inside.

There's even a cathedral vibe in here: the high ceilings and ornate stained-glass windows give an air of reverence and importance. The purpose of this school is to provide each class, or race, the opportunity to hone their powers and skills. It's necessary if you don't want your powers or Shifting ability to spiral out of control.

At least for me, my Air Affinity isn't in that 'danger zone area', according to Dad. I just need to figure out how to activate the electrical component of my Affinity. It took me until the age of fifteen to activate my wings. Dad, who is half-Nymph and has the Air Affinity, tells me that electricity is usually the more challenging part of the Air Affinity to control.

That's another thing I'm afraid of: not being able to

perform or control my Affinity during training. I guess that can happen tomorrow, during the first day of classes.

Nora told me that the Enchanter-slash-Nymph's Field is just off-campus, past the wooded area, near the Gomada Mountains. I guess our training field is further secluded, just in case we can't get a grip on our powers.

The academy is a winding, complicated sea of different doors and hallways. I have no idea where we're going, but the trickling mob of students in front of us seems to, so we follow them. Eventually, we get to a large fork off one of the main halls, with a large wooden sign boarded onto the wall. Gold lettering displays '**AUDITORIUM**' in bold letters.

The inside of the auditorium is massive. Rafter seating along the walls and the aisled seats that seem to go on forever make it look more like a movie theatre than a school auditorium.

"Move it, already!"

Nora and I turn around, surprised that our one second of staring, away from the entrance, caused such a disruption. I know I shouldn't be surprised when I see who's behind us.

Désirée Chapin and a girl with short blonde hair and blue eyes stare down at us. It was actually the blonde who snapped at us, but I'm sure if she's anything like her friend, she's just as dangerous.

Then, I remembered what Nora had said earlier. This must be Désirée's cousin, Lucille. Désirée holds Ebony in her arms while a white fox drapes over Lucille's left shoulder. I have to say, that white fox sure is cute. It's even nibbling affectionately on Lucille's blonde locks, who is letting it happen. I guess Enchantresses, even mean ones like these two, let their Familiars do what they want, because they love them. I don't know too much about Familiars – though I wish I had my own pet.

Nora frowns at Lucille. "We weren't even in the way," she

protests quietly. Even though Nora spoke softly, it's clear that she got the two Enchantress' attention.

"Excuse me?" Désirée snaps. "Do you know who you're speaking to, Nymph?"

Again, the way she says 'Nymph' is laced with venom and callousness.

Nora folds her arms and rolls her eyes. "Back off, both of you," she counters.

Not wanting her to fight them all by herself, I add, "We're not trying to start anything. We're just trying to find a seat."

Lucy looks down at me. "So, this is the pipsqueak from before?" she asks, looking over at her cousin in a jeering way, as if I'm a sideshow.

Why is everyone calling me that?

"Seven hundred of us, and I still run into you three times," Désirée cuts me down to size by spitting at me.

"Then you can leave," I find myself suggesting.

Désirée gives me a smug smile. "I hope we meet a fourth time, Nymph. Maybe then, I can teach you to respect your superiors."

Superiors?

We're both Freshmen. We're both new to the academy. Why is she being so condescending?

Thankfully, Désirée and Lucille walk away from us and toward the front of the auditorium. Figures as much. Girls like them think everyone wants to notice them, so they congregate where they think they'll be most seen.

"Bitches," Nora grumbles, causing me to chuckle.

"Ladies and gentlemen, please turn off your phones and find a seat," a strong male voice speaks out into the auditorium – maybe by using a PA system of some kind.

Nora and I quickly make our way down the first few steps and sit at the fourth-last row of chairs. I'm sitting on the aisle seat, so I quickly make myself smaller, so no one else bumps into me.

A sudden chill spins down my spine. As soon as I look up, a pair of green eyes stare down at me. Cole Hudson gives me a smile that matches the cold feeling I just felt, and I jump a mile when he suddenly smooshes his still-lit cigarette against my arm. Even with my jean jacket on, it still burns me.

"Thanks, Willow," he tells me darkly as tears well up in my eyes.

"What a jerk!" Nora gasps as Cole follows that long-haired friend of his down the steps.

I rub my arm, aghast when I notice a burn mark on the arm of my jacket. The threads are badly loosened, and I'm sure a hole will form there. I know how to sew, so maybe I can fix it with a patch or a cute design – but that's not the point. I can't afford to buy a new jacket, and that hurt, too!

"You really are having bad luck today," Nora observes, rubbing my right arm as tears fall down my cheeks.

Maybe if I was more extroverted, I would've followed him and told him off. But all I want to do right now is use my grandpa's pocket watch (back in my dorm room) to bring me back to San Francisco.

The already-hushed student chatter dies as soon as a woman approaches the steps to the stage below, climbing them purposefully and walking onto the raised platform. There's a wooden stand with a microphone poised and at the ready. I haven't seen pictures or anything like that. Still, I'm betting the woman on-stage, who must be in her late thirties, is Leona Frow, the Headmistress of Gomada Academy.

Beyond the podium and the Headmistress are two rows of chairs where the staff and faculty must sit. I don't know any of their names, and I don't recognize any of them, either. I do notice that some professors have Familiars either sitting with them or on their laps. I spot an owl, a snake, a goose (they scare me), and a lion.

The Headmistress is beautiful and gives off this vibe of *importance*, even from far away. She has long black hair tied into a loose knot at the nape of her neck. With the overhead lights shining on her, it also looks like she has blue lowlights in her hair. A red hawk flies behind her, floating above her head and sitting on the wooden podium as if it were a perch. She must be an Enchantress.

She adjusts the microphone on its stand with no interference from the PA system. "Good afternoon, students, faculty, and staff," she announces. Her voice is smooth like velvet. It seems the audience settles when she speaks. What is her Affinity – or, Affinities?

"Welcome to another year at Gomada Academy. My name is Leona Frow. Most of you older students may not recognize me. I am your new Headmistress. This is my first term as your guide. It's a pleasure to meet the next generation of promising young people to lead Gomada and the four realms in truth, integrity, and honour.

"Now, onto some housekeeping rules. Please ensure your phones are turned off. No photographs or recording, please. The staff and I frown on technology as a distraction."

Shuffling sounds are heard as some students likely turn off their phones or, like me, ensure that they're definitely powered off.

"As Headmaster Leopold Granton taught you last year, this

is a space for learning, personal growth, and camaraderie. Gomada as a realm and Gomada Academy as an institution want to foster a relationship between the three races. We want to look past socialized and inherent biases and learn to work together. That is exactly why you Freshmen and Sophomores have been paired with a student from a different class. Everyone is equal at Gomada Academy."

Applause swells from all corners of the auditorium. I clap, too, but I don't believe it. It hasn't even been six hours yet, and I've already made enemies from two different classes. I didn't mean for it to happen, but it did, anyway. I can't help but wonder if people like Désirée Chapin and Cole Hudson believe in this mandate from the academy. But how much better am I if I don't believe it?

Maybe I want to believe it, but it's proving to be much harder than I expected.

Leona adjusts her sparkling black blouse. "Now, curfew is ten o'clock. If you wish to leave campus, you must gain the permission of a professor or myself. Remember to remain on campus at all times, where we can protect you."

'Where we can protect you'? What else is out there?

I glance at Nora, horrified. Does she know what the Headmistress is talking about? Nora currently lives on Earth (or the Overworld); but used to live in Gomada. I think she was born here. Maybe she knows more about this than others coming to the academy from other realms.

Nora must have sensed me looking at her, because she turns slightly and makes eye contact.

"There are some creatures out in the Gomada Thicket," she whispers.

Oh. The Gomada Thicket must be the name of that wooded area I had to walk through to get here. But more important than that, what kind of *creatures* are out there?

I'm missing the assembly now, and Nora has gone back to paying attention, so I will thank her later and look back at the Headmistress.

"There will be a host of different classes you will all be expected to take. Yes, we will help you hone your Affinities, Shifting powers, and overall skill as a supernatural entity. You'll have in-class learning sessions and hands-on, outdoor training. But we'll also instruct you in the areas of literature, arithmetic, and history."

Groans echo through the auditorium – and mine is more of an internal, emotional wail at the realization that I'll still have to take math class here.

Leona surprises me by smiling, which is visible even all the way at the back of the auditorium.

"I do love shocking students with that message," she states off-hand.

"Classes will start at eight o'clock in the morning and will end by four. You will see a mixture of all three races in your math, history, and literature classes. Do not miss the opportunity to learn from your other peers."

I hate to think this way, but the only thing I've learnt from Enchantresses and Shifters so far is that they aren't to be trusted, and they don't want anything to do with me.

COLE'S FIRST NIGHT

The damned assembly went on forever. It didn't help much that I was craving a cig the entire time. And I guess it didn't help that I didn't sleep well last night. The night before the first day of school is always the worst. All those thoughts about who others want me to be, who I am, and why I can't just do what I want. It was bad last year, but it's worse now – maybe because Professor Qadir lectured me this morning about being a slacker.

When the assembly is *finally* over, I get up sooner than most people in my row and leave. Diego sat next to Taylor. She's a Shifter and a Freshman. Apparently, her Mentor is that jackass Lukas Crabtree. He was a total dick to me last year. Taylor's stuck with him now – and isn't very happy about it. I understand – but more to the point, maybe if Diego hangs out with his own kind, he may start to like her instead of that Enchantress snob. Not that I'm a matchmaker, or anything, but I'd just rather not see my buddy get his soul crushed by that Dark Bitch.

I sneak out through the side way before anyone like

Professor Qadir can corner me and make me do extra-credit work. It's no secret to the professors here that I passed through the skin of my teeth last year. I'm sure the standards this year will be much higher. I'm not looking forward to that.

As I walk briskly down the now-empty hall more oxygen fills my lungs, and I feel safer. Fewer people equals more freedom. But it doesn't last long, because my back is suddenly up. Someone else is coming up from behind me. Maybe it's the Tedla inside me forcing me to stay on alert, or maybe it's my paranoia of being watched – but whatever it is, I turn.

Stepping out from the shadows is the jackass himself. Lukas Crabtree is standing behind me, and that annoying black dingo Familiar is pacing behind him. It looked like he was trying to stalk me. Too bad, so sad for him. He squared off against Diego and I last year, but just like the others, he sensed the creatures inside us and didn't push too hard.

From what I remember about Crabtree – I never forget an enemy – he specializes in Poison and Earth Affinities. He's jacked, too, and taller than Diego and I. But all that doesn't mean much when he's up against two monsters – and he knows it. This makes me wonder why he's following me now.

"Got a problem, Crabtree?" I ask off-hand, like talking to him is a waste of time. And it is. But I'm also cautious. God knows what this asshole is up to. It's not just Diego and I who hate him. Most of the Freshman class from last year wanted to see his head on a spike.

His green eyes stare back at me. He's not intimidated.

"Just wanted to catch up, Hudson," he responds just as easily, folding his arms and leaning against one of the black pillars that hold up the second floor.

"How creepy of you," I respond flatly.

His stupid pet dog bares his teeth at me – I can see it in my peripheral vision – but I ignore it.

He shrugs under his folded-arms stance. "Well, I see you haven't changed much. Still a drug-obsessed loser, aren't you?"

My jaw clenches, but I say nothing.

Lukas raises a blonde eyebrow. "Well? Am I wrong? Or is this the year you'll finally make something of yourself?"

I don't know why this baiting thing he's doing is working. But it is, and I'm annoyed.

"Maybe, if assholes like you are in the way," I counter evenly.

Lukas smirks at that. "I'm no expert, but I know something particularly devil-like is inside of you. Don't want to bring it out by aggravating you."

I hate it when people label the Tedla as evil or devil-like, even if they don't know what it is. They can sense something dark inside of me, sure, but they have no right to judge it.

"Think what you like," is all I say. "Besides, if you *aggravate* me enough, maybe it'll have a chomp at that mutt behind you."

I love threatening Enchanter and Enchantress' Familiars. It's hilarious how riled up they get because of it. But to this day, I haven't touched any of them. Animal abuse isn't really my thing. Though after that fucking fleabag slashing up my face today, I was seriously rethinking that.

Unlike Lucy and Désirée, Lukas rolls his eyes and scoffs at that threat from me. Weird. "I'm sure Fang will enjoy your attempt," he tells me. The dingo behind him opens its mouth, revealing its teeth to me. I've seen sharper. The dog is just as fucked up as his master.

"If that's all," I end the conversation by sighing, hoping to let him know that this whole thing was boring and pointless to me, beginning to turn on my heel.

"There's something fucked up about you, Hudson."

I turn to face him. "What?" I snarl.

Lukas smiles at me, knowing he got my goat good this time. He usually doesn't talk like that, so I know now that he was trying to bait me. Too late.

"You're hiding something. Something big." He frowns at me as if he's trying to figure me out.

I don't really know what he's talking about. Does he mean my Tedla or my family secret? They're kind of the same thing. Whatever. This shit doesn't scare me.

"Have fun with your detective work," I huff. "You'll need to take your head out of your ass to do it, though."

Lukas glares at me, and I glare right back. No way in Hell is Lukas figuring out where I come from, what I could be capable of. And even though I'm acting like his goal doesn't scare me, it does. If anyone can figure out my family secret, it's this smart-ass and brown-nosed bastard.

I feel like killing him with my bare hands, so I turn around and walk to the school exit so I don't get expelled and thrown in jail. I don't know if it's the Tedla inside me feeling threatened by Lukas, or if I'm the one who's feeling attacked – or maybe it's both – but I'm so mad that I see red.

Walking around this ghost town of a campus, because most students are still hanging out in the auditorium like a bunch of suck-ups, I try to take in a few deep breaths to steady myself.

The anger inside me slowly fades. The more I inhale and exhale deeply like this, the easier it is to control. All that talk inside about sunshine and rainbows and loving the other races? It's bullshit. Enchanters and Nymphs are moronic. I have no desire to ever get close to any of them. It's clear they can't be trusted.

I pull my phone out of my pocket when it vibrates (like I ever turned it off in the first place).

Want to get lunch with me and Taylor?

I'm still reeling from what happened with Lukas inside, even if I'm starting to feel better. I don't think I can be near other people right now.

Some other time. Peace.

I answer quickly so Diego doesn't think I'm being a dick.

Getting back to my dorm, I throw myself on my bed and rub my temples. I'm tired. I'm angry. I'm a walking time bomb if anyone else pisses me off. And if I explode, Tedla will take over. I'm still trying to control it, but it's much harder to do when I'm angry.

When I finally feel like I'm not going to rip anyone's head off, I get up and head back to Gomada Academy. Their dining hall is the only place to get food here and there's a ticking clock on that, so I know I need to eat now. From what I remember about last year, lunch is from twelve to two – and with the assembly, they extend it until three.

When I get to the Dining Hall, it's loaded up with students. I'm already annoyed, but I'm not as red as I once was. The line is long. I spend the time looking at random shit on my phone. When I'm finally inside the kitchen area of the Dining Hall, I discover that it's stir fry day. Whatever. I'm not picky. I'll eat anything and everything.

I have the lady behind the counter load up my plate and walk out into the seating area of the Dining Hall. I find a secluded table near a window. It's cold – the heating sucks in here – but I'd rather be cold and alone than toasty and pissed off by the chit-chat.

Just as I'm about to take a bite of my meal – which actually smells better than I thought it would – a shadow looms over me.

What now?

Arya Willow is standing across from me. How the fuck did she find me in a room this large, that probably has all seven hundred students in it?

I put my fork down. "What do you want?" I challenge her. I'm seriously not in the mood to be fucked with by anyone else. And just because this pipsqueak is a girl doesn't mean she'll be safe if she pushes me close to the edge.

"You ruined my jacket," she accuses. Her arms are folded, and her dark brown eyes stare at me angrily.

Ah. She's referring to my stunt from earlier.

I shrug. "Your point?"

She gapes. "You really can't guess why I'm mad?"

I laugh, leaning back in my chair. "I can guess. I just don't care."

She's fuming now. This is great. This is just the medicine I needed after squaring off against Lukas.

"You burnt my arm!" she exclaims. "You can't just go around treating people like–"

"What are you going to do about it, Pixie?" I cut her off simply. "You're a wet blanket. Go drip on somebody else."

Her jaw clenches. She's really mad now. I'm about to smile with glee when her eyes suddenly go white. With a flick of her hand, my entire tray flies up, and my lunch smashes me in the face.

"You *bitch!*" I exclaim, shoving out my chair just as the tray attacks me, but it's too late. It's all over me. It's hot, and I'm so mad I could leap across the table and smash her face through this window to my right.

"Leave me alone!" she counters. Tears are in her eyes, but she's still mad. Her eyes are still white. She was channelling her Air Affinity before and after this trick of hers.

I jump up from my chair so fast that it skids across the floor and falls over. I grind my teeth together as I wipe the food off me. She just stares right back at me. Maybe she's scared, but she's had enough, because she's still shaking, and I see a pulse of white energy surrounding her.

"Mess with me again," I snarl, "and you'll be fucking sorry."

It looks like my threat scares her because she gives me one final *stare* before walking away from my table. I watch her go, trying to inhale and exhale to get my anger under control.

No dice.

I want to rip her head off.

But I know I can't do that, so I take in another breath and turn around, picking up my chair and slamming it onto the floor. People around me are snickering about the fact that food is all over me. I'm starving, but I'm too mad to go back in there and ask for more food. I leave my mess where it is and just stalk out of the Dining Hall, ready to throw myself into the Gomada Pond off-campus so I can cool down.

Pacing the width of my dorm room, I'm pushing back against throwing my laptop through the window above my desk. I want to yank her brown hair out of her head. I want to go find her and scare the shit out of her. She's such a mousey little bitch. My temples are flaring again. She's lucky she's a girl. If it was Lukas who did that, he'd be shipped off to the infirmary.

I can't stay in this room, either. I'm probably going to end up doing something I regret.

Once I'm outside again, I walk in the general direction of the Shifter's Field, behind Feara. I know I'll have privacy with the professors' dorm being out of sight from the Field. Just as I suspected, no one is out here. Nobody wants to train on the first day. I don't, either, but I want the freedom, the empty space.

Sitting on the grass that must have been mown before

today, I look up at the sky. It's overcast. Maybe it will rain. The sky is also darker than before, so I look at my phone. Huh. It's past four. How long was I stewing in my room, trying not to kill the little Pixie?

Whatever. Now that I'm alone, I'll be good in a matter of minutes.

I'm surprised when my phone goes off again.

> Bro, I heard you wore your lunch. You
> good?

> Fuck! Who else knows about that?

It's a big-ass school, yet shit like this still flies around campus, anyway. And it burns me that the little Pixie Bitch did it to me.

The rage hits me again, but it's not going to boil over this time. I take a deep breath and answer Diego.

> I'm fine

Is that a lie? Maybe. Or maybe it isn't.

I close my texting app and find myself on social media. I type in 'Arya Willow' in the search bar, and sure enough, her fucking face appears. Of course, her profile is set to private. But I can find out a few things about her.

She's sixteen. She's from the Overworld – a place called San Francisco. Figures as much, since she didn't have a clue about anything when she sought me out today. She doesn't have any friends in her profile pictures. She doesn't have a ton of friends. She's either very picky or super-shy. I think it's the second one. She likes pink and stupid girly shit. She's single and straight.

I don't care about most of this shit, but it'll help me if I ever want to put the screws to her. I like knowing *little things* like this about my enemies. You never know when so-called little things could be useful.

I usually don't consider Pixies like Arya as 'enemies' – but this is different. She crossed the line this afternoon in the Dining Hall.

She's an enemy. And she's going to regret going up against me. I vow, right here, right now, to make her life a living Hell.

It's weird but doing this cyber-stalking or whatever it's called helped calm me down. After just breathing in the fading afternoon sky, I feel like I can head back to campus without murdering anyone. I'm usually not an angry guy – not unless I'm pushed. Normally, I could care less about everyone and everything. But one wrong move at the wrong time–

I shake off those thoughts. It's not good for me to dive into my rage. It's one thing when I'm in human form. But when I'm the Tedla, if I'm already pissed, all sorts of shit could hit the fan.

Circling around Feara now, I look at my phone again. It's almost five o'clock. Dinner is usually from six until eight. I just have one hour to kill until I finally eat – for the first time today.

Dinner is uneventful. I'm finally allowed some peace by myself. That annoying Pixie Bitch doesn't find me; neither does Lukas. Once dinner is over, I weave in and out of the clusters of students who just like to stand in random places and talk. I'm going to have to get used to being surrounded by stupid people.

I'm facing Feara again. It's close to eight o'clock now. I'm just about to approach the dorms – because I'm more tired now than before – but Diego and Lucy suddenly walk out from around the side of the building.

Were they at the Shifter's Field?

Why is he wasting time with that Witch?

He couldn't care less about what I said earlier. I mean, it's not like I listen to *him* when he calls me things like 'judge-mental douche', but...

This is about *him*. I don't want anything to happen to him. And if someone like Lucy Chapin has her claws in him, well...

There's no way I can go over there now – even though I want to know what the hell they're talking about. I turn around and begin to walk the campus grounds aimlessly. And then, it hits me.

Fuck this place! I think. *Just hop the fence and go get some real air.*

A human can't hop the wrought-iron fences without getting shish kabobed. But a Shifter who's completed a transition can, no problem.

I'm in the Shifter's Field at nine PM. I made sure to wait long enough to have no witnesses. I scour the field before finally accepting the fact that it's deserted. No one has seen my Shifting yet – and I don't want to start now. It's better if they don't know.

I started getting the *urge* to Shift when I was around five years old. By ten I was able to Shift on my own, no problem. At seventeen, I can Shift in no time at all. Sure, I experience extreme pain, but my transition time is shorter after years of practicing. Less time in pain is a good compromise after years of perfecting my Shifting techniques. It's one thing to want to Shift. You also have to *feel* the Shift – 'connect mind and body', like Dad says.

I duck into the shadows of trees and tap into the darkest

part of my being to trigger my Shift. Every Shifter taps into different parts of themselves to trigger their transition. Diego taps into his determination and resolve. I tap into the parts of myself that aren't so pretty. Anger, frustration.

I have to think about Lucy egging me on this morning.

I have to think about Désirée and her cat attacking me.

I have to think about Lukas stalking me after the assembly to push me to my breaking point.

And I gladly think about Arya dumping my own lunch onto my face.

In seconds, snapping sounds hit the Fall air. I sink to my knees, giving in to the pain. As a kid, I cried when I Shifted. Now, I almost *welcome* the pain. Yeah, it kills, but at least it's a tangible pain. And it distracts me from whatever else I have going on that I always try to push to the back-burner.

I used to black out when the pain got this bad. Tendons snap, my spine dislocates and realigns, my teeth clench together so I don't scream. My clothes are ripped from my body. I forgot to remove them, or I didn't care to do it earlier.

The crescent moon above me begins to waver. It's suddenly super-clear. I'm now seeing life through the Tedla's eyes. My vision is better when I can summon his eyes in human form, but this is different. Everything is sharp and focused. I'm fully Shifted now.

The Tedla is eight feet tall on two legs, and his hearing is better than any wolf's. His teeth can break through cars. I could kill someone with one paw swipe of black, intimidating claws.

I throw my body in the opposite direction and charge head-long for the wrought-iron fence that wraps around all of campus – even the Shifter's Field. I can run fast on two legs, but four would have been doable, too. I prefer two feet. It freaks people out the most.

I jump as soon as I'm a handful of feet away from the fence. Soaring through the night air, feeling the cold Fall breeze through my fur, the invincible and powerful adrenaline pumping through my veins–

Yeah. I like being a Tedla.

It's hard to determine whether he's me or I'm him. I think about him as a separate creature – but sometimes, I'm also him. This is a good thing: it means that the Shifter has accepted his creature alter ego.

Whatever. If we can work together, I don't really care who's who.

I now drop to all fours and race through the Gomada Thicket. It's dark, shadowy, and deserted here. One of the good things about being a Shifter: any other creatures or 'monsters' out here don't fuck with you if you're higher-up on the Shifter Creep List.

The terrain rises to form small hills as I reach higher. The vegetation and trees get thicker here. It's weird, though. Even though I'm a big-ass monster, there's usually some kind of wildlife here. It's not usually this quiet. Even the crickets aren't chirping. I don't like thinking this way, but that's weird.

Just as I'm thinking this, something strange and bright gets my attention from the corners of my peripheral vision. I turn my head to the left, not going too quickly, just in case this *thing*, whatever it is, spots me.

But it doesn't.

I see this creepy-as-fuck (and that's saying something, because I'm fucked up, too), bright white *figure* standing on one of the lower hills that overlooks campus. You can see the outline of the academy from here, and the outline of the fence.

My eyes zero in on this *thing*. It looks see-through, like it's not tangible or made up of solid matter. There's even a sort of *steam* or some other kind of air-like thing surrounding the creature.

I freeze.

Well? I think. *What is this thing, buddy?*

I don't talk to my Tedla self very often. But I suddenly get this damp, scared feeling.

The fuck?

The Tedla's not *scared* of anything!

But when the *thing* turns around and its large, hole-like yellow eyes look at me, I get that damp feeling times a trillion.

Too bad! I'm not backing down from some weird matter-less creep!

I crouch and snarl, opening my arms wide and showing my claws. I bare my teeth, showing him I've come to fight if he tries anything.

But just as soon as this thing sees me, it vanishes, and all that's left is the damp feeling from before. And cold sweat. I'm sweating.

I'm scared as fuck!

I'm so stunned and freaked that I don't move a muscle from before. I don't know if whatever I saw has anything to do with it, or if I'm just so scared shitless that I can't move on my own.

I'm still crouched, arms open wide. I stay like that, because I'm not a hundred percent sure the thing won't come back. I'm also shitting myself.

What kind of thing was that, if the *Tedla* was scared of it?

Five

ARYA'S GUILT

It's hard for me to sleep. I keep tossing and turning, hoping and waiting, but nothing happens. I think I finally drifted off around five AM – but when my alarm gets me up at six-thirty, I'm exhausted and restless. I feel like I didn't sleep at all. And I know why.

Nora is already awake: she told me last night that she likes to go for a jog every morning to be closer to nature. I imagine with her Earth Affinity, she'd take any and every opportunity to be outdoors.

Speaking of exercise, I should have just given up on sleep and gone jogging with her. I have a few pounds I need to lose, but I'm always so busy doing something or other that it's hard to exercise.

I step into the shower, hoping steam and hot water will wake me up. I guess it helps, but not as much as I'd hoped.

I towel-dry my hair, not really in the mood to go to the trouble to blow-dry and style it. I wanted to look put-together and professional for my first official day at Gomada Academy – but a cloud of tiredness and *guilt* eats away at my resolve.

I pull on my black mini-skirt and pink long-sleeved top. I guess I'm still trying to look *somewhat* collected or appropriate for my first day of school – but at the same time, I'm not going that extra mile. I brush the wet tangles from my long brown hair. I apply black eyeliner, mascara, and colourless lip gloss. I find my brown leather boots and make sure I have all my school supplies together.

The Freshman class all have the same schedule – with accommodations for their race. First period, we all have History. Second period is our specific race class. Third period is Literature. Fourth period is our hands-on, in-the-field race class. I'm not happy that I have to wait all day to humiliate myself in the Nymph's Field. And, with the Enchanters and Enchantresses sharing that same field, I'm sure everyone will be able to mock me when my eventual screw-ups happen.

Maybe I'm not having a very good outlook for my very first day – but it's a realistic one. I'd rather be realistic today instead of daydreaming.

Dreaming.

I *wish* I was dreaming right now. Even a nightmare. Sleeping would be better than dealing with school now. I was so excited to transfer here, but now–

At least I have enough notebooks for my classes today. After school, I need to try and find that stationery store on the campus map Nora and I got at the Student Services section of the school.

I grab a quick hold of my jean jacket before I unlock and open my dorm room. I take one last look at my safety net, taking in my quickly made bed and Nora's sunny living section. Her green duvet and flower throw pillows make me feel safe – but tired, too.

When I close my door and lock it, I see other Nymphs walking through the hallway. Most of them are on their phones. Some look for things in backpacks and bookbags as they make their way to the exit – probably to go to class. Some are drinking coffee in to-go cups. I'm not a coffee fan, but I need one today. I'm tired and stressed to the max.

I tap the arm of a passing Nymph with a large to-go coffee cup.

"Excuse me. Where did you get the coffee?" I ask him.

He looks down at me. "There's a café in the school," he reports.

As he walks away, I call out a surprised, "Thank you!"

There's a coffee shop in the school?

Well, that's all I needed to hear. I'm walking briskly for the exit to the double doors to Meera. I need caffeine if I want to have a prayer of surviving this day. Thankfully, according to my grandpa's pocket watch that I'm holding in my hand, it's seven forty-five, so I have plenty of time (I hope) to get my coffee and then find my first class.

It's a crisp Fall day when I get outside. Leaves are already falling from the trees surrounding the dormitory. The naturescape here is beautiful for a school with intimidating and cruel students. Nora must be in her element.

That reminds me.

I pull my phone out of my bookbag.

See you in History. Want a coffee?

Oh, my God, that'd be great. Thanks! I just take cream in mine. Xo.

I smile at Nora's quick and happy message. I really want to become good friends with her. Hopefully, shared dorms and classes will help. And if I can do nice things for her, the better.

Doing something nice for someone makes me think about the terrible thing I did to somebody else...

I'm not usually a confrontational person. I hate fighting with people. But Cole does something to me that makes me want to fight back. But in any case, I know what I did was wrong. Even though this makes my skin crawl, I should apologize to him. It's the right thing to do – even if it is Cole. Besides, I don't want to make an enemy – not right now. Not so soon into the school year. Or ever, really.

The walk to Gomada Academy – the first I'll ever take to school – sure beats taking public transit to my former high school, Primeston Collegiate Institute. But it's still brisk, and I'm on a time crunch, so I don't dawdle and look at the scenery like I might have done if I'd had more time.

Maybe it's my bad luck coming back to bite me again, but I take note of Cole leaning against one of the jutted-out large pillars that make up part of the castle-like building. I'm labelling this as 'bad luck' because I'll have to face him without caffeine and a good night's sleep as armour. Looking back at the size of the academy, it must have numerous floors. I don't remember seeing any elevators yesterday while Nora and I were walking to and from the assembly.

I know I have to face Cole now, so I still have time to get to the café (and I still have to find it) and then locate my first-ever class.

Maybe I should do this after school.

No! Don't be a coward!

The only thing is, I really ticked him off yesterday afternoon. If he's anything as frightening as whatever creature is inside of him, I poked the bear big time.

Finally, I suck in a lungful of cold Fall air – which is more painful than helpful – and begin to approach him. Of course, Cole is smoking – though I don't know how he's getting away with it, being so close to school grounds.

He looks in my direction when I'm about ten feet away

from him. I already see his facial expression sour. Even with a beanie and a black jacket with the collars pulled up, I can still tell he's mad.

Looks like time didn't do anything to cool him down – though I know what I did to him was mean.

He lets me get in front of him before he gives me a dissatisfied look. "Do you have a death wish or something, Pixie Bitch?" he snaps.

I immediately bristle at his insult, but maybe I deserve it after what I did, so I try to let it go.

"I just came over to apologize. For yesterday," I tack on as he takes a drag of his cigarette. How repulsive!

He frowns at me as he continues to suck on his cancer stick. I don't understand how Cole's lung capacity is so good if he's constantly polluting his respiratory system with that garbage.

He gives me a look that would probably hurt more than the 'death wish' he mentioned earlier, then blows a cloud of cigarette smoke in my face. I bristle again but try to hold it back – and a cough.

The Shifter laughs openly. "An apology?" he rephrases. "Please. You've come back to settle the score."

"No," I protest.

Cole looks me up and down as if he's scrutinizing me. Is he looking for weapons or something? What is he expecting?

When his eyes land on my grandfather's pocket watch that I've been carrying all this time (and forgotten about), he snatches it from me.

"Give it back!" I immediately insist as Cole examines it.

"What the fuck is this?" he asks, turning it over in his hand, as if he's inspecting it.

"It's mine. Please give it back," I try again.

Cole withdraws his arm when I reach out for the pocket watch, a spooky gleam in his green eyes.

"This means something to you, huh?" he muses.

I frown. "It was my grandpa's," I admit – only because I'm hoping even Cole has a soul, and it will prompt him to give the pocket watch back to me.

Cole glances down at it. "Oh, yeah? Is Grandpa excited for your first day of school?"

"He's dead," I answer.

"Probably wanted to get away from you, too," Cole smirks at me.

When I say nothing, Cole looks down at the pocket watch again. "My lunch meant something to me, too," he thinks out loud.

Uh oh. This can't be good.

"I'm sorry about that," I attempt to apologize again.

Cole glances at the overcast sky as if he's considering my two apologies. "Yeah. I don't care," he responds, suddenly dropping my grandfather's antique to the ground and stomping on it with his hiking boots.

I scream as soon as the glass housing the timepiece shatters.

"What's wrong with you?" I exclaim, tears pouring down my cheeks.

But instead of looking even the tiniest bit guilty, Cole sneers down at me as I cry, like a true bully. How could I have even *considered* apologizing to this horrible person?

"You're such a crybaby," he hurls down at me.

I'm clenching my fists at my sides as he laughs at me. All I want to do right now is punch him in the face. I've never hit someone before, but now–

I put my hands on his chest and push him – but only so he steps back from the pocket watch and I can scoop it up from the asphalt. It's in pieces.

As I turn on my heel to walk – no, *run* – for the school, Cole takes a firm hold of my arm and swings me backward.

"Don't ever try to pull one over on me again, Pixie," he spits at me, suddenly taking his cigarette and swinging it toward my left cheek.

I scream and dart out of the way just as he lets go of me, and I topple to the ground. I'm still crying, so my vision is blurry – but not so blurry that I don't see the huge shadow looming over me. Cole snatches the pocket watch from my hand even though I try to fight him off.

"Go join Grandpa in Hell," he snaps at me, walking past me now. I'm too distraught from everything that's happened to register where he's going.

Rushing to class, I barely have time to find Nora before the chiming of the antique bells goes off, signalling the start of first period. I hand over her coffee and sink into the empty space beside her. Thankfully, she saved me a seat.

History class is in the auditorium, where we had the assembly. Because it's a required class for all Freshmen, the school needed a larger space to hold the course. The auditorium looks different than it did yesterday afternoon. Even though the room looks full, there aren't nearly as many students here now as there were before.

I'm a complete mess. I feel like the entire world has shifted to a topsy-turvy angle, and I'm just free-falling. It looks like Nora wants to say something to me, but when the professor walks into the classroom, we know we have to remain silent. Even though this professor seems to command respect, he doesn't look like an overly harsh teacher. He has red hair and blue eyes, with glasses that he adjusts.

"Good morning, class," he greets us. "I'm Professor Miles Szorenyi. I'll be your History guru for the next four months. This course may be required, but I try to make it as fun as possible. You'll learn everything from ancient Gomada to the four other realms you may travel to one day. Take lots of notes. I may look like a nice guy, but my exams are extensive.

"With that being said, I only give out one midterm and one final exam. The rest are all papers. I don't believe in group projects or oral examinations. You can thank my introversion for that. Let's begin, shall we?"

Well, at least one thing is going right for me today! I sigh inwardly, pulling my notebook and pencil case out of my pink bookbag.

Thankfully, Nora's and my Nymph Studies course is really interesting and takes my mind off my troubles – for the most part. Our professor, Seamus Gallagher, is a lively speaker, and it was easy to pay attention. Lunch was uneventful. Nora and I went to the Dining Hall for our one-hour break and had pasta alfredo. It was nice to see other people and to get out of the classroom – but I was terrified that I would see Cole again. Literature class was different – we had a substitute professor. I'm unsure where our 'real' one is, or when they will attend campus.

When the multi-bell chime finally signalled the travel time for fourth period classes, Nora and I packed up our things and began to head out of the confines of Gomada Academy. According to our class schedules, our fourth period classes would always take place in the Nymph's Field – rain or shine.

As we walked, we noticed that students from our second period Nymph Studies class were ahead of us. Instead of asking anyone for directions (which we both considered), we decided to follow them. Sure enough, they led us to the gates of Gomada Academy, where a cluster of Enchanter and Enchantress students were also waiting. I could tell they were of that race because Désirée and Lucy were with them.

Nora looks at the two of them and closes her eyes halfway, trying to suppress an eye-roll. Even though Nora's quiet, like me, she's definitely able to roll with the punches better than I am. Hopefully in a few weeks, I'll feel more settled.

Maybe I'll feel more settled with my classes, the dorm, and the campus – but what about me being in an entirely new *realm*, with people who clearly want to see me fail, or worse?

My doomsday thoughts are interrupted when a tall woman of Asian descent saunters up to the other side of the gate. She's off-campus. There's a certain *air* about her that makes me realize that she's a Nymph, and likely our Field Practice professor. She's wearing a long white blouse, a black blazer overtop, and heeled boots. It looks like she is a well-seasoned professor, making me nervous.

"Good afternoon, class," she greets us, just as another professor crosses behind her and approaches the group of Enchanter and Enchantress students. "My name is Professor Lilith Xhao. I am your Field Practice educator. We will meet here every afternoon for training. Please do not be late unless the excuse is, shall we say, justifiable."

I usually try to never be late for things, but the way she said that makes me anxious.

"Follow me," is all Professor Xhao states now, pushing the gate open. The students toward the front of the group follow her first, and the rest of us trickle along.

The walk to the Nymph's Field takes about ten minutes. Professor Xhao seems to take shortcuts through the Gomada Thicket to reach our destination faster. I notice that the closer we get to the field, the colder it becomes. When we finally approach the open-concept field with no fence, I'm shocked to see the peaks of mountains jutting out of the treeline beyond us. I guess that's why I'm so cold now.

"There are ninety of you enrolled in this course," Professor Xhao states, turning around, arms folded behind her, looking out at us calmly. She's projecting her voice slightly. The thinness of the air this close to the mountains is making me dizzy, so I don't know how Professor Xhao can withstand the pressure to talk louder to us now.

"By the end of the month, I am sure some of you will leave. And by the end of the term, most of you will have considered it."

Quiet murmurs erupt from either end of the cluster of Nymphs.

"Fostering an Affinity is a daunting task. It's not for the faint of heart. You will have to be determined. You will have to work hard. You will need to step out of your comfort zone."

Stepping out of my comfort zone...

I know I need to work on this part of myself, but at the same time, hearing these words out of Professor Xhao's mouth scares me. A lot.

"As of today, I won't be evaluating each of you. But as of next week, we will begin the process. By this point in time, you've had sixteen years to develop your one Affinity. This is much easier than Enchanters and Enchantresses, who have attempted the mastery of *two* Affinities in the same amount of time. You should have already made impressive strides with your *one* Affinity."

The way she's talking, it sounds like she expects us to be leagues ahead of where I actually am at the moment. Looking around at the dozens of students in the Field, I try to hold back a shudder. How many of these Freshmen Nymphs are like me – half-Human, half-Nymph? When you're *half* of something, it's much harder to control, develop, and sustain your Affinity. Even if I do manage to one day activate my Air Affinity's lightning component, it may not come back the next time I try to use it. My powers are very temperamental. I'm assuming Professor Xhao won't see that as an excuse; perhaps she won't like the half part of my identity, and things will be even tougher for me.

What a horrible thought!

I can't tell anyone about this. It's not that I'm ashamed of where I come from or my family. I can't help being a half-Nymph, and neither can Dad. He's not sure where the bloodline truly severed – but it's definitely not a recent generation of his. I just don't want anyone using this secret against me – and, based on what I know about some of the people here, that's not a paranoid thought to have.

Nora nudges me suddenly, snapping me out of my trance. "Want to be partners?" she whispers as if she's nervous to talk at a normal volume. I can understand why. Crossing Professor Xhao isn't high on my to-do list, either.

"Partners?" I all but wheeze. This tells me I missed the last part of Professor Xhao's lecture, which fills me with dread.

Nora frowns at me confusedly. "She wants us to pair up to see what we can do," she adds. Maybe she's trying to jog my memory.

"Oh. Right. Sure," I agree quickly, not wanting Nora – my only friend here – to think that I was trying to ignore her.

Nora and I walk to a more secluded part of the Nymph's Field. It's so enormous that all forty-five pairs of Freshmen Nymphs can practice here, with space to spare, without bumping into one another. The Enchanter and Enchantress' side of the field is sectioned off by high foliage – maybe for privacy and concentration purposes. I wonder how those high trees and bushes have remained intact for so many years, with so many Enchanters, Enchantresses, and Nymphs having Fire Affinities.

Nora doesn't look concerned as she walks across from me – about fifteen or twenty feet, maybe – adjusting her stance so her feet are further apart. It looks like Nora has done this type of thing before. I guess I've tried with Dad, but those 'practices' weren't the same as the ones we're going to have at school.

Nora adjusts her black leather jacket, but it dawns on me that she's exposing her hands through its sleeves, so they have more freedom. I wonder what she's going to do – and quickly find out when a faint and then almost-*vibrating* green glow pulses from her palms. Her eyes aren't tightly shut, but it's clear that she's concentrating. This small detail shows me that Nora is comfortable enough with controlling her Affinity that she's not stressing out her body to the max.

She suddenly propels the green beams at me, or past me. I watch them sail around and above other groups of students – what control she has! – and *absorb* into the foliage separating the two Fields. Beautiful flowers of different colours spring up from previously empty green spaces.

What an impressive and beneficial Affinity to have! Thanks to Nora, I know how and why those high trees and bushes have been sustained for so long. I guess I should have known that earlier.

"Wow," I breathe. "That was–"

"Very impressive, Miss... Leith," comes a voice from my left. I whip my head around, seeing Professor Xhao in the middle of our patch of practice grass, looking at a clipboard she's carrying. I didn't notice it until now. Maybe all of her students' names are somewhere on those pages.

Nora adjusts her black ponytail that's swaying in the breeze. She looks embarrassed that someone saw that moment between her and her Affinity. "Thank you, Professor Xhao," she responds.

The professor looks from Nora to me, and then back at her clipboard as if she's trying to place me. This sends a shiver down my spine, but I try not to let it show. What if something she has on me tells her I'm half-Nymph? But that can't be possible. That was never a part of the application I filled out in January.

"And you're... Miss Arya Willow," she reads, finally putting a name to the face. For a second time, I think she's figured it out – but instead, she just looks up from her clipboard, her hazel eyes studying me.

"You have an Air Affinity," is all she says – but it still freaks me out. "Demonstrate your abilities, as Miss Leith did."

I hesitate. It's usually easiest for me to tap into my Affinity when I'm 'emotionally charged', as Dad says. If I'm really excited, scared, or angry, it's easier to draw on my Affinity. Even though I'm really nervous now, I'm afraid it won't be enough of a *draw*. But I know I have to try, especially because a professor is watching.

I fix my stance on the grass and hold my hands palm-up instead of forward. I close my eyes and try to concentrate. I'm trying to visualize the air and wind pumping through my body and the breeze blowing my hair; trying to make my own body tap into it–

"You are concentrating too hard, Miss Willow. Your Affinity won't be able to connect with your mind if you are too stressed."

I'm immediately embarrassed. I feel tears sting the backs of my eyes – but thankfully, they're closed, so no one sees. Doubts fill my mind, too. What if I can't do this because I'm half-human? What if everyone finds out?

But at that moment, I feel the smooth, almost-cool energy flowing through my veins, like gentle water filling a rain bucket, and I feel pulses of wind shoot out of my palms. I open my eyes just as my homemade gusts blow through the trees surrounding Nora and I. They ruffle the leaves, tug at the grass, and disperse into the skies above.

Nora watches the gusts up above with a smile on her face. "That felt good, Arya," she commends me. I smile at her shyly in response.

"Hmm. Good," Professor Xhao comments, but how she says that makes me wonder if she truly feels that way. At least I was able to actually summon up my Affinity without too much of a delay. I hope this doesn't affect my grades.

Six

COLE CRIED WOLF

I can't get that damned *ghost* out of my mind all day. I shouldn't have gone out last night – which is weird because I never regret breaking the rules, especially here. If I'd never snuck out, I wouldn't have seen that fucked up thing.

I tossed and turned all night long. I kept thinking it was going to *come for me* – but I kept telling myself that if it did, it would regret going up against the Tedla. The thing was, I don't know if it was my fear talking or my own gut feeling, but I wasn't sure if I would have been able to take it last night. And as I'm finishing up my first Field Practice with the other Shifters, I still think I wouldn't have been okay in that fight.

At least the Shifter's Field practice thing was okay. Because there are a bunch of Freshmen (I wasn't paying attention when one of the other Shifter profs told us numbers), a lot of it was review. How to tap into the emotions required to Shift, using your ability wisely, blah-blah-blah. I was more annoyed than interested.

As I'm returning to Diego, someone suddenly clears their

throat behind me. I turn around, knowing a ghost wouldn't get my attention like that, so I shouldn't be so freaked, and realize that Professor Qadir is behind me.

"Mister Hudson," he states, all-business. "I'm relieved, yet actually surprised, that you showed up this afternoon."

At first, I'm confused by this. But then, I remember. Last year, I skipped the first few days of classes. I'm not sure how I wasn't suspended or expelled for that. Well, I guess I *know* why, after all.

I don't know what to say, so I don't answer him. He folds his arms and studies me – just like Lukas did. Why can't everyone just leave me the fuck alone? Since when am I that interesting?

But I don't say any of *that* to Professor Qadir, either. I know what's inside of him – and I'm not messing with any of that shit. He didn't even Shift this afternoon – probably to spare the Freshmen. Last year, he only Shifted for us around the end of first term. That was the first time I began to respect him a bit more. He's dangerous and crazed as fuck, like I am – but I think he's able to control it way better.

"I do hope you will eventually Shift in front of your peers," he tells me, leaning forward a bit. It's like he thinks he needs to keep this conversation private. I don't care if people know I don't want to Shift in a public place, even if it is a training ground.

"I understand wanting to keep your lineage and Shifter's Identity private," he adds, "but it has been a year, Mr. Hudson."

Right. Our alter egos have personalities and all that shit – a 'Shifter's Identity'. I'm really not sure about that. The Tedla and I are pretty similar. Maybe he's more insane than I am, but it's not like when I'm pushed to the limit, I don't push back.

"I'll think about it," I tell him, making eye contact so he

knows I'm listening. I may not be serious – hell, I may be lying through the skin of my teeth – but I want him to at least see that I heard him. And if he believes me? So much, the better.

But the way he's looking at me now, with his brown eyes practically digging a hole into my chest, I know he wasn't tricked.

"Hmm," he responds, turning on his heel and walking away from me.

It's not like I want to hang around here any longer than I have to, so I walk up to Diego, who's looking at his phone. As soon as he hears me coming – and based on who's inside him, I know his senses are jacked, maybe even better than mine – he shoves his phone into his front jeans pocket. Weird. I thought nothing of what Diego was doing until he did that.

Am I just being – what's the word, *paranoid*? – after what happened last night? Or is something else going on here, too?

"Hey, bro," Diego greets me, his black hair blowing in a strong breeze as he slaps my shoulder. "Didn't grace the world with your Shift, eh?"

I roll my eyes as Diego grins at me, clearly tickled pink that he rubbed me the wrong way – not that that's hard to do.

Diego hasn't really 'graced anyone' with his Shifting, though rumours have hit him from all four corners of the school about his alter ego. It has been known for decades that the Jasper family has a lineage of one of the most powerful creatures of all time – the Phoenix. Diego has never denied or agreed with the rumours, but he's still careful about when and where he Shifts. We've both seen each other's alter egos – and I can get why Diego is careful with his. The Phoenix causes a lot of attention – even at night. It can light up a black sky with its fiery body – while I can just slip into the shadows, and no one can see me.

This is one reason I applied to Gomada Academy using

Mom's last name. If I'd used 'Germain', I'd be suffering from the same kind of rumour shit as Diego.

Speaking of suffering...

"Neither have you, asshole," I snap back, giving him a small smile as he gives me some goofy facial expression.

"What's your deal, anyway, Hudson?" Diego asks as we make our way off the Shifter's Field. We don't wait for anyone else. Like me, Diego doesn't really see the need for school and crap like that. We both like to break the rules or bend them until there's nothing left. But sometimes, even Diego and I have to fall in line – like when Professor Qadir is watching.

"I didn't sleep well last night," I admit, wondering if I should actually 'fess up to him about the weird ghost thing I saw.

Would he believe me? Would he think I was nuts? Then again, Diego and I transform into monsters. It's probably a safe bet to say he won't judge me – like I do to everyone else.

"That's typical for you," Diego teases me, causing me to roll my eyes. They hurt from sleeplessness.

"I went for a little stroll off-campus," I try to say, folding my arms as we get closer to the trees that fringe the Shifter's Field. Even if anyone else has super-hearing, they won't be able to overhear this conversation – not with the wind and the way we're speaking now.

Diego frowns at me – maybe because he suspects something is up, for real. Even his hazel eyes squint down at me as if they are (again, fuck) trying to figure me out. Me sneaking out is nothing new, but the way I'm saying it–

"What happened?" he asks, looking down at me with this weird look on his face. It's halfway between curious and worried. He's not that much taller than me, but the way he's looking down at me is more extreme because of it.

"I dunno," I finally sigh. "I Shifted. Just needed some air."

No need to tell him that I was trying to stop myself from killing a Nymph.

Diego smirks at me. "You? Breaking the rules and Shifting off-campus? Big whoop."

"I saw something out there, dumbass!" I exclaim, instantly feeling like shit because I cut him down for no reason. But Diego is really hard to piss off, so he rolls his eyes and continues to listen.

"It was... A ghost or something," I groan, knowing how crazy I sound. There's no way he'll believe me now. "But the way it moved and looked at me... It was like it wasn't made of anything solid. Had two creepy yellow eyes, and a weird residue or whatever was steaming off of it."

Diego stares at me for a long time. Great. This isn't good. "Are you sure you weren't–" he begins.

"I wasn't dreaming! Or high!" I protest. I knew from the get-go that I shouldn't have said anything! "This happened, Jasper! I wish it didn't, but it did! Even the fucking Tedla was scared of it!" I lower my voice as quickly as possible because more Shifters are walking out of the Field and will pass us soon.

Diego looks freaked by my little outburst – maybe because I'm being serious about something, for once, or maybe because he knows as well as I do that the Tedla isn't scared of anything.

"You serious?" he all but whispers. Shifters are passing us now. Taylor is one of them. She gives us a look as she passes us. She knows we're talking about something crazy. You need to be careful when talking about this kind of stuff around other Shifters.

As soon as she's gone, Diego looks back to me and folds his arms, looking confident now. "Well, maybe we should go out tonight and see if it comes back," he suggests.

I feel good that Diego believes me, that he believes me enough to *check it out*. But part of me also feels *scared* again –

like even the thought of seeing that ghost thing a second time will make me sick.

But I don't say anything like that to Diego. I just nod at him and agree, "Let's do it."

I'm not a coward. I don't get scared very easily. Usually, I'm the one doing the scaring. But what I saw last night was way worse than any horror movie or stunt I've ever pulled on someone else.

I guess I should be working on my Sophomore History reading, or I should be tracking down that stupid Pixie Bitch, so Professor Qadir doesn't catch me slacking. But I really want to sit here on my bed and nap. I'm sitting with my pillows against the bed's headboard, arms folded. I'm freaked as fuck, and tired as hell. I wish my mind would shut up for even just a minute, so I could sleep.

Something in my hoodie pocket makes a jingling sound when I slouch down into a half-laying-down position. Weird. I reach a hand inside, wondering what I stashed in there. I pull out the broken-up pocket watch I took from the Nymph earlier today. Having her go from raging bitch to crybaby was the highlight of my week. It fuelled me and made me forget about what I saw last night – at least, for a little while. Or what I saw last night made me lash out at her, big-time. But even if I *hadn't* seen anything last night, making her miserable was just what I needed.

I stare at the pocket watch a little harder when I notice that the smashed-up glass is *glowing*.

Huh. That's weird. Unless this watch isn't normal, typical crap like this shouldn't be giving off magic.

Does the Pixie have a Trinket? Why would she need something like that, made from an Enchanter or Enchantress? What–

Wait. I remember now. She's from the Overworld. I can't remember the place exactly, but I remember that she's not from around here. I guess that makes sense. Why else would she have a Trinket?

So, this was her grandfather's, *and* it's a Trinket – or, was a Trinket. No wonder she freaked when I broke it.

A small wave of guilt crashes over me. I hate feeling shit like this. The Nymph deserved it. She pissed me off on Monday, and today she was trying to even the score. She shouldn't have messed with me.

But I still feel a little bad that I wrecked a Trinket. And I guess I know a thing or two about heirlooms from grandparents. Fuck.

I hate that I feel bad about something I did to a *Nymph*, but there's nothing I can do about that. It's probably because of what happened last night. Everything's out of whack now. I shouldn't be too worried about feeling guilty. Once Diego and I look for that fucked up creature, all this will be over.

But that doesn't solve my problem now. I want to stop feeling guilty for breaking the stupid Pixie's pocket watch. I turn the watch over in my hand. I'm good with fixing things, but I'm no watchmaker. This looks pretty busted to me. I don't think there's a way out of this.

Wait a minute.

There *is* a way out of this – it'll just suck to get there. And I'd rather not go this route, but maybe there's a way I can without suffering too much grief.

I pace as I wait for the door to open. I hate being in Gleera.

The dorm got its name because of some well-known Enchanter called Michel Gleera. I remember that from my Freshman History class last year – even though I wish I could forget a lot of the stuff I learned in that class. I have a good memory, only when it serves me wrong.

The door flings open, and I'm face-to-face with Ryker Johnson. I haven't seen him since June of last year, but I'd still be able to place him, and the same's probably true for him because his brown eyes widen a bit when he sees me, like he's shocked I'm at his door. I'm still surprised by this, too.

"Hudson, what the hell!" Ryker laughs, smacking me on the shoulder.

Damn, that hurt.

Ryker quickly looks from left to right. I made sure the coast was clear before I knocked, but he didn't know. He jerks his head in the direction of his dorm.

"Come in," he orders.

I step into his dorm room and Ryker closes the door quickly. Ryker and I aren't *exactly* friends, but we're also not enemies. Diego and I began to respect Ryker a wee bit last year when we saw him cut down Lukas after a tough training day out on the Field. We don't know what happened between them, but Ryker was pretty clear about hating him. And so, every now and then, we'd nod in his direction or speak to him if no one else was around.

From what I can remember, Ryker's Affinities are Darkness and Light. A combo like that makes him *special* – we heard of him before we saw him rile up Erik – so maybe Diego and I felt sorry for him, too. We get the pressure – even if he is an Enchanter.

Ryker steps in front of me just as his big-ass black panther opens one eye to stare at me. Holy shit, that thing is just as scary now as it was last year.

"Don't worry. Zola already ate."

When I turn to stare down at him in shitting-my-pants mode, Ryker throws his head back and laughs, his black cornrows moving as he goes.

"Shut up," I order as he waves his hand at me.

"She's fine. Anyway," the Enchanter says, approaching his bed and petting the big thing. "I'm pretty sure you didn't come here to chit-chat, Hudson."

I look around Ryker's dorm room. I don't know how, but he managed to get a single. It's usually hard to do around here, but I shouldn't be surprised that he could pull it off. Even though he's not a total tool, Enchanters and Enchantresses seem to have golden horseshoes shoved up their asses. Or, maybe no one else wanted to share a dorm room with a fucking black panther.

Like the thing – Zola – knows I was thinking that, she opens both eyes and stares at me again.

"I need a favour," I finally say, feeling stupid and angry that I even dragged myself here in the first place. But I hate feeling stupid shit like guilt. The sooner I get rid of it, the better I'll feel. I'll be more focused for tonight.

Ryker raises a black eyebrow at me. "A favour? Did I hear you right?" he mocks.

"Johnson," I all but growl.

He shakes his head, like he can't believe his ears. Maybe he won't help me, after all. This keeps getting better and better!

"Fine. A favour. Okay. What kind of favour?" Ryker asks.

Before he can change his mind, I dig into my jeans pocket and pull out the Trinket. "Can you fix this?" I ask.

Ryker frowns at the glowing object in my hand. The glow isn't as strong now as it was before. I think it's beginning to fade because the magic in the Trinket is dying, or whatever.

Ryker knows more about this than I do since his race can use any Affinity they want to make a Trinket, well, *work*.

"Probably," he answers, sounding just as cocky as I remember him. "For a price."

I roll my eyes. Of course there's gonna be a price. I should have known that Ryker would ask for something. "What do you want?" I ask, wondering if I'll be able to *afford* this. If he asks for money, I'm out. A Nymph isn't worth that much.

"Some answers." Ryker sits close to Zola and looks at me with this dumb *smirk*. "Who's it for?" he asks without waiting for me to answer.

I shrug. "Some girl. It's her dead grandpa's," I add, to give him context, or whatever that word is.

Ryker laughs. "Went too far, eh?"

"Is that it?" I ask instead.

Ryker looks to the side, like he's deep in thought. "No," he answers. "You and Jasper are always so hush-hush about your Shifts. I want to know why."

How does he know about that?

"Our alter egos are dangerous as fuck," is all I respond, which makes Ryker grin at me.

"Figured as much," he replies. "And I guess I wanna know if you'll help me."

"That's not a question," I frown, making Ryker scoff. "With what?" I add.

Ryker grins at me. Maybe he thinks I'll like what he's about to say. "With putting Crabtree in his place," he finishes.

Huh. I knew Ryker didn't like Lukas, but I didn't know he needed help taking him down. I didn't know he wanted to do that. You know Crabtree is a dick when even other Enchanters want him to shut his yap.

"I can't speak for Jasper," I respond, "but I'm in. No deal necessary."

Ryker looks thrilled (a feeling I don't get that often) about my response. "Then you have a deal, Hudson," he affirms.

I hate walking into Meera even more than I hate walking into Gleera. I yank my hood over my head, so no one will see me. Even though I know the Nymphs here will sense I'm not one of them, why add to the humiliation by having one of them recognize me?

As I walk through the halls, trying to remember where the Pixie's room is, I decide on a plan of attack. There's no way in Hell I'm ever telling her this fixing-up thing was my idea. That was something I worked out with Ryker. If my own grandfather wasn't dead and buried, I probably wouldn't have gone to so much trouble for a fucking Nymph. She's not even worth the air I breathe.

I finally find her and Nora's room. From what I can remember, Nora wasn't as easy to squash as the Pixie. Still, I don't want to run into either of them while completing this *drop-off*.

Even though I want to book it out of here as quickly as possible, I look down at the golden pocket watch. It's probably an antique, expensive – and anyone with a brain would see the now-healthy glow shining from it and know it was a Trinket. Those things are fucking expensive. I'm sure this one takes you to the Overworld. I'd never go there in a million years, but others would. It'd suck if this got stolen if it belonged to a grandfather – even a grandfather Nymph.

I finally look right and left, seeing no one is down here. Perfect. But I need to do this quickly because I can hear what I think are two girls chit-chatting from one of the side stairwells. They'll be up here any minute. I pound on the door twice, leave the Trinket on the carpeted floor in front of the dorm, and dart to the right. I'm gone within seconds, before the door can be opened.

A wave of fear makes me start to sweat as Diego and I cross the cold, empty grasses fringing the front of campus. It's well past ten PM, and no one else is out here. Typical. At the beginning of the school year, everyone's always paranoid about breaking the rules. Boring.

We've already made it past the prof dorms with no issues – typical, too. Getting caught isn't what I'm afraid of, anyway. Finger-wagging and lectures don't freak me out – but that creepy-as-fuck thing does.

Diego never told me outright that he didn't believe me, but I can tell that he thinks this is just something fun to do – sneaking out at the beginning of term. Maybe he's excited about looking for something creepier than us. Maybe I would have felt the same way if I hadn't seen the thing before. I see it whenever I close my eyes now. I feel like a coward! But there's no way I can escape it. It's like it's bored a hole into my brain.

We lean against the fence, looking back at the campus. "We could just Shift here, you know," Diego tells me. "No one's around. And we both know the security guards change at ten. Cameras won't be watched for, what? Five minutes?"

I frown at him. "Your fucking fire wings can light up all of Upper Gomada," I remind him.

Diego laughs happily at my comment. "Aw, what? You scared of getting caught, Hudson?" he teases me.

Maybe, I reply in my head. *If we get caught, there's no way we can investigate that thing again.*

Even though part of me never wants to see that ghost thing again, the other part wants to know what it is and if it's a threat to us. If it was watching the school – or, at least, that's what it looked like the ghost was doing – then it may be planning to do something on-campus. And that affects me and Diego.

"Nah," I dismiss. "Just don't want anyone getting in the way of this."

Diego turns his head from side to side, considering. "Fine," he agrees. "I see your point – if the thing's really out there." He grins at me now, showing me he's not fully convinced about the *thing* in the first place.

I glare at him. "D'you think I'd make this up, Jasper?"

"No idea," he smirks, causing me to glare harder at him. "Anyway, you have a point, for once. Let's circle the outer perimeter and shift from there."

Now mid-air over the fence, just like Monday night, I dump my clothes behind a big tree that I'll recognize on my way back before sprinting to where I was about twenty-four hours ago. My heart is thumping in my chest as I run on all fours. I can feel an angry or frustrated kind of sensation inside me as I go.

The Tedla's mad. He's mad that I'm going back.

I'm surprised. Usually, the Tedla and I don't fight like this. But he's clearly pissed that I'm putting us both in danger again. This is more evidence that this thing we're going after is fucked up and not just some typical Shifter or ghost. It disappeared into thin air. I don't know of any Enchanter or Shifter who can do that. But it's not like I'm super-smart in Enchanter 101. Maybe Ryker would know – but I'm not about to let anyone else in on this. Diego is more than enough, especially since he's suspicious of what's happening in the Gomada Thicket.

I'm ignoring the Tedla as much as I can when a sudden *flash* rips the black sky from up ahead. Diego's Shift must be finished. Case in point: I look up and a big-ass firebird is flying over the treetops. Diego and I would sometimes spar or scrimmage together, but always off-campus and never with any witnesses. He usually has the advantage because of flight – but there have been a few times when I've taken him down because of the height of my jumps.

I run faster to catch up with him, even though he's actually following me. As soon as I get to the hilled area and see a peek of campus from where I'm standing, tree branches crack and split above me. When I look up, Diego swings his body down to where I'm positioned. He lands beside me, folding his wings. His dark brown eyes frown at me – maybe he can sense that I'm freaked, even though I don't think I'm showing anything right now.

We wait.

Minutes turn into a half hour, but we don't see, hear, or sense anything. Even the wildlife in the Gomada Thicket seems to be back to life. Crickets hum. Animals rush through the bushes. Things are normal – or they feel that way. It's too weird. It's too different. Not like it was last night. The thicket seemed dead; scared to make a sound last night. And now – what? Everything's just hunky-dory?

We eventually decide to split up and explore the area by ourselves. The only thing is, a ghost like that – if that's what the creature was – isn't gonna leave any kind of clues. No foot-prints, no odours, no signs of life. When Diego and I meet up again an hour later, we both shake our heads in resignation. When I see his face, I'm worried that he may actually think I made everything up – maybe to distract him or just be a dick. And honestly, now that we're back here, at the scene of the crime, or whatever, and nothing's happened, I'm kind of wondering if it was all in my head.

But if it *was* all in my head, why was the Tedla so scared before and even now? What's the reason, if I was imagining things? The Tedla's never bullshitted me before. What I saw last night has to mean something. Maybe it sensed that two Shifters were out looking for it and didn't want to mess with us. Maybe it's out haunting somebody else.

I have to trust the Tedla, even if I don't trust myself. That damp feeling from last night is still being felt by him. Something fucked up is out here, and I need to find out what it is. And if it knows that we're after it, we *really* need to get our shit together and find it before it finds us.

Something above my head lights up part of the night sky, causing me to look up immediately.

What the fuck is that? I wonder as the white flash shoots over the treetops. It's going fast, but not so fast that we can't follow it with our eyes. It's not normal, but I don't have the same feeling I did last night. But I still sense that the *flash* isn't like me.

Nymph.

What the fuck is a *Nymph* doing out here?

Diego and I look at each other, shooting after it like bullets. Diego will probably catch it first because he's faster than me and has the wings, to boot. I'll be on foot, but I can get to it if it lands. This may not be the ghost, but at least it's something to do.

Seven

ARYA'S FLIGHT

Opening the door, I'm shocked to see Grandpa's pocket watch sitting on the floor outside my dorm room. I reach down and pick it up immediately, causing the folded-up note on top of it to fall. I inspect the pocket watch, even opening it up for good measure. It's completely fixed. How could this have happened?

I bend down to pick up the note. I'm surprised by what it says, especially since I don't know who wrote it.

Arya,

I saw what happened this morning and felt bad for you. I fixed your Trinket.
No thanks necessary.
Ryker Johnson

For the first time this week (and it's only Tuesday night), I feel there could be more than a handful of good people at Gomada Academy. Who is this Ryker person? If he could fix my grandfather's Trinket, that means he's an Enchanter. Nymphs may be able to fix them, but based on the damage this Trinket suffered, there's no way one of us would have been strong enough to fix it. That's a complicated sort of magic that Enchanters or Enchantresses with two Affinities can tap into. When Nymphs only have one, that makes that kind of 'summoning power' more difficult.

I'm filled with relief and gratitude to the point that my eyes fill with tears. Even though this Ryker person says I don't need to thank him, I still want to try.

Stepping back into the dorm, I close the door and place the antique into my pocket. Cole was such a jerk to break it the way he did. He's a violent, out-of-control bully who clearly needs to undergo some form of therapy or anger management class. I hate that I have to even be in the same school as him, let alone have him as my Mentor!

Crossing back to my bed, I sit at the foot and think about what to do. I've already finished my homework – and not just because I like to keep up with my studies. I needed something to distract me from how gutted I felt. But I'm still angry, riled up, and helpless even hours later. I'm not used to feeling these negative emotions, but I desperately need to figure out how to stop Cole from tormenting me. It's only been two days, and he's clearly got it out for me – even when I've apologized.

There's only one thing I can think of that could fix this.

Get stronger.

I wonder if going to a teacher or even the Headmistress would do much good. I'm sure the school has rules against bullying and discrimination against others based on their race – but someone like Cole would never listen to authority. In fact,

I bet he'd retaliate against me even more if I 'tattled' on him. That leaves me with taking care of it myself – which terrifies me, but maybe it will help me activate my electrical abilities. This would also help me to improve in field classes with Professor Xhao. Maybe, in a warped way, this could help me succeed in school.

Nora comes home from her early-evening jog, and we get dinner together. I begin to get antsy when it's close to nine o'clock at night. If I want to start training, I know I need to do so where no one else can see me. I can't let anyone else know I have a weakness – that I'm a half-Nymph. If that means going to the edge of campus, I have to do it.

While Nora is finishing her homework, I tell her I'm going to go for a walk and then grab my jean jacket. Seeing the burn mark on its right sleeve makes me even more determined to get tougher – not just with my Affinity, but with my backbone, too. It's only been two days, but I'm tired of him already. And I don't want to take three years of abuse from him.

I need to fix this now!

It's cold and dark as I walk away from Meera and to the edge of campus, where the wrought-iron fence surrounds Gomada Academy. There are a few students around, but not many. I feel damp embarrassment as they walk across the school grounds. Any one of them could see me practicing and figure out my secret for themselves. Maybe I'm being paranoid, and I'm sure people aren't watching me – but I can't be too careful. Maybe I can just go to the Nymph's Field and practice there. It's off-campus, yes, but maybe going there would still be allowed since it's technically still a part of the school. That makes me feel less worried about leaving the school grounds – but only a little bit.

I finally make it to the gates that signal the entrance and exit to campus. They're still open – maybe because it's before curfew. I expected security guards here, but maybe the giant security cameras stationed at different sections of the fence mean that they're not always necessary.

I cross through the open gates, feeling a damp sweat hit the back of my neck as I go. The wind is picking up – or is it just my imagination? – as I officially make my way off-campus. When I see the security camera stationed at the top of one of the gates behind me, I desperately want to scream, 'I'm just going to the Nymph's Field to practice,' at the camera. I don't want my teachers or the security guards watching the cameras to think I'm doing anything wrong (and I'm not... Right?).

Shivering as I begin to make my way to the Nymph's Field, trying to remember where I went just a few hours earlier, I try to get my bearings and look for landmarks. Okay. I saw that tree earlier... This must be the right way.

Finally, I get that same intense chill I got the last time I came to this part of the grounds near the Gomada Thicket. I see the familiar outline of the Nymph's Field. The Gomada Mountains are beyond it. Those are good landmarks. I should've just remembered to look for those. I feel dumb thinking about that.

Leaves crunch under my feet as I approach the still-open gates. Phew! I guess they close at ten. I may try and get here earlier next time (tomorrow?) because I need to hurry up and get some training in before someone comes to lock up the Field for the night. Looking at Grandpa's pocket watch, at least I have a good half hour of training time before I need to quickly make my way back. Walking here took much longer than I thought. It took about ten minutes before, but because I was so unsure of myself this time and didn't have students to follow, the walk took me about twenty minutes. I bet leaving campus also caused some foot-dragging. I hate breaking or even *thinking* I'm breaking the rules.

Walking deeper into the abandoned field, I decide to cross close to the other side in case someone else shows up. Now that I know the way, I feel more comfortable here. I must tap into my surroundings and the wind to fully perform my Affinity. If I'm cold and scared, it won't work well. I need to be calmer. So I keep walking.

I stop mid-step when I notice a strange mist or fog pooling up from around the grass. It's at my feet and as far as I can see. I know fog comes from clouds, so I'm confused by what I'm seeing. This fog wasn't here just a minute ago.

This is scary. I'm all alone and didn't bring my phone. I look left and right, feeling my heart pumping madly in my ears. "It's like my face is covered in plastic wrap, because it's hard to breathe or even form a coherent thought. It's the same feeling of helplessness.

When I turn around, my mouth hangs open. I want to scream but can't. A strange *figure* is about twenty feet behind me, with large, brilliant yellow eyes. It's staring at me. I get a very odd, horrifying feeling that creeps down my spine and doesn't stop until it reaches my toes. I can't move.

It has limbs but doesn't look like it's touching the ground. Is it floating? There's a strange mist pooling from its frame, which might be what surrounds me now.

Is this a ghost? I've never seen one before – and I never really wanted to, either. I don't believe in ghosts, or just don't like them. I've never really thought much about them – but it's hard to fight what's staring at you, plain as day.

The ghost, or creature, begins to hover over the ground. It's coming closer!

My God!

Thunder cracks from above my head. The wind picks up in speed, whipping my hair past my shoulders and in various directions. At first, I think my electrical ability is finally taking shape – what perfect timing that would be! – but instead, warmth spreads down my back, and sparkling white wings appear. I see the vibrant glittering in my peripheral vision.

I've practiced flying at home with Dad. I've improved over the years, but it's still hard to do. There's no time to think about that now. The ghost is still *coming for me*, and I have to get out of here!

I jump as hard and as high as I can after taking a running start to the left. My wings immediately take control, like they have a life of their own, and I'm already airborne. I don't know how fast or how high this ghost can float or fly, so I quickly make my way as high up as I can. Even though I hate to do this, I know I need to fly *over* the ghost to escape the Gomada Mountains. I'm losing too much air up here, and less breathing means I'll be in less control of my flying.

I soar past the ghost, who is looking up and watching me escape. How scary! My entire body is trembling as I shoot past it. I'm so scared that it will follow me that I forget about my logic and senses and just catapult myself over the Gomada Thicket. I don't know where I'm going or what I'm doing, but I'm way too scared to go close to the school again.

What if the creature *waits* for me at the gates to Gomada Academy? What if it finds me? I need to get as far away from the Nymph's Field as possible!

Wind and electricity pulse through me as I glide over the treetops. I look up to either side of me, seeing dark clouds churning around me. I don't know if my terror is causing this or if a real storm is coming. My hair is flying behind me. My arms are pinned to my sides. I'm too scared to move anything other than my wings and eyes.

So far, the Gomada Thicket looks okay – at least, from above. I wonder if the ghost can follow me from this high or teleport. I don't know much about paranormal stuff like that – but I don't want to take any chances.

After flying for a while, I suddenly realize that if I go too far, I may be too tired to make it back to campus. And if I fly too far, I may get lost. I finally swing myself down to the tree-tops, ready to find a place to rest – maybe a branch or something. I need to save my energy. If I get too tired, my wings may disappear. And if I'm too scared, I may not be able to activate my wings again.

I hate being in this position. If I was tougher, things would be easier for me.

Landing clumsily onto a thick tree branch, I try my best to control my thoughts and feelings.

It was coming for me!

It was looking straight at me!

*What was a **ghost** doing so close to campus?*

Was it looking for me or someone else?

These thoughts of mine are *not* helping me calm down!

I don't know how long I stay frozen on this tree branch, looking down at the world below. The only comforting thing about my situation right now is that the Gomada Thicket *seems* to be normal. I see owls much lower down. I hear crickets chirping, even against the harsh wind. I can almost feel nature here – something Nymphs can usually tap into, especially if they have an Affinity like Earth, Wind, and Water. If the forest life here is acting normally, does that mean the ghost isn't here?

Just as I think that, a frightening *red glow* breaks the clouds from overhead at the other end of the forest. My wings flicker.

Oh, no! I'm tired and terrified! If I stay here any longer, I may lose my wings and be unable to return to my dorm!

I take a few deep breaths. *The ghost wasn't red,* I try to tell myself. *I don't know what that is, but it's definitely not the creature I saw at the Nymph's Field.*

But still, what *is* that?

I'm never coming to the Nymph's Field or the Gomada Thicket again! I don't care if I'm the weakest Nymph to ever enter the academy, or if Cole beats me up every day! This will *not* happen again!

I jump off the branch, and for a split second, I'm afraid I will fall to my death. But my wings flap, and I'm pushing myself farther into the sky. I think I'm more desperate to survive and be in a comfortable place than I am afraid – at least right now. Or, maybe it's a firm fifty-fifty. But whatever I'm feeling, I tap into it and surge it through my being as I fixate on one destination: Gomada Academy.

As I fly in the opposite direction, I realize that the fiery red thing is nowhere to be seen. Where did it go? I guess it doesn't matter because I need to get out of here, and if no other monsters are around, maybe I have a fighting chance after all.

I barrel over the last few rows of dark trees, feeling the weight and hearing the tremor of the thunder from above me. Clouds are heavy with the threat of rain, but I don't care. I need to be somewhere safe. And rain, getting caught in a storm, isn't nearly as scary as being attacked by a ghost or a fiery red thing.

Soaring over what seems to be a familiar black rectangle, I register the wrought-iron fence that houses the academy. I quickly descend, hoping no one sees or catches me. But getting caught or detention is much better than being hunted down by an evil ghost! Still, I choose to land away from Meera, where trees fringe the outer part of campus.

It seems darker as I finally land on two feet – or is it just my imagination? I fall down as soon as my boots touch the ground. I always get dizzy when I feel the earth beneath me after flying – and I've never flown for so long. Both flights knocked me out, making me weak and disoriented. If that ghost comes for me now—

I struggle to my feet when the rustling of nearby bushes and low-lying tree branches catches my attention. Oh, my God! The thing really is coming back!

I back away, still panicking. I'm way too tired to fight, or run. There's no way I'll be able to fly away again, even summon my wings, or generate any air and wind to use against an enemy.

I'm a sitting duck!

I flinch when a shadow steps out from the cover of the foliage – and I'm not even a hair less terrified when I see Cole coming into view of the moonlight. I'm weak and dizzy – no match against a ghost, a fiery red thing, or a bully.

Cole stops when we make eye contact.

"The fuck are you doing out here, past curfew?" he asks – or demands.

I'm surprised that I still have the strength for things like frustration and annoyance, but I tense up as soon as he speaks. His nails-on-a-chalkboard voice is enough to send me through the roof, even if I'm wiped out.

"I don't have time for your bullshit!" I snap, surprised by my tone and language – but unable to help either. I'm probably so exhausted and horrified by all I saw that I'm not acting like myself.

Cole looks caught off guard by my counterattack but suddenly throws his head back and laughs. As if the sound of his voice wasn't bad enough, the loud laughter, like he's some kind of sick hyena—

"Shut up!" I quickly blurt out, terrified that his insane laughter will attract the spirit or ghost from the Nymph's Field.

"What the hell is your–" he begins, in-between guffaws, as I finally find my feet and approach him.

"Shut up!" I demand, pushing him to get his attention because two warnings aren't enough.

Cole looks down at me, very much annoyed now. "What the fuck is your–"

"There's a ghost walking around here!" I hiss. "So shut up, so it doesn't find us and eat us!"

Cole's green eyes widen with alarm (I've never seen him wear *that* expression before) as he stares down at me. I would have thought that he would have made endless fun of me for talking about ghosts, but instead, he looks like this – like he believes me.

"A ghost? Where?" he asks, which throws me off the rails. No mocking or belittling or 'dumb Pixie' comments, like I thought he'd make. He's asking a legitimate question!

"The Nymph's Field," I report.

Cole's head whips forward, probably in the general direction of the Nymph's Field.

"Why do you look like that?" I finally demand.

His green eyes look down at me tiredly. It looks like he doesn't want to talk to me anymore. "Look like what?" he asks angrily.

Cole probably thinks I'm going to insult him. And maybe I would have, under different circumstances.

"Like you believe me," I explain, as he folds his arms defensively.

Cole looks left and right – and I realize that he's making sure the coast is clear before he bends his head down (which sends a chill down my spine) and murmurs,

"Because I saw it last night."

I gape at what he tells me. A part of me was hoping that what I saw at the Nymph's Field was some sort of weird illusion. I was clinging to any and every possibility that what I saw wasn't real. But someone else – a tough bully like Cole – has also seen the ghost. That means it can't be fake or some figment of my imagination.

Cole frowns at me. "What? Cat got your tongue, Pixie?"

"Where did you see it?" I ask instead, frowning back at him in return.

He shrugs. "None of your business."

When I seethe – which might be more obvious than I would have wanted – Cole rolls his eyes and adds, "Off-campus. In the thicket."

"Were you in there just now?" I gasp, realizing that the red glow I saw before could be–

"None of your business," he repeats abruptly, which screams a big fat 'yes' to me.

I fold my arms. "Don't you think we should maybe work together to figure this out if we both saw a ghost on and around campus?"

Cole looks at me as if I've sprouted a new head. "I don't need any help," he dismisses.

I scoff at that. "Fine. When you get eaten by that ghost, I'm sure you'll at least give it indigestion."

Cole grabs my arm as I turn around to head back to Meera. I turn around, bracing myself for him to attack me again. His green eyes are firm and angry.

"Don't fucking go out there again, Pixie," he tells me. "I know you were flying over there. You're gonna get yourself killed."

Yanking my arm away, I shoot back, "As if you care about that."

He laughs once. "I don't give a shit about you."

"I don't care about you, either!" I counter gruffly – or as gruffly as I can muster.

We glare at one another for a long time. The fire in his green eyes scares me, but I don't want to show him I'm afraid. Instead, I try to look as mad at him as he is at me.

Cole causes me to jump back when he yanks his white hoodie over his head and breezes past me. He moves with agility, even though he's probably weighing himself down with nicotine and tar from the plethora of cigarettes he sucks on all day.

Even though he's an obnoxious jerk, I know he's right about one thing. If I go out to the thicket or the Nymph's Field again, I may not make it out alive.

I can't sleep. Thankfully, my tossing and turning does nothing to wake Nora, who seems to be a deep sleeper. I was thankful I didn't wake her up when I returned to Meera. When I finally close my eyes, exhaustion taking over my fear; it's past four AM.

Even though I only got two hours of sleep, I get out of bed at six o'clock and start to get ready for my day, same as usual. I make my bed. I pack my bookbag. I get dressed. I brush my teeth. Every little thing I do, though, just seems off, and damaged. Nothing can erase the fact that I saw a real-life ghost last night. I wish I could talk to Nora about it, but I worry that she wouldn't believe me. She is already up and out of the dorm. Nora's bed is made, and her bookbag is taken off the back of the chair at her workstation. I couldn't tell her, even if I wanted to be honest about what happened to me last night.

I'm surprised to see a text from Nora when I lock up the dorm and check my phone for the first time since unplugging it from the wall. Each morning, I usually check my phone for messages from my parents, and I also scroll through some social media pages. But today, I just don't feel like *looking at anything*.

Where were you last night?

I wanted to go get some practice in before class today

I know this isn't a lie. Even though it didn't happen the way I wanted it to, I got some training last night. And I never want to go through anything like that again.

I feel guilty for only giving Nora a partial truth. If I want us to be so close, how can we get that far with me keeping things from her? Maybe this isn't a typical thing to share, but–

I stop my train of thought. I need to get to school before History class starts. All my teachers seem to have the same zero-tolerance policy for things like lateness and truancy.

I'm met with an overcast and dreary sky as soon as I open one of the double doors to Meera. Not many students were in the lobby – and now, I see why. Everyone assumes that it will rain soon – no one is hanging around. I walk a bit faster to get to the academy before I'm rained on.

When I follow the Nymph students ahead, someone suddenly clears their throat behind me. It's loud enough that I think it's meant for me – but that can't be possible. I haven't made any friends yet, besides Nora. I still turn around, though, just in case. As I turn, I smell the disgusting odour of cigarette smoke, and my shoulders tense.

Cole frowns at me. "You're slower than usual this morning, Pixie."

I narrow my eyes at him. "What are you doing over here?" I

find myself demanding. "You've made it pretty obvious you think we're all trash."

Cole shrugs under his arms as he places his cigarette to his lips. Gross! I don't know how he can smoke all day. "No. Just you," he dismisses, breathing the smoke through his mouth as he insults me.

"What are you doing here?" I ask again, trying not to become baited by him, as he leans off the brick building and approaches me.

"We need to talk," is all he says.

I gape at him before continuing to make my way to the academy. I don't have very much time to spare, and I was hoping to get some coffee before first period. I'll need it more than ever if I plan to get through this day without falling asleep in class.

"You want to talk to me?" I rephrase without turning around.

Cole catches up to me without batting an eye – even though I question how he can do anything physical after inhaling so much poison.

"Don't flatter yourself," he snaps, yanking his green hoodie over his head – probably so no one sees him with me. Jerk. "I want to know what you saw last night," he adds.

I can't help myself. "None of your business," I quote.

Cole laughs once. "Knee-slapper," he states dryly.

Maybe last night, when I was terrified of what I saw and realized that Cole and I witnessed the same horrible thing, I wanted to work with him. But after everything he's done and continues to do, I want nothing to do with him. Being in the Mentorship Program with him is awful enough – I refuse to add anything else to the mix.

"I don't owe you anything," I dismiss as we border the academy.

Cole grunts something that sounds like 'stupid bitch' under his breath, so I shoot him a glare. He stares right back at me.

"What happened to your little sing-song last night?" he asks, probably referring to me wanting to work with him to figure out what we saw off-campus.

"I remembered how obnoxious you are," I counter.

Cole rolls his eyes. "By the way, ghosts don't eat people, Pixie," he suddenly tells me, as if he's picking apart every little thing I've said to him over the past three days – which isn't much.

"Hudson? You're up before noon?"

Cole turns immediately with a greeting of sorts from behind him. The person who calls out to him steps to the side, which causes me to see him for the first time. He's not as tall as Cole, but way taller than me. He has cornrows, brown eyes, and a deep voice. One look at the enormous black panther following at his side tells me he's an Enchanter.

"Hey, Johnson," Cole responds casually, which surprises me. I thought Cole wanted nothing to do with any race other than his own.

The boy, whose last name must be Johnson, jerks his head in my direction after giving me a smile in greeting. When he smiles at me, I feel my legs shake.

"Who's this? Girlfriend? When's the apocalypse?" he jokes.

Cole snorts a laugh at that. "In her dreams," he spits.

"Never," I remark at the same time.

The boy laughs hard at that. "Forget I said anything," he states, holding his hands up, as if we have a badge and a gun. "I'm Ryker. Ryker Johnson," he tells me, holding out his hand to me now.

Oh, my God! This is the boy who fixed my Trinket! And

he's super nice, funny, and cute! The fact that he seems to know Cole is a minor misstep that I can overlook.

I hold out my hand and shake his. As soon as I touch him, I feel a jolt pulse through my chest. "Hi," I breathe. "Um, I'm Arya Willow," I add, temporarily forgetting who I am.

"Oh! Right. Putting a name to the face, finally," Ryker nods. We let go of each other at about the same time. "Nice to meet you. Hope your Trinket's working again."

"Yes, it is. Thank you so much," I gush, even though I don't know if my grandpa's pocket watch is functioning now. For some reason, I just don't want to tell him that it may not be.

Ryker turns his left wrist to face him, pulling up his leather jacket's cuff. His black leather jacket is a perfect match to his dark jeans, skin, and Familiar. Everything about him screams *smooth*.

"Well, I gotta get to class. Nice to meet you," the Enchanter tells me, slapping Cole's shoulder as he passes us. "Catch you later, Hudson," he calls over his shoulder as his black panther Familiar follows.

As the panther walks away, it turns and eyes Cole. How bad of a person he must be if Familiars and animals dislike him?

Cole stares right back at the black panther – figures as much – and folds his arms when Ryker is gone.

"What the fuck was *that*?" he asks me, causing me to squirm in place.

Oh, no! If someone like Cole discovers that I think Ryker is cute and fascinating, there's no telling what kind of evil he'll unleash on me!

"What are you talking about?" I try to sigh.

Cole rolls his eyes. "God, you're so pathetic," he scoffs, turning on his heel and walking away from me.

As soon as Cole leaves – finally giving me peace – I'm suddenly okay with the fact that he made fun of me, that I'm so tired I can't see straight, that I'm dreading my fourth period Field Practice class.

This Ryker Johnson boy has suddenly changed everything for me – and at the perfect time, too.

COLE'S BIND

For the rest of the week, I'm in a really shitty mood. The only good thing about this shitshow of a week is that I'm finally able to sleep on Wednesday – maybe because that's the first night I don't sneak out to be a ghost hunter. But even when I'm sleeping, I see the figure in my messed-up dreams. I just can't get away from it, even if I sleep. Even if I'm in class, listening to stupid shit I'll never need to remember once I graduate.

I'm pretty sure Diego is unconvinced about the ghost. I know he believes that I didn't make anything up – and when I told him that the Pixie saw the ghost, too, that gets him going – but I think not seeing it is what's making him think twice. I don't know how else to convince him. If the ghost was in the Gomada Thicket on Monday but suddenly decided to visit the Nymph's-slash-Enchanter's Field on Tuesday, doesn't that mean something?

It's getting closer and closer to campus. What's it looking for? Why haunt a school? Or is it going to do more than just scare students?

It would sure help if Diego and the Pixie worked with me on this. Diego is gone from the dorm more than ever, and I don't care enough about the Pixie to know where she is. All I know is that I'm the only one who seems to give a shit about what's happening, what could happen.

It's Friday afternoon during Literature class, where I already want to end my life, when I get an idea. If the ghost is getting closer to campus, maybe it's been captured on the security cameras. Diego and I know where they're positioned and can usually avoid getting caught – but a ghost wouldn't know how to do any of that. Maybe getting into the computers in the Headmistress' office or the security station is the way to go. The only thing is, I doubt the Headmistress will let me walk in and make myself at home. I may have to settle for the security station on the school's faculty level. And tonight would be the perfect night to do it, because everyone will be at that stupid 'welcome to Gomada Academy' mixer.

It's not like I haven't done this kind of thing before – but I'm usually with Diego when I pull this kind of shit. Even though I hate thinking this way, I'm not sure if I can pull it off without his help. I'm pretty sure that Diego actually wants to go to this party. It used to be that he and I would mock this kind of stuff and ditch as soon as no one was watching. Now, though...

Does it have something to do with Lucy? I'm so fed up with these Enchanters who keep thinking they're better than the rest of us.

But this gives me an idea as I finish up my Field Practice sparring with Diego. Maybe I need to show up to the mixer so my absence isn't so obvious. It's not like people notice me – but I know Professor Qadir would notice if I was there. If I go for a little while and then slip out, it may be less weird than me not going at all. Besides, these beginning-of-the-year things are always mandatory. I can't afford to get into any more trouble with Professor Qadir if I skip this thing.

I leave my dorm with Diego in front of me. I lock up, trying to brace myself for what will happen. I hate social things like this. I always feel like I don't belong. And I guess it makes me feel even worse that Diego seems to be looking forward to this *mixer*. That makes me even more on edge about explaining my mission to him. He won't want any part of it if he's already gung-ho about this stupid party.

"So, you're looking forward to this, eh?" I ask, trying to sound as casual as possible, as Diego and I make our way down the hallway.

Looks like lots of Shifters are looking forward to tonight, too, because the girls are dressed up, and the guys look like they put in an effort. A few hot girls watch us walk by them – but I know they're looking at Diego. It doesn't bother me. I don't have the time or the energy for girls.

Diego shrugs as we walk. "Not really," he responds, which fills me with hope, even though I hate admitting it. Diego has changed a lot over the school break – and I want to find out why.

"Just something to do," he finishes, causing me to nod, but I'm still not convinced.

"Yeah," is all I say.

We're quiet until we get to the lobby of Feara – and that's when it happens. Diego looks down at me, and once I take in his black dress shirt with the sleeves rolled up, I know he's a goner.

"So, don't get all war lord on me, but–" Diego starts to say, adding off-hand as he pushes open one of the double doors to the dorm, "I have a date tonight. With Lucy."

Even though I knew this was coming, I still feel like I've been punched in the gut by someone wearing a spiked glove.

"Huh," I finally comment because I don't know what else to say. There's really nothing to say right now. Diego knows how I feel about him getting close to an Enchantress. He doesn't need me to spell it out for him again. I just think he's signing his own death certificate.

"What? No comments? No judgements?" Diego teases, as we walk toward Gomada Academy. The party is in the Reception Hall, one level up from the Dining Hall. I don't go up there very often – but the thing is, the Reception Hall is on the same level as the faculty offices and the security station.

I pause. Is Diego baiting me, or legit surprised that I'm not shitting all over his plans? He's looking at me intently now, so I think he's waiting for an attack. But I don't have the energy to keep confronting him about this. If he's going to shoot himself in the foot, he's going to have to do it. If I, his best friend, can't stop him, then no one else will.

"No. Do what you gotta do," is all I respond.

"Huh. I'm surprised you're actually cool with this," Diego breathes, as we follow a few Enchanters (fuck) into the school. "Or maybe I shouldn't be," he states weirdly, like he's hoping I'll bite. Which I do.

"What is that supposed to mean?" I demand, looking up at him in shock. What the fuck is he getting at now? Maybe he is pissed that I've been shitting all over his hang-outs with Lucy, and now it's payback time.

"Just that you're spending a ton of time with that Nymph, when you were riding my ass about Lucy the entire time," Diego responds, some fire behind the mocking in his voice. He means business.

I groan. "Good God, Jasper. I'm torturing her, not hanging on her every word. There's a fucking difference."

What the literal fuck is wrong with Diego? Has Lucy really gotten to him that badly that now he's not even thinking straight? No wonder he doesn't have the same interest in the ghost as I do. Maybe he's more interested in getting with Lucy than ensuring the school doesn't explode.

"Really?" Diego challenges me, folding his arms now. He looks way bigger than me – more than just a couple of inches. "Taking her Trinket? Trying to light her hair on fire? Making her cry every day?"

"All for my own personal amusement," I reply easily.

"Sure. If that's the story you wanna stick with," Diego answers gruffly, baiting me a second time. I bite – again.

I glare up at Diego. "What the fuck is your–" I begin, just as he steps in front of me. We're inside the academy now, and students are prancing past us, looking forward to food and underage drinking when no one's looking. I'm more concerned about my best friend's mind, which seems so far up his ass that he can't see straight.

"I don't care who you spend time with, Hudson," Diego tells me firmly, his hazel eyes ripping through me the way they do when he's pissed as hell at me. This isn't good. "But don't be a fucking hypocrite and expect me to be cool with it."

Diego turns on his heel and marches away from me. I watch him go, feeling so angry that I have to stop myself from throwing myself down the hall and jumping him. I know it's not really Diego that's pissing me off. It's that he's being so easily manipulated by Lucy Chapin that's rubbing me the wrong way.

I may have to get over it. If Diego's feelings for Lucy are as strong as they seem, there's no getting through to him – not until she dumps his ass and he realizes how dumb he's been. Until then, I just hope that's the worst thing she does to him.

Walking into the Reception Hall alone feels shitty. Me against all these freaks? This sounds about right. Or am I the freak?

Diego and I don't square off often – and when we do, it's never over a girl. She's already changing him – why can't he see that? At least I know why he was so weird over Break, why he's been weird this week. They've probably been talking and texting the entire time. There's no point in trying to talk him out of it. He's gonna do what he's gonna do.

"Mister Hudson. I'm surprised you're in attendance."

I turn around fast. Professor Qadir is behind me, dressed in a black suit. He's always wearing fancy crap like this. It's like he's on his way to the runway or something. I still think the suit-wearing and proper language are because his alter ego is fucking crazy.

"Attendance is mandatory," I respond.

Professor Qadir arches an eyebrow. "And that sort of thing works on you now, Mr. Hudson?" he asks. He's making a joke. Hilarious.

But at least now that he's seen me, all I have to do is just hang out here for a little while longer before ducking out. That was easier than I thought. Maybe I *can* pull this off by myself.

I hold in an eye roll as Professor Qadir steps to the side and passes me. "Enjoy your evening," he tells me, turning around and heading to the drinks table.

I'm just about to follow him and see if the drinks and food will be enough to keep me here for an extra five minutes when I suddenly spot Ryker. He's without Zola – thank God. Enchanters and Enchantresses usually leave their pets at home for things like this. He's dressed up a little bit, too. Good God, is no one safe from this kind of shit?

I suddenly realize *why* Ryker looks so *put-together*. He's talking to the Pixie. She's looking up at him like he's the smartest and most charming dude she's ever met, twirling her hair in her fingers and giggling about something he must have said. I'd throw up if I'd eaten anything today.

Walking over to the crystal punch bowl, I pick up one of the matching glasses to use. I'm suddenly thirsty. I frown when the glass shatters in my right hand, cutting me. Glass and blood are everywhere. Fuck.

"Slow down, there, tiger."

I look behind me, seeing Taylor Hayden. She looks pretty good tonight, too. I think Taylor's hot as Hell, but I'd never do anything about it. Diego and I know Taylor, because we're all from Houssan. We met on a class trip to Sunset Hills, where Taylor lives. We're friends – sort of – but I don't really like to associate much with girls. They're kind of annoying, whether they're just a friend or more than that.

"Did I get you?" I ask.

Taylor shakes her head 'no', her high red ponytail swishing as she goes. Her favourite colour is red – something anyone and everyone knows, even if they're not her friend. Her red mini skirt and white blouse would turn me on if I wasn't in such a bad mood.

"What's your deal?" Taylor frowns, folding her arms as I grab one of the paper cups near the bowl and leave my mess for someone else to clean up.

"Nothing," I respond, scooping punch into my cup, trying not to break anything else.

"Uh-huh," Taylor comments, clearly unconvinced, as she suddenly picks up a crystal cup and shakes it for me. "See? Still works," she grins, causing me to roll my eyes.

"Did you come here just to annoy me?" I ask, crossing over to the food table and grabbing a (paper) plate.

"Of course. My entire life is to be at your beck and call, Hudson," Taylor scoffs, picking up a plate from behind me and taking some salad. I don't care enough to find out what kind of salad it is – though I'm so hungry I could eat the entire bowl without blinking.

"I guess you're mad about your BFF and Chapin," Taylor states, causing me to stare at her, surprised. I know she's smart, but–

"How do you know that?" I can't help but gasp.

Taylor smirks at me with her red lips and green eyes, happy that she caught me off-guard. I roll my eyes at that. Taylor thinks she knows everything. When she points behind me, I turn to see Lucy and Diego talking. Of course, Lucy didn't get the memo: her stupid white fox is hanging over her shoulder.

I sigh. "And, what? You're all for it?" I ask gruffly.

Taylor shrugs in my peripheral vision. "Whatever makes him happy," she comments, causing me to frown down at her.

"Come on, Hudson," Taylor frowns, poking at me with the clean-ish end of her paper plate that isn't loaded with food. The sight of Diego and Lucy made me lose my appetite. "Why are you so bent on just hanging out with Shifters? The rest of us aren't that bad."

"You mean, the rest of them," I correct her.

She frowns at me before answering, "Sure."

I turn around and decide I need to eat something, so I grab an apple and leave my unused plate at the end of the table, tossing the apple around in my hand as I make my way back to the doors to the Reception Hall. I mingled. I spoke to people. I even got punch and food. I can probably bail in a few minutes.

I notice that the Pixie is just now leaving Ryker's side and is heading in the same general direction as I am. It annoys me that people think it's okay to associate with Enchanters and Enchantresses – like it's no big deal. Am I the only normal person here?

I suddenly get an idea and begin to approach her. It's obvious that the Pixie is trying really hard tonight. Between the goofy look on her face before and the pink blouse and black mini skirt, I bet she's trying to sink her claws into Johnson – poor bastard.

Like a typical Pixie, she doesn't notice me coming until I'm maybe three feet away. She stiffens up as soon as she sees me. Good. I want her to be afraid of me. I want her to see me as the enemy. And if Diego is watching – even better. His accusations are still ringing through my ears.

"What do you want?" she demands, though it sounds like she's more scared than trying to threaten me. As if she could ever threaten me!

"Nothing," I dismiss, looking around at the event. Students and teachers are everywhere, so I can't do much more than this. The best news is, Ryker is talking to Lucy now: they're both within earshot and view of this moment.

"Enjoying the party?" I mockingly ask her.

She frowns at me. "I was, until you showed up," she shoots back.

I sigh at that. "Oh, come on," I respond. "Loosen up a bit and have some punch."

She screams as soon as I toss my punch all over her outfit. It's impossible not to throw my head back and laugh happily. Her reaction is priceless!

"You *asshole*!" she weeps, smacking my chest as I'm still laughing my head off. Oh, my God, I feel so much better now!

She narrows her eyes at me. I can tell that she's mad, even through her tears and smudged makeup. This is amazing!

Suddenly, her eyes go white and the apple flies out of my hand and is now in hers.

"What the fuck are you going to–" I begin, but suddenly keel backward and choke when she shoots the apple right at my trachea.

"Aw, you bitch!" I wheeze, still clasping my throat and trying to suck in a normal breath as my apple falls to the floor beside me. She must have used her damned Air Affinity to shoot the apple right at my throat, because there's no way her aim is that good.

The Pixie stomps away from me – I can tell from my super-hearing and the fact that I smell her leaving. That vanilla scent makes me gag now.

But at least this means I've cheered myself up and stayed at the party a little longer than I intended – good news all around. I can eat my apple and then take off – for good.

Sneaking out of the mixer is easy. Everyone is busy with their own crap and doesn't notice me. I should've known this would be the easier part of the mission. The only problem is, I noticed that Headmistress Frow wasn't at the party – or, at least, I didn't see her when I looked. This may put her on the faculty side of this floor of the academy, making my job a little more difficult.

At least the hallway is empty as I walk through it. My throat is sore now, and I'm trying hard not to cough or clear my throat as I get closer to the faculty side of the building. Fuck that irritating and crybaby Pixie! She's using her stupid Air Affinity to mess with me! If she ever does that again, I'm gonna Shift and scare the shit out of her – girl or not. I hate that she keeps trying to one-up me, but next time, she won't have a prayer of getting past me.

Anyway, I have bigger, more important problems than a

wet blanket. Case in point: the door to the far left of the floor reads, '**SECURITY STATION**'.

I turn left and right, looking all the way down the hall. No one is here – but part of me thinks that I'm not alone. And then, I hear it clearly.

"I don't want anyone else getting wind of this, Mr. Greyson. It's the beginning of the term. The students will go into a frenzy if they catch even a whisper of this."

I recognize that voice. That's why I couldn't find the Headmistress. She's here, with the head of security, Mr. Dumb-As-Fuck Henry Greyson. I know I have to hide, so I duck into one of the little alcove things in the brick wall with a little bench. The wall juts out just enough for me to flatten myself against it. Hopefully, she doesn't hear me. I don't care about Greyson, though. He's fully human and fully clueless.

"I understand, Headmistress."

Their voices aren't carrying anymore. They're probably out in the open now. I hear the door close. They're definitely out here.

"Something is clearly watching the academy, Mr. Greyson," Headmistress Frow practically whispers – but since my senses are so strong, I can hear everything she says. "Why can't our cameras get a decent read on it?"

Holy shit. They're definitely talking about the ghost. And if their cameras aren't doing a good job of picking it up, there's no point in me trying to break in and see for myself. Maybe it's a good idea if I just listen to them. They may know something I don't.

"I don't know, Miss Frow. My guards are just as confused. It's always hidden in shadow or fog. Even our cameras positioned at different angles can't get a good read on it."

"It has to be a spirit or paranormal entity," the Headmistress suggests. She sounds worried. Well, if the most powerful Enchantress here is freaked, we're probably in deep shit. I may not like their race, but I know enough to understand the shittiness of the situation if the Headmistress, herself, is spooked by the ghost.

"We can put up more cameras. Increase security at the gates," Greyson suggests. What a loser.

"I'm afraid more cameras and security guards won't fix the issue, Mr. Greyson. Whatever is out there is clearly impervious to both. We'll have to ensure the students do not venture out past curfew."

Now's the time to see if they've caught anything on their cameras over the past few days.

"We haven't seen anyone sneak out past curfew," Greyson reports. Moron. "Some strange lights and flashing, but that's about it."

Diego.

The Pixie.

"Well, we may have to exacerbate the consequences of breaking curfew," Headmistress Frow decides.

Great. Not that things like detention or suspension scare me, but still. Way to ruin a good time, Leona. Or, I guess, us trying to figure out what the hell this thing is, what it's capable of, why it's here.

"That sounds like a plan, Miss Frow. I'll tell the guards to be on the alert."

They walk right up to the alcove. With a small turn of the head, I see them pass me. I'm surprised Leona didn't sense me. Maybe she's so freaked by the ghost to pay attention. I don't expect Clueless Grey to notice me, that's for damn sure.

I'm just about to hide and figure out my next move when I hear the Headmistress say, from all the way down the hall,

"I think the time has come for me to see if I can discover the creature, myself, Mr. Greyson. Perhaps tomorrow night."

"Oh, Miss Frow, do you think that's safe? Necessary?" I hear Greyson suck up – but I'm no longer listening now.

Headmistress Frow is checking this out. And I want to be there when she does. The thing is, I may want some back-up if I'm tailing her. I'm sure Diego won't want to get in on this – not after our confrontation about Lucy.

That leaves me with one last option.

Fuck my life.

Nine

ARYA AND NORA'S FIELD TRIP

Nora looks excited as we approach the gates to Gomada Academy. Come to think of it, I'm pretty excited, too. I will be teleporting to Florida – specifically, the city of Lakeland, where Nora lives – to shop with Nora. She suggested the idea to me last night, after the party.

Maybe she was planning to go by herself and only offered to take me with her because she knew I had an awful time at the mixer last night – but regardless of the reason, I was really happy that she wanted to spend more time with me. Maybe Nora and I can become good friends sooner than later – which I really want to happen.

Nora picks up the sapphire pendant around her neck, rubbing the faintly-glowing gem with her index finger. This must be her Trinket that will transport us back to the Overworld. I'm so excited to be able to head back to Earth – even if it's to a place I've never been before. Anything will feel better than Gomada. I need an escape – and something tells me that Nora does, too.

I don't know much about Trinkets. I've only used them a couple of times – and only once alone. But Nora, who seems to do this kind of thing often, holds her hand out to me, showing her black-painted fingernails.

"Take my hand," she tells me. "And don't let go."

As soon as my hand clasps hers, a strong blue light envelopes us. Just like when I teleported from San Francisco to Gomada, the warmth that holds me now is not too hot but still startling. I feel like I'm being rocked back and forth – which is weird, because this didn't happen last time. Maybe it's happening now because two people are using one Trinket?

Like when I used Grandma's topaz ring (which I'll never wear, thanks to what Cole did to Grandpa's pocket watch) to teleport from San Francisco to Gomada, the 'travel time' is quick and painless – just uncomfortable. I imagine with more practice, it'll feel like riding the bus or driving. It's how many different people get from realm to realm – human or not. I guess I need to get used to it.

Seconds ago, we were standing on campus, experiencing the Fall breeze. Now, we're positioned next to a row of houses in a quiet, family-oriented subdivision. Palm trees and warm winds greet us instead of frosty chills.

"This is my street," Nora reports, pointing behind her. "That's my house," she adds, causing me to turn quickly. A beautiful two-storey home with a wide veranda meets us.

The garden and pond out front seem very Nora. It makes me wonder if one or both of Nora's parents are Earth Nymphs. Usually, Affinities are genetic – but sometimes, according to Dad, children of Nymphs can possess different abilities.

"It's a beautiful house," I comment. "You must miss home a lot," I add, hoping I'm not being too nosy.

Nora nods easily, though, as if I didn't offend her or make

her feel bad. "Yeah," she agrees, moving her black side braid from her shoulder. "I like school, but I miss home a lot."

I'm surprised when she turns away from her house and continues to walk down the street – but when I follow her, I recall that there are no cars in the driveway. Maybe her parents are doing errands, and no one is home. Hoping to distract her from that if she's disappointed, I ask,

"Do you have any siblings?"

"Nope," Nora responds, sighing slightly. *Good job, Arya.* "I've always wanted a little sister or brother. I think Mom and Dad did, too, but–" she trails off, not finishing her sentence. I can get the gist.

"I get it," I agree, as Nora plants her feet in front of what looks to be a bus stop. Thankfully, I think I have enough change in my purse to pay for a ticket. "My parents wanted to have a second child, too – and after a long time, it finally happened."

When Nora looks at me excitedly, I add, "You can borrow my little sister anytime."

Nora frowns at me after laughing. "Why? Is she particularly annoying?" she asks.

I smile. "In a way. She's really into sports and building things. We're not much alike, other than reading. But I do miss her a lot."

Nora begins to dig into her cream-coloured purse, which is more of a tote bag than a small handbag. One quick look to the left tells me that a city bus is currently driving in our direction.

Looking back at Nora and her purse, I admire its design. It's decorated with roses and long vines. She pulls out what looks like a roll of bus tickets. She rips off two and hands me one.

Touched, I murmur, "You don't have to–"

"No way!" Nora dismisses, a smile on her face. "You're on my turf now, Arya. You can show me around when we go to San Francisco next weekend."

I smile excitedly at that. "Okay," I affirm as the bus slows to a stop in front of us.

"Where are we going?" I ask Nora as we take two aisle seats in the middle of the already-crowded bus. It is Saturday morning, so I shouldn't be surprised about the people on the bus.

"Lakeland Square Mall," Nora reports. "They have great stores and a movie theatre. We can watch a movie later if you want."

"I can't remember the last time I saw a movie," I breathe. "That sounds like a good idea."

We ride in silence for a while. Nora seems to know the route, so I don't bother to ask her any questions. For someone who calls herself shy and introverted, I think Nora is still on another level than someone like me, who took years to have the confidence to ride public transit alone.

"How's your Mentorship Program going?" Nora surprises me by asking. "Or do I want to know?" she adds, giving me a small smile in response to her comment.

I sigh. "It's horrible, Nora," I admit as the bus drives over a bump in the road. "He's so obnoxious and cruel. Thank God it's only for a couple of weeks."

Nora rubs my arm. "Well, at least he hasn't set you on fire yet," she tries to assure me.

"He tried on Thursday," I confess causing her to arch both eyebrows at once.

"Seriously?" she gasps. "What a loser! You should tell a teacher."

As the bus draws to a stop, allowing passengers to disembark and board, I consider Nora's suggestion. I've considered telling someone earlier, it's true, but I just don't think it would help me. I'm afraid it would do more harm than good, actually. But I don't voice my thoughts to Nora. She's trying to help, and I don't want her to think that I'm being ungrateful.

"Maybe," I respond. "That's a good idea."

When the bus continues down a busier section of town, I ask, "How about you? I hope your Mentor is nice."

"He sure is," Nora agrees quickly. Based on the way she's talking, it sounds like she's relieved by that discovery of hers. "He's an Enchanter, but he has no airs or judgements about him. He's really great."

A nice Enchanter? They're rare, I thought. *The only nice one I know of is–*

"What's his name?" I question.

"Ryker. Ryker Johnson," Nora embellishes.

As soon as she says his name, my chest squeezes together. It's only been a few days, but I have a crush on him. I'd wanted to get to know him since he penned that note. Meeting him just when Cole was trying to squash me like an annoying bug was fate. The only bad thing about the entire thing was that Cole embarrassed me right in front of Ryker at the mixer. I could have punched him for that!

"Oh," I try to comment calmly, but my voice shakes slightly. "I've met him. He does seem really cool."

Nora gives me a nudge with her elbow. "Cute, too, right?" she adds knowingly.

I blush – I never blush! "Yeah," I respond helplessly.

"I think so, too," Nora seems to begin, "but there's someone else I'm kind of *mulling* over."

"Really? Who?" I ask, elated that Nora and I are talking about school, family life, and boys. Maybe things will be a bit easier at school if we have a closer bond.

Nora looks uncomfortable for a split second before clearing her throat. "Well, it's not a 'he'. It's a 'she'," she confesses to me, her blue eyes looking from the floor to me almost bashfully. "I kind of like guys and girls," she adds, almost like she's waiting for a negative comment from me.

I'm touched that Nora trusts me enough to tell me this about her. I also know this isn't about me, though. I take her arm as the bus comes to another stop. She's not making any move to get up, so I'm assuming we'll be staying on board for a while.

"That's great, Nora. And totally okay with me," I tell her -- only because it seems like Nora wants some kind of confirmation, one way or the other. It shouldn't matter what other people think – but that's the kind of world we live in now.

Nora gives me a grateful smile. "Great," she breathes. "Um, I don't think you know her," she confesses. "She's a Nymph in her Sophomore Year. Her name is Anja Berina."

I frown, trying to match the name to a face. "I don't think I know her," I admit. "Tell me about her," I request, just as Nora begins to get her things together. I do the same. Our stop must be coming up soon! This makes me nervous.

"Maybe. If you're good," Nora teases, causing me to laugh softly.

Nora lets out a small breath as the shimmering light from the Trinket vanishes. We're now back in Gomada – specifically, right in front of the gates to the school. Trinkets seem to remember where you were standing the last time you were in that specific realm. I'm not sure how it all works – but Nymphs like Nora seem to be experts.

"Phew," Nora sighs, making me swing my head back to look at her. "I'm beat. Shopping for a new outfit always takes a lot out of me." She shifts the bags she's holding in her right hand as if her body and mind are tired. I'm feeling the same way.

Nora bought a new outfit to wear to a special dinner organized by Nymphs from the Master Class. It's being held at Meera toward the end of September. It suited her: a black dress with a slit up the back hem. Nora may be shy and quiet, but she's beautiful – and I notice that wherever we go, looks from strangers always follow her.

"I'm glad you found something. It'll look great on you," I tell her, moving my hair away from my right shoulder.

I'm overheated – maybe because we rushed to get our bus back to Nora's side of town. It was good, though, because we got to see Nora's parents, Patrick and Dayna. We stayed for a little while. Dayna made coffee for us. Even though coffee isn't my favourite drink, I happily took a mug, not wanting to be rude.

"Thanks!" Nora smiles at me. "Fifth time's the charm, right?" she teases, causing me to laugh.

"It took me just as long to find a new blouse," I remind her – though it's hard to keep the bitterness out of my voice, knowing that my favourite pink blouse was completely ruined. Cranberry punch will never come out of that blouse. I might as well set it on fire or shred it with a chainsaw.

Nora grins at me knowingly. "Well, we both have something nice to wear to that dinner party. Think positive thoughts, Arya," she encourages me, suddenly yanking her phone out of the pocket of her leather jacket.

"Everything okay?" I ask when her brow wrinkles.

"Oh, yeah. Ryker and I are going to meet up soon. Mentor stuff. I want to pick his brain about clubs. Maybe there's a gardening club or an introverts society." Nora winks at me, and I giggle helplessly.

"Speaking of which–" Nora shakes her phone in front of

me in a leading way. "Want me to give you Ryker's phone number? That way, you won't have to wait until the next September mixer to talk to him."

I bite my lip. I'd love to have Ryker's phone number. The only thing is, I don't want him to think I was being sneaky in trying to get it. Some people are very private about who has their personal contact information. And if I suddenly have his phone number, it may look like I'm trying too hard – or I like him. I'm not sure I'm ready to shout that from the rooftops.

"Thanks," I murmur quietly, "but I think I'll hold off for now."

Nora frowns at me. "Why?" she asks. "Strike while the iron's hot – that's what my grandma always says."

"Your grandma?" I gape, astonished. A smile breaks through my surprise, though.

Nora grins at me. "Yeah. Grandma Leith is pretty awesome."

When someone makes what sounds like an exasperated sound from in front of us, Nora and I turn to face forward. My entire body tenses as soon as I see Cole. Nora, on the other hand, looks annoyed that he's here – as if he's ruining our outing (and he is).

"I thought they already sprayed for pests," Nora shocks me by stating, looking at Cole like he belongs on a 'wanted' poster.

Even though I'm shocked by her comment, it's so hilarious that it's hard for me to keep a straight face. What's even funnier is the fact that Cole, himself, is surprised by her statement.

"All you need is a brick wall and a mic," he tells her sourly.

Even though I know it won't happen again (I won't let it), I take a firmer hold of my purse slung over my shoulder. Grandpa's pocket watch is in there. I don't just keep it on me because it's a Trinket – I have it with me because it was his. It's a memory of him. And I don't want Cole ruining my last connection with my grandfather.

Nora says nothing to counter Cole, but she gives him a *look* that is a mixture of annoyance mixed with wariness. Everyone here is either afraid of or wary of Cole Hudson. And now, more than ever, I can understand why. I've only seen one or two people – his friend with the black ponytail and Ryker – who seem to be able to tolerate him.

"Are you done, Leith?" Cole asks Nora.

She seems surprised that he knows her last name but doesn't answer him. I'm curious about how he knows her last name, too. Maybe when he came to Meera on the first day of school, he paid attention to the signage on each dorm room door (we soon took ours down, for privacy reasons). Or, he asked someone. Either way, it's creepy.

I'm terrified, but I try to make it look like I'm irritated by it when Cole looks at me quickly – if a look can last less than a second – and jerks his head away from the students walking and talking around the front part of campus.

"A word, Pixie?" he asks – but it's not really a question.

I narrow my eyes at him. "That's not my name," I snap.

Cole scrunches his face, like he's just stepped in something that smells bad. "*Arya*," he recites as if my name is some kind of virus that is super-contagious if spoken out loud.

Cole shoves his hands into his jeans pockets, looking left and right. We're at a secluded part of campus, along the fence-line. It freaks me out. I know people can see us right now, but no one is close enough to stop him if he decides to try and set my hair on fire again.

When he looks down at me and says, "We're going to trail the Headmistress tonight," I know he was also making sure that no one would hear our conversation.

"What?" I gasp.

"She's looking for the ghost," Cole explains – but he does it in such a way that makes it sound like I'm stupid or brainless. I tense up at that, wanting to punch him all over again.

I'm never this aggressive or rude. But Cole does something to me. It's like a fire I can't put out. I just wish he'd evaporate or leave me alone for good. Since he hates Nymphs, I thought he would have avoided me like the plague. But no such luck.

"She's tracking the *ghost*?" I all but whisper.

Cole rolls his eyes. "Yes, Pixie. Good God, you're slower than usual today. Too much shopping?"

"Why do you need *my* help, anyway?" I ask him. "Last I checked, you didn't want or need it." Even though that's not entirely true, I'm not about to split hairs over anything to do with Cole Hudson.

Either way, Cole looks unhappy about that. "If I'm tailing the fucking Headmistress, I wouldn't mind back-up – even if it's you," he adds sourly.

I sigh. "Well, thank you for the flattery. That makes me want to help so much more than before."

Cole folds his arms and gives me a pointed look with his green eyes. "So, you want the ghost to just rip through school and start killing people?" he counters.

"I'm sure the Headmistress can handle it," I respond.

I don't bother telling him this, but there's no way two students can help a Headmistress who is one of the most powerful Enchantresses in all of Gomada. Even I know this about Headmistress Leona Frow, and I've only been living in Gomada for six days.

Cole seems to somehow know what I'm thinking because he rolls his eyes at the overcast afternoon sky and mutters, "You keep thinking that, Pixie. Just let other people run the show."

Do I let people do that to me?

No! Don't let him get to you!

The thing is, I really *don't* want to find, track, or see that ghost ever again. On the other hand, I can't stop thinking about it. The only time I could stop was when Nora and I were in the Overworld. Things felt safer, *normal*, there. But as soon as we got back to Gomada–

What if Headmistress Frow encounters the ghost and needs help? Not to mention that my nightmares and day-terrors (which I didn't think existed) will never go away until this *ghost thing* is taken care of, one way or another.

"Fine," I respond, knowing that the second I agree, crap could hit the fan like nobody's business.

Cole looks surprised, but the expression only lasts a second. "Meet me right here, at ten," he reports, suddenly pulling a box of cigarettes out of the wide pocket of his hoodie. Gross!

"At ten?" I repeat, nervous already.

He frowns at me. "D'you really think she's gonna track a spirit in broad daylight, Pixie?"

I guess he has a point – but does he have to be so obnoxious about it?

"If I agree to do this," I find myself telling him firmly, "you have to stop berating me and calling me degrading names."

Cole sighs, digging a lighter out of his jeans pocket.

"Well?" I prompt, when he lights his cigarette and says nothing.

"For one night," he responds, bringing his cigarette to his lips. "It's not like it's gonna happen again," he states with venom, probably taking advantage of the opportunity to speak and also blow cigarette smoke in my face. When I make a disgusted grimace at that, he smiles triumphantly.

Thank God, I wheeze internally, thinking about only having to deal with Cole for one night. I suddenly become nervous when Cole glares at me. I must have spoken that thought without realizing it.

I can't believe I will be breaking curfew (the last time was an honest mistake, and I'd sworn that it would never happen again), with the least likeable person I've ever met. But I guess I'm doing it for the Headmistress, and to ensure that the ghost doesn't scare or hurt anyone else. I just hope that no one gets hurt tonight – that Headmistress Frow takes care of the ghost for good.

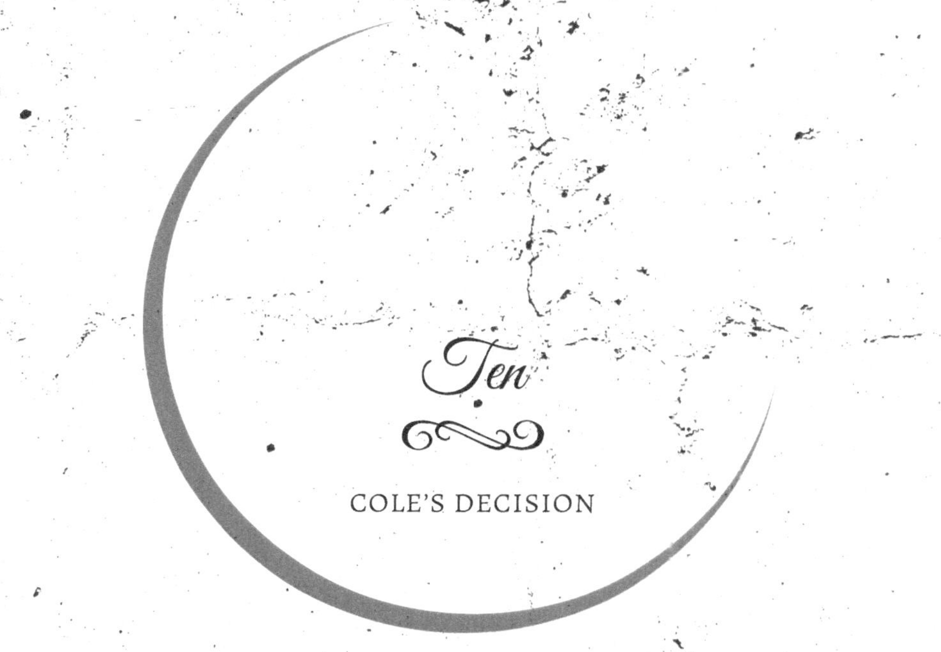

COLE'S DECISION

Diego and I are still not talking much. If we ever square off against the other like this, we usually have it out and then it's over. But this time is different. He's either convinced that Lucy is good for him, or he is so wrapped around her Enchantress fingers that he can't make up his own mind. Or maybe it's both. Either way, I can't worry about that tonight.

At 9:45, I'm yanking on my black leather jacket and my beanie. I dress in all-black tonight, just in case. Even though I'm good at sneaking out and following people (the Tedla's an expert at that stuff, too, so together, we're pretty unstoppable), the Pixie isn't used to any of that stuff. I'll have to be extra careful in case she screws anything up. Maybe I could've done this alone, but honestly, an Enchantress and Headmistress combo – and a ghost – tells me I need back-up. And I know Diego won't be in the mood to help.

I spot Diego's head lifting from the top of his bed. He's reading a book (weird for him), and it's not even something for school. That's about the only time I've ever seen him reading something.

Before I can grumble about that damned Enchantress again, Diego asks, "Going out?"

"Yeah," is all I say, knowing I can't be honest with my closest friend – even if I wanted to be, which is true. If I tell him I'm tailing the Headmistress with the Pixie, he'll spout more bullshit about me being a 'hypocrite'. And now that he's pissed at me, he may not even want to hear about any ghost stuff. Part of me still thinks he doesn't believe me.

To my surprise, though, Diego doesn't even answer me or ask about *where* I'm going. Maybe it's because he's used to me sneaking out. I'm used to him sneaking out, too. It's not like we always tell each other where we're going. But it still feels weird now, after everything that's happened. I guess girls can do a lot of damage to a friendship – especially Enchantress girls.

That bitch!

"Later," I call over my shoulder, walking to the door after tugging on my hiking boots.

I'm not much for sports and shit like that, but due to my *lineage*, Dad had me get '*used to the bush*' as a kid. '*The Tedla thrives in the bush*,' he'd say. '*You need to, as well. If you both excel at something, it'll be exacerbated.*'

I definitely didn't get my dad's way with words, or his work ethic – but whatever. I don't have time to think about that now.

"Later," I hear Diego respond just as I unlock and open the door.

Stepping out into the hallway, of course no one is out here. I close the door and lock it, swerving to the left. The door at this end of the hall will take me down steps that will eventually lead to a side exit. Technically, Master Class Shifters enforce things like curfew and shit like that, but the Masters here don't give a fuck what the Sophomores, Juniors, and Seniors do. They pick on the Freshmen – something I had to deal with last year. I even pass by a Master's Shifter on my way to the side door. She doesn't even look up from her phone as I pass. Then again, she's out in the hall close to ten, too. I wonder what she's up to that she doesn't want anyone to know about.

Shifters take care of each other. I'm not gonna rat her out, and she won't say anything about me.

I'm outside, the cold air hitting me square in the face. I'm kind of surprised that it's already fucking cold like this. Usually, the weather here isn't so – *extreme*.

Whatever. I have more important things to worry about than stuff like global warming. If the ghost kills all of us, no one will be around to complain about the weather.

I never thought this would happen, but I actually wish I had the Pixie's number. I'm at the spot with the big-ass tree, and I don't see her anywhere. Did the bitch chicken out? I should've known she'd be too spineless to help me. Fuck! Am I the only one who cares about this damned school? And since when do I care about *school*?

I hear an unnatural sound behind me so I turn around, expecting to see the Headmistress, arms folded and lecture-ready. Instead I see the Nymph.

Well, she's still a coward because she looks like she's gonna barf, but at least she showed up. I hate to say it, but it's more than Diego would've done now.

"You're late," I tell her when she gets close enough that no one will hear us.

She gapes. "It's only nine-fifty–" she begins, at a normal fucking volume!

"*Shut up!*" I snap, causing her to snap her mouth shut. "Do you know what 'sneaking out' even means?"

She glares up at me. "You said you'd–" she tries again.

"That was before I found out you were gonna be an idiot," I counter.

She opens her mouth again, probably to say something Pixie-like and dumb to me, but I hear something else from far away and hide entirely behind the large tree. The Pixie scoots behind it, too.

"What?" she asks. She sounds scared now. Great. Am I the only take-charge person here? Since when did I become that responsible?

"Someone's coming," I whisper.

Sure enough, a few seconds later, we see Leona Frow walking through the black grass, as if she's taking a lah-di-dah stroll in the afternoon. Figures. Nothing scares Enchanters. And when you're as powerful as the Headmistress, nothing ever scares you.

I can feel the Pixie tense up beside me. She's probably afraid of getting caught. What would Diego call her – an 'amateur'?

Thankfully, the Pixie doesn't move or say anything as Leona passes through our field of vision. From what I can remember, Leona has Water and Air affinities. She may be able to detect heavy breathing if we're close enough. So if we stay calm and quiet, she may not notice us. Plus, she's on a mission. I doubt she's thinking about being watched by students right now. If anything, whatever she's feeling now comes from the ghost.

Leona approaches the gate. I frown at this as we slowly creep into the shadows and surrounding trees to follow her. I didn't think faculty had keys to the school gates. Maybe the Headmistress does?

Suddenly, two large silver wings sprout out from her back like a fucking fairy, and I almost shit myself. I forgot about the fact that Air Affinities equals flying. I glance at the Pixie, who looks in awe of the situation.

Right. She can fly, too.

So, *that's* how Frow is going to get out of here. The problem is, if she flies off, we won't be able to track her. Unless–

"Fly after her," I whisper to Arya.

"What? I can't!" she whispers back. She's useless, but at least she's being quiet this time. "It's hard to control. And the wings stand out. She'll sense or see me."

Fuck. I guess that's true – even though I'd never admit that to her.

"Then move your ass," I order, just as Leona sails over the fenceline like a triathlete with a hurdle.

We get to the fence, far enough away from the gates that the cameras won't see us. And where we are now, the shadows and shit will keep us out of view. For now.

"You gotta fly or whatever," I tell the Pixie "Just for five seconds. Can't you manage that?"

She glares at me again, her angry brown eyes visible even though we're in the dark. I roll my own eyes in response.

"I can do it," she sighs. "But what about you?"

When I stare down at her expectantly, she breathes, "Oh, no," in defiance.

"Just do it," I order. "The longer we stall, the further she'll get, and I won't be able to track her."

It's not like I'm a fan of this plan, either, but it's not like there's time for stalling. If the Pixie and I waste more time, we won't be able to track Frow – me and the Tedla. But I don't say that to the Pixie.

"I can't lift you," she protests. "But I have another idea."

I was so close to telling her to fuck off until she said that last part. "Fine," I sigh, hoping that her bright idea is actually *bright*.

The Pixie shuts her eyes. It looks like she's trying hard to concentrate. I would've made fun of her for this, but now isn't the time.

The wind suddenly picks up around us, hitting the tree branches and blowing the grass. I'm surprised: it's a more brutal gust of wind than I would've thought possible for her. Maybe when she tries, she isn't such a wet blanket.

My eyes hurt for a split second when sparkly white wings jut out from her back. I would be more worried about someone finding us, but there's no way Leona will be able to see this. And we're still hidden from the cameras – for the most part.

The Pixie stops my thoughts by jumping into the air. Her wings start flapping, and she's already gliding like a fucking eagle over the fence. I'm mad because I'm impressed – and I'm impressed that I'm mad about it. But I'd never tell her. This is only a one-time thing. No need for team-building.

More wind suddenly throws itself against me – no, around me. I suddenly feel nauseous as the wind tugs at my feet and arms, and I'm suddenly up in the air!

"What the fuck?" I splutter as the wind pushes me up higher until I'm way more than five inches off the ground. I'm approaching the fence – oh, God, I'm flying over it!

I've never told anyone this before – not even Diego – but heights freak me out. Ten feet and higher will make me want to puke. And right now, I want to hurl, big-time!

As soon as I'm on the taller grass on the other side of the fence, I grip the wrought-iron behind me and heave in a shaky breath.

"Cole?"

I look up from my crouched-over position and glare at her quickly when she gives me a knowing smile.

"Are you scared of heights?" she asks, her white wings disappearing. Weird sparkles fall off of her as it happens.

"No," I snap, straightening out and adjusting my beanie. "Let's go," I add, so she knows I'm still in charge and I'm not scared of anything. The last thing I need is a damned Pixie running the show, trying to turn the tables on me again.

I can track just as well (or almost as well) in human form as I can as the Tedla. Hopefully, we won't be too far behind Frow–

"It's okay if you're scared of heights."

I jerk my head to look over at her. "I'm not scared of–" I counter.

She looks super stoked about this *discovery* of hers. "I just didn't think you had fears. Or a soul," she interrupts me – pissing me off all the more – but surprises me by adding, "Oh, sorry. We had a truce."

I look away from her and down at the ground. The plan was for me to stop hassling her – not the other way around – but I don't say anything about that. Whatever makes us do this in silence works for me.

We're now walking around the outer perimeter of the fence. We're getting close to where Leona would've flown when she hopped the fence – but since I'm trying to keep us out of sight of the security cameras, we have to do some zig-zagging around. Good thing Diego and I spent most of last year figuring that out.

Fuck.

"She never landed," I breathe, furious now. "She just kept flying. This is fucking great."

"I can go up there and look for her."

I look down at her. "And get the Headmistress on your ass?" I shoot back. "Just give me a minute. Stop talking."

She gives me a pissed-off look but says nothing as we get to the edge of the Gomada Thicket.

There is **one** *way for me to find her – find the ghost – and not waste time. I could've done this if I had been working with Diego.*

I keep my idea to myself for a while. If I'm going to do this, I need to be in the safety of the thicket long before I carry out my plan. I'm surprised, but as we keep walking and tracking (or, as I keep tracking), the Pixie looks around but stays quiet.

Huh. Nymphs are much easier to tolerate when they're like this. But I have a feeling all that is going to change very soon.

I step in front of her when we're knee-deep in shrubs and shadows. Even though it's dark, she suddenly looks scared. Scared of me.

You have no idea, Pixie.

"I'm gonna Shift," I say.

She frowns at me. "What?" she gasps. "Into, um–" she stops, maybe because she doesn't know what to call my alter ego. Figures. Nymphs don't know much about any race but their own.

"None of your business," I respond, even if she wasn't trying to guess at my Shifter's form. "Just hang back here in case you see anything."

"All by myself? No way!" she whines as if she's a five-year-old and I'm her god-forsaken babysitter.

"Too bad, so sad," I respond quickly. "It'll be the fastest way for me to track the Headmistress and that ghoul."

I'm ready for more arguing – isn't that what I always get with her? – when the Pixie's head suddenly snaps to the left. I frown, confused. It's not like her to get distracted from a fight to just enjoy the scenery.

This isn't good.

"I feel something," she suddenly tells me, but she's not looking at me. She's still looking into the dark, almost-moving shadows ahead of us. It's too dark to see into that part of the thicket. That's why I want to Shift. The Tedla's vision will be a thousand times better than mine – even if my current vision is better than the average person's.

Wait a minute.

If the Pixie has an Air Affinity, and that's a real ghost that isn't attached to shit like gravity and is made up of that steamy stuff I saw the other night–

And then, I feel it, too. That damp, fucked up feeling I couldn't shake the night I saw it. When I look back at the Pixie, she looks like a deer caught in headlights.

"Move it!" I order. There's a large tree surrounded by bushes right next to her, but she doesn't budge.

I'm not sure how good that ghost's vision would be; or if it would sense us. Whatever. We must keep ourselves as hidden as possible until we know what we're dealing with.

The damp feeling gets worse.

It's coming.

Damn it! This could ruin everything!

I grab hold of her shoulders and shove her backward without letting go, forcing her to sit or crouch or whatever she's going to do behind the tree. She's shaking like a fucking leaf now, so I doubt she'd fight me off if she could.

Nymphs are such babies! Do I have to do everything around here?

Eleven

ARYA'S FIRST INDISCRETION

I don't know what happened. One minute, Cole and I are arguing about him Shifting and leaving me behind. The next, I'm frozen solid to the grass and can't move. Even now, I'm so scared that I'm having trouble breathing. That odd and horrifying feeling from before hits me so hard that I wish I could cry or evaporate. I'm sitting on the cold, damp ground, feeling like I've been run over by a transport truck.

Besides being scared out of my mind, I'm also shocked that Cole *isn't* scared. He's still standing in front of me. He's not craning his neck to see around the tree. He's standing still and straight. It looks like he's listening. After a few terrifying moments of quiet, he slowly crouches, placing his hands on either side of the large tree trunk for support.

Did he hear something? I didn't hear a thing!

When a sudden rustling sound cuts through the eerie quiet, Cole pulls on a lock of my probably-crazy hair – probably to get my attention – then puts his finger to his lips. His green eyes look annoyed, like he's panicked I'll mess everything up any second. I'm too scared to hate him now. I'm worried I'll mess up, too.

Why did I agree to this?

For a long while, everything is spooky and quiet again. It's almost like what we heard before never existed – or that it was just an animal or the wind. But I don't think we're that lucky.

It has to be the ghost. There's no way I could recreate that awful feeling from earlier this week on my own. And based on the way Cole's looking right now, he's not playing around, either.

"Children."

Cole snaps his head down and shakes his head at me firmly. I can't really see anymore – I think I'm going to faint. The voice seems close – but not near the tree. I think that's the only thing we have going for us right now.

"I know you're here."

My shaking gets worse. Cole takes one of his hands away from the tree and holds it out to me as if he's trying to steady me.

"Come out and play with me."

I stare up at Cole, open-mouthed and horrified. The voice – the ghost – sounds so much closer now! He knows where we are!

Cole removes his other hand from the trunk and mouths, "Don't move" to me. That's not really a problem.

"I sense one of you is a Nymph. Those are especially delicious."

The colour drains from my face. I'm cold. Thunder suddenly ripples from high above the trees.

Oh, no! Now I've blown our cover, for sure!

A deep chuckle rings out from close behind us.

He's right near the tree!

I look up at Cole. It's no secret that we don't get along. If

Cole had his way, I'm sure he'd just offer me up as bait to the ghost so he could get away scot-free. And who knows, maybe that's what he's going to do right now.

We make accidental eye contact. I notice that he doesn't look angry or annoyed with me anymore. I'm not sure *what* he's thinking – and it's not like I spend my spare time wondering about those things. His face is inches from mine. His jaw is clenched. It looks like he's concentrating.

What do we do? And how can the ghost *sense* that one of us is a Nymph? I know supernatural creatures can sense differences in other races, but I didn't think ghosts could, too. What else is this ghost capable of that I don't know about – besides wanting to eat me?

Cole's eyes are now straight ahead. Before I can even blink, they change into those terrifying oval-shaped eyes from the first day I met him. He backs away from the tree, and I flatten my back against the tree and scream when a *crack* splits the quiet in the thicket.

Maybe this is a cowardly thing to do, but I cover my eyes and cry as more snapping and cracking noises cut through the tension. I can't hear the ghost. I can't hear anything over what sounds like trees ripping in half.

When quiet floods my system, I open my ears and shriek so loudly that my voice cuts off, my throat feeling split in two.

Standing in front of me is an enormous wolf on two legs. In an instant, it's mid-air. Then, it's gone.

Roaring and snarling pound through the air as I try to get to my feet. When I finally step around the tree, holding onto the trunk for support, I see the wolf-man standing in the small clearing of the Gomada Thicket.

Where did the ghost go?

What about the Headmistress? Did the ghost – did the ghost kill her?

The wolf-man turns around. I step backward and trip on an undergrowth as soon as it looks at me. When it begins to approach me, thunder cracks through the sky. I look down at my hands, shocked. My palms are white. Electricity crackles from them, growing in its intensity.

My God! My electrical ability!

I look up at the horrifying creature. I can't know for sure if I summoned my electricity willingly or otherwise – but it's here, its warmth making me feel more in control of myself, but not by very much.

"Arya."

I rush to my feet, even if it hurts to move. Maybe I injured myself when I fell. The electricity in my palms sparks and cracks in – defense? I've never experienced this power before. I have no idea what to do with it. But I'm just terrified enough to lose control.

"It's me. Relax."

I recognize the obnoxious, condescending voice and the creepy, low-pitched growl.

It's Cole.

How could he be both? I knew his Shifting form must be something as cruel and ruthless as him, but this–

"Don't electrocute me. That would suck."

As soon as he holds out his arms – arms that could probably break every bone in my body with one swat – the electricity absorbs back into my palms, and there's blackness.

Nausea hits the pit in my stomach when I open my eyes. The memories from the evening flood back to me like a tsunami, and I jerk upright. Looking around, I realize that the odd, damp feeling I felt before is no longer there. I feel cold from the weather and the gentle mist that'll probably turn into rain soon. I feel exhausted and drained but no longer *under attack.*

Where am I?

Where are the ghost and Headmistress Frow?

Where is Cole – and is he human again?

I look around again as if the first time wasn't enough to jog my memory. I still don't know where I am. At least this time, I brought my phone with me. Hopefully, it still works. One quick look at the time fills me with horror.

It's almost midnight!

How is that possible? That means I have over an hour that's unaccounted for. Maybe I don't remember everything that happened tonight. I can't, if it should still be before eleven, and it's now before midnight!

Trying hard not to panic, I try to remember.

The rustling sound put us on alert.

The creepy ghost voice kept on getting closer and closer.

The ghost saying he'd eat me.

Headmistress Frow being nowhere to be found.

Cole Shifting into that wolf-man creature.

What else am I missing? That can't be everything – or else, how would I have gotten here?

A strong night breeze picks up my messy hair and flings it up at my shoulders, causing the mist to hit me square in the face. I try to blink it away, but it's cold and uncomfortable against my skin. My back is pressed against something hard, but my head is down low, and I feel dizzy. I finally turn to have a look.

Brick. A brick wall. I turn around again, and see a black object lining the area in front of me.

Wait. I'm at the school. I recognize the brick and the wrought-iron fenceline. How did I get back here?

I must have fainted. That's the only logical explanation. I never pass out, so I don't know what it feels like – but this has to be it.

I can't believe I'm feeling this way, but real guilt tugs at me for fainting, leaving Cole to deal with the ghost alone.

Wait!

Did Cole die? Is he okay? And if he didn't die, where is he now?

Did he bring me back here and then *leave* me here? Or did I get back here on my own and then fall asleep?

Angry tears fill my eyes. I would have thought that working together to track down a ghost clearly closing in on the school would've forced Cole and I to not kill each other. But if he just left me out there or dumped me out here in the cold–

Why would I expect anything less from him? He's a selfish bully and an obnoxious jerk with no compassion for anyone other than himself. I guess I thought he'd Shifted to protect me – but that's a laughable thought. He probably only Shifted to attack the ghost. I'm sure it had nothing to do with me and everything to do with getting rid of the ghost – if that's a thing that can happen in this realm.

My thoughts scatter away from me when a dark shadow looms over me. My throbbing throat stops me from screaming.

But it's not a ghost or a monster in front of me. It's the Headmistress herself. If I wasn't pale already, I'm white as a ghost (bad choice of words) now.

Even with the mist slowly turning into rain and the darkness that could have made it harder to see, I can make out the Headmistress clearly – maybe because I'm terrified, all over again. She's wearing the same brown trenchcoat that she was wearing when Cole and I saw her walking through the front part of campus. The difference is that her long black hair that was pulled up is now unkempt and spilling out of her navy blue clip. Small scrapes and cuts are on her face. Even though her blue eyes are staring down at me angrily, a part of me still worries that she got into a fight with the ghost and got hurt.

"Miss Willow," she states – how does she know my name? – her tone *disappointed* as if she knows this isn't something I normally do. "What are you doing outside of your dorm past midnight?"

*It's past **midnight** now?*

"This is unacceptable behaviour. Detention and community service will be assigned, and your parents will be telephoned on Monday. I'm very disappointed, Miss Willow."

I stumble to my feet now because it looks like she wants me to do that. When I open my mouth to apologize, the look on Headmistress Frow's face tells me I should think twice, so I close it and don't say anything.

The first time I ever break the rules, and I get into big trouble! I should've known this would happen!

Why did I think I ever would have gotten away with this? Why did I agree to help Cole in the first place? I'm sure he's at home, safe and sound, while I'm getting detention and whatever community service means as punishment for breaking curfew. Unbelievable!

From now on, I should just let the grown-ups handle everything. Headmistress Frow is a powerful Enchantress. I'm sure she can handle one ghost. It was dumb of me to think I could be of any help at all – and it was stupid of me to think I could ever work with Cole.

Sunday morning is cold and dreary. It's raining. I hear the rain before I see it. Usually, I like rainy days, but today, I feel like it adds to my gloomy mood. Maybe I should be happy, relieved, that I survived a ghost attack and a horrific Shifter monster whose alter ego hates my guts – but this morning, all I feel is despondence.

When I lift my head off my pillow, the window that over-looks Nora's bed is dark. Rain is coming down in thick sheets. The wind hits the window pane, threatening anyone who decides to venture outside.

Rain does nothing to stop Nora, though. She is probably running in rainboots. Plus, with her love of the land and plants, I'm sure she welcomes this kind of weather. I just hope she doesn't get hurt out there.

I finally reach over to my left – I'm on my stomach, with my head facing the headboard of my single bed – and reach out blindly to take hold of my phone. I almost drop it along the way. I finally look at the time. It's about nine o'clock in the morning. This is usually the latest I ever sleep in, so even with a bad mood to suffer through, I know I shouldn't make things worse by staying in bed any longer than I usually do.

I shower in an attempt to wake up. I know I need to be awake and ready, because I need to tell my parents about what happened last night before Headmistress Frow calls them on Monday morning. I want them to hear about my bad decision from me. I'm sure they'll be disappointed in me.

The worst thing is, I'm unsure if I should tell them why I was out so late last night. Based on what happened between us outside, I don't think Headmistress Frow knows why I was breaking curfew. I guess that is a good thing, because ghost hunting and tailing a faculty member would have warranted a much bigger punishment. At the same time, I don't want to tell my parents about the ghost, because I don't want them to worry about me. They're already concerned that I'm being bullied at school by a Shifter and an Enchantress (that kind of came out the night Cole tried to set my hair on fire) – I don't want them panicking over any other supernatural threats.

It's still raining when I step outside. I'm wearing my favourite pink rain jacket – but now I feel like it's just a big pastel target on my back. If Cole – or, even worse, the ghost – wants to find me, it won't be very easy for me to hide.

I'm heading to the library. I need a change of scenery. I don't think doing my homework alone in my dorm will do anything to calm my nerves and ease my guilt. I may feel safer if I'm in a big building within the academy, full of people. At least, I'm *hoping* I'll feel safer.

The library takes up both the second and third floors of Gomada Academy. It's a big place, Nora says, but I haven't had the chance to visit yet. I was planning to go Wednesday evening, but a pyromaniac changed my mind.

Just as I'm getting close to the large, beautiful door with an antique handle leading to the library, it opens from the inside. At first, I feel my heart quicken and my palms become sweaty. What if it's–

When I see Ryker Johnson (what are the odds?) instead of an evil spirit, I could cry in, or jump up and down with, relief. But now isn't the time for those things. This could be my chance to make up for the embarrassing mixer fiasco that Ryker witnessed. If only I wasn't soaking wet from outside, which means my hair must be a mess under my hood!

I pull my pink hood down quickly, just as Ryker turns to

his left and spots me. "Hey," I blurt out, hoping I'm not being too forward by saying 'hi' to him first.

I've never had a boyfriend before – I don't think my one outing across the playground with Phineas Vern in Grade Three counts – and none of my crushes have ever led to anything more than that, so I don't really know how to act around boys.

To my relief, Ryker doesn't look at me with annoyance or pity. His brown eyes smile at me before his lips do – and for a minute, I forget about ghosts, monsters, and my punishment from the Headmistress.

"Hey! Good morning, Arya," he greets me.

I'm surprised he remembers my name. It's not like I'm very memorable. I guess I'm sort of okay-looking, but I'm definitely not on the same level as Désirée and Lucy Chapin. I'm just happy he remembers me, and the sight of me doesn't make him violently sick.

Unlike me, Ryker is totally dry. He's wearing a black v-neck long-sleeved shirt that blends nicely with his dark skin and cornrows. He's carrying books against his side. The fact that he seems to care about his studies or reading makes him all the more appealing to me.

Now's your chance! Don't mess it up!

"What are you up to?" I ask casually, but then realize that it's quite obvious what he's up to – he just came out of a library! – so I'm immediately embarrassed.

But Ryker doesn't take my question in the same way. He shrugs. "Just doing some last-minute studying. I got swamped with other stuff yesterday, and time just got away from me. Know what I mean?"

More than ever, I answer in my own head, thankful that it doesn't look like I voice my inner thoughts out loud, for once.

"Yeah, I do," I agree. "So, um, I hear you're Nora's Mentor," I try to continue the conversation by saying.

He nods once, but it's an enthusiastic one. "Sure am!" he affirms. "She's pretty awesome. I've never worked with someone with an Earth Affinity before. I'm learning a lot."

Wow. He just seems so perfect! Not only is he a really nice guy, but he also seems to care for my friend. I don't think I could have continued liking him if he'd wanted nothing to do with Nora. Or, it would have made things really difficult. On the other hand, the fact that he seems to be so perfect makes me even more freaked out about potentially messing things up.

"She is really great," I agree. "I've been learning a lot from her, too."

Ryker shifts his stance and frowns down at me suddenly. I'm about to panic until he asks, "Who's your Mentor, Arya? I don't think I've asked you that yet."

I'm surprised that I'm blushing again. Great! I really hope he doesn't notice. "Cole Hudson," I answer, hoping my tone sounds polite and not bitter. For some odd reason, Ryker seems friendly with Cole, so I don't want to ruin anything between him and me by bad-mouthing Cole.

Ryker's frown deepens. "Oh," is all he says. "Well, is he treating you right?" he asks after a brief pause, startling me with the sincerity behind his question. "I know he can be a little rough around the edges," Ryker adds.

I hesitate. I need to explain this properly. If I say the wrong thing–

But now that I'm hesitating, I bet Ryker knows my answer, so I can't sugarcoat it too much. I also can't say 'he's a horrible person, and I wish I had never met him'.

"Um, things have been... Difficult," I finally finish, realizing that with his brown eyes on me, it's hard to be anything but honest with him.

Ryker looks concerned – which sends me through the roof with excitement – but also not surprised about what I've said. "Well, want me to have a word with him?" he inquires. "We're friends – sort of. I wouldn't mind."

I still can't feel my face. "That would be great," I gush, a little embarrassed.

The fact that Ryker would want to set Cole straight must mean that he cares about me in *some* way, right? Or is he just being nice? I don't want to assume things, but I don't want to second-guess myself.

This isn't complicated at all.

"Thank you," I add, just so he doesn't think I'm being ungrateful.

"Hey, no worries," Ryker seems to dismiss, as students walk past us as if we're not there. I guess this must have been happening this whole time, but I never noticed.

Does that mean he *doesn't* care? Is he just doing a favour for a friend, or is it more than that? It's not like we've spent a ton of time together yet. There may not be anything for him to feel.

"Well, I gotta go," Ryker tells me. "Catch you later, Arya."

"Bye," I call, just as he's passing me. Along the way, Ryker touches my left shoulder. Sparks run up and down my left arm. The feeling of his large hand on me–

I try to shake that heavy and intense feeling as I open the door to the library. I have to focus on my homework now – the history of a realm I barely know anything about – and on my looming sentence from Headmistress Frow. I don't have the time to think about a cute, nice boy.

Or do I?

COLE IS DIFFERENT

I don't care about things.

I don't care that Diego's probably still pissed at me. I don't care that I almost got caught by Frow last night. I just don't give two shits about stuff.

I don't care that it's raining or that I have a test in Literature tomorrow. I just don't care.

But sitting in bed in the dark, not wanting to get up or even move, I know I care about one thing.

I *do care* that I lost the ghost last night. I was so close! My Shifting time was the fastest it's ever been. Usually, it's just a minute, maybe two. In the beginning, it was longer – but once I got used to things, everything went faster. But last night, it was like I was lightning.

Even with my fast transformation time, that fucking ghost still got away! Why make a show of cornering us, threatening us, and then – *poof*, disappear? It just doesn't make sense.

Not only that, the Tedla was not happy about coming out like I wanted. I guess I was using a lot of willpower to push him out because even after I Shifted, I could feel resistance when I went for the ghost. I think the Tedla was relieved that the ghost had disappeared. And that's fucked up, because the Tedla's not scared of anything. The Tedla's the one that does the scaring.

Case in point: the Pixie. Good God, she didn't scream at the ghost, but she screamed at me? I guess it just further proves my point that people can't know about the monster inside me. There's a reason why I've kept it a secret for over a year.

So why Shift last night? Why expose my darkest family secret to some bitch who's probably blabbed it to everyone she knows by now? Why put the Tedla, my family legacy, in danger?

I needed to show the ghost I wasn't afraid of it. I needed to try and attack it somehow, get it weakened. If I turned tail and ran, it would've known it had the upper hand. I was trying to keep the school safe – Diego, Taylor, even Ryker.

I was protecting myself and protecting my friends, plain and simple. No debate needed. I don't need to keep thinking about it.

I hear a shuffling sound from my right. Diego is waking up. He's usually up by now. I think it's around eight AM. It's hard to tell when the sky is so dark.

"Cole?" he grumbles. He's not himself first thing in the morning. I guess I'm not, either. I don't feel like myself right now, no matter what time it is.

"Hey," I respond gruffly. My voice is scratchy – maybe from roaring and growling last night. Making a big show to try and intimidate a ghost who ended up running off, anyway. Coward.

More shuffling. Since my eyes are adjusted to the dark now, when I look over for the first time, Diego's sitting up, too. He rubs his messy hair and gives me a frown.

"You got back late as fuck last night," he growls at me.

I roll my eyes. Diego's back – sort of. "Past midnight isn't 'late as fuck', Grandpa," I shoot back.

He eyes me as he throws his tangled-up blankets off himself and stands. "What'd you do, anyway?" he asks, turning around to pick up a fallen pillow from the floor.

I sigh. "Nothing earth-shattering, Jasper."

I wish it was.

Diego begins to get dressed in the dark. We don't care about shit like privacy. Most Shifters don't because our clothes tear off when we turn, anyway. It's not like we make a show of watching each other, though. It's just a cultural thing. Probably not something the others would understand.

Looking down at my blankets, I know I need to suck it up and say something, so I do.

"So, uh – sorry," I finally admit. "If you wanna date her or whatever – I'll just stay out of it."

"Didn't think I needed your permission," Diego responds, as I hear drawers closing to my right. Great. That sure as hell didn't work.

After a weird pause, Diego clears his throat and turns. I can feel his eyes on me, so I look up at him. He could still kick my ass, so I know better than to do anything more to piss him off.

"Thanks," he responds. Good. He heard me.

I nod. We don't have to talk about this anymore. I just wanted to apologize for being – what was it? A 'judgemental douche'?

Fully dressed and more himself than he was a minute or two ago, Diego folds his arms and asks curiously, "Why the change of heart, Hudson?"

I frown up at him. "What?"

He shrugs. "You lost your mind at the mixer – and now, you're right as rain about it."

I shake my head in response. "Nothing happened. It's just not my business."

Diego raises an eyebrow. "Since when?" he teases. "You make everything your business, Hudson." He's giving me that damned smile I always want to punch off his face. He's back to his old self – so why am I not feeling the way I used to?

Is it because a ghost almost killed me last night? Am I so freaked that my family secret could be outed that I'm not thinking straight?

Fuck. I need to fix that, ASAP.

I suddenly feel a bit better as I throw off my blankets and walk to the dresser that Diego and I share. We also share the closet. We don't have a ton of clothes, so everything fits nicely. We don't care about crap like that.

"Where's the fire? It's only nine AM."

Huh. My hunch was off, I guess.

"Gotta go take care of something," I call over my shoulder, shoving my still-wet and half-ripped-apart shirt from last night into the already-full laundry hamper we haven't taken care of yet.

Yanking on jeans and a gray shirt, I'm going fast because I don't know how much time I have. The sooner I get this taken care of, the better.

"That's not suss at all," Diego comments as I unlock and open the door to our dorm.

I ignore what he says because if he has a right to his shit, I have a right to mine. I don't want to tell him that a damn Pixie knows about the Tedla. Just thinking about this makes me sick. No Shifter here (besides Diego) knows about my other identity, but she does? It's too much for me to handle, which is probably why I'm going fast first thing in the morning with no coffee or cigarettes to help me.

I don't care about showering or brushing my teeth right

now. I only care about fixing this mess before it blows up in my face.

I'd never admit this to anyone, but after a week of getting messed with by me, I'm worried the Pixie will do anything she can to fuck with me – and that may be revealing my Tedla secret to as many people as possible.

Fuck my life – again.

Pouring rain falls on top of me. I'm cold and soaked already, but I don't care. As I walk past Feara and head for Meera, a lot of people stare at me like I'm nuts – maybe because I don't have a jacket on, or maybe because I probably look nuts. I don't care, though. That makes me feel good, more like myself. Once I get all this taken care of, things will get better.

It takes longer for me to get to the Nymph dorm – or, at least, it feels that way. I'm really angry and on edge as I get to the steps and throw myself up. I swing open one of the double doors and almost bump into a Nymph along the way. He gives me a glare when we almost smash into each other. But I'm not in the mood to be stared down by some Pixie, so I glare right back and push past him. What's the worst he can do to me? I'm so mad now that I'm less worried than I would have been earlier – and that wouldn't have been a lot, anyway.

It takes me seconds to get to the fourth floor – I go fast when I'm angry, and I guess I'm anxious too, but I'd never admit that to anyone – and even less time to get to Room 407. I bang on the door. No one answers.

Fuck!

She's probably blabbing about my wolf-guy alter ego to

everyone. No wonder she's not at home. Little bitch. I should've left her unconscious out in the Gomada Thicket instead of carrying her back here. I had felt sorry for her – something else I'd never admit. She's such a coward. Clearly, I made the wrong choice. She's scum, just like the rest of them.

I knock again. Nothing.

I'm fuming now. I want to bash through the door and tear apart the place. I know I need to calm down. If I get too angry, I may push the Tedla to come out.

I should have gotten her number somehow, or at least figured out her routine, so I could track her down like the idiot mouse she is and make her pay for what she's done. Now, I have to find her like some crazy moron. I take a deep breath, turn around and retrace my steps.

I can track her based on her scent. Now that I'm not as pissed off – and I was pretty angry when I got in here just a minute ago – I can smell her stupid vanilla perfume in between the other scents floating around here.

Disgusting aftershave. The Pixie's vanilla scent. What seems to be flowers – maybe roses. And pot. That's the only aroma I like as I follow the Pixie's scent. I'm on a mission now, and no one can stop me.

What if I underestimated the Pixie? What if she knows more about Shifters than she lets on? I know that's impossible – Nymphs aren't that bright, and the Pixie seems to be the dullest bulb in the box – but you never know.

Sometimes, it's the stupid ones that surprise you. I can't take any chances – especially with the Germain family secret.

I follow the vanilla scent the best I can. The rain and the competing scents from everyone else around me – why are people running around doing shit on a Sunday morning? – make it harder than usual to trail someone. Maybe it's because I'm determined. Maybe it's because I still want to make up for my *fail* from last night. But whatever it is, I push myself to follow the scent, even if I get turned around once or twice. Even though I'm fucking drenched and will probably die of pneumonia (who would miss me?), at least I'm doing everything I can to keep my shit together.

I shouldn't be surprised when her trail leads me to the library within Gomada Academy. She's a goody-two-shoes: where else would she be on a Sunday morning besides Sunday School? Of course she'd be here. This should have been my first clue.

The library spans two floors, so the Pixie could be anywhere here. At least with the lack of rain, it'll be easier to follow her trail. That makes me feel less freaked as I head inside.

I'm dripping everywhere as I go. The librarian – I forget her name – gives me the evil eye from under her weird glasses. Some Freshmen girls who are probably Enchantresses because they look like little Chapins In Training giggle at me with eye-rolls and whispers. They're so pathetic that I don't even bother to tell them they're going nowhere as I pass them. I still have a firm grip on the Pixie's scent, and it's leading me to the other end of the library – near the stairs leading to the third floor.

I'm about to do the stairs when I spot her. She's sitting at a small table in the shape of a circle. She's reading something from a textbook. Looks like Freshman History.

Well, at least she's sitting in the library doing homework, not in the Dining Hall, telling everyone about my story. Maybe she doesn't care about my secret – which makes sense since we've already said that we mean jack shit to each other – so maybe she hasn't told anyone about me, after all. But I can't take any chances. Even though I'm a disappointment, I can't take any chances with my grandfather's legacy.

I walk over to her. It's not hard to spot me here: I'm drenched, and I never come to the library, especially on the weekend. I must stick out like a sore– something. I forget about how that saying works. All I can think about is making sure she keeps her mouth shut.

She looks up when I'm close, but not right up to the table. Either her instincts are getting better (fat chance), or she's just so scared over what happened that she's on hyper-alert now. I'm betting on the second thing, but I don't care enough to find out.

As soon as she sees me, she hardens. It's funny. I like it when people tense up when they see me. It's about time she respected me.

"What do you want?" she asks. Of course she's whispering, because we're in a library. She doesn't seem to notice that I'm soaking wet and dripping everywhere. Does she have tunnel vision or something? But then again, all Nymphs are stuck-up and stupid. I'm not surprised that all she can see is herself.

I'm so mad I can't whisper, even if I tried. Plus, rules are there for a reason: to be broken.

"Who did you tell?" I growl.

The Pixie frowns up at me, looking confused now. "About the ghost?" she responds, her voice quieter when she says 'ghost'. Pathetic. "Nobody."

I'm pissed that she'd jump to that conclusion right away, instead of the obvious one. Is she messing with me, trying to piss me off all the more by giving me the run-around? I keep underestimating how fucking annoying and calculated this little Nymph can be.

"No," I snap, causing her to look even more confused and scared, too. Good. "About me."

The frown leaves her face. She definitely knows what I'm talking about. She stands up from the wooden chair and approaches me. Close, but not too close. She has her back almost touching the table, as if she's using it as some sort of defence against me. Hilarious!

"No one," she counters through almost-clenched teeth. She seems mad now. "Everyone knows you're a monster. Why do I have to say anything?"

I'm stunned by her comeback. I thought I would have been thankful (and I don't get that way very often) that the Pixie hadn't opened her big mouth and told everyone about my family secret. But part of me wants to know why. She finally has the ammunition to take me down, make me suffer, and does *nothing with it*? Crazy!

I'm also not crazy about what she said. For some reason, it really gets under my skin. Sure, I'm used to people being afraid of me – sometimes, sensing there's danger is freakier than knowing about it for sure – but this is different, for some reason.

"We can't all have wings and magic wands," I can't help but fire back at her.

I'm sure my parents would be mad that I'm doing this to a Nymph – they've always told me not to use 'derogatory language' – but I can't help it. Getting a rise out of her gives me a rush. Even though I'm craving my morning smoke, I still feel awesome, knowing I've made her mad.

She gapes up at me. "I shouldn't expect anything kind or sincere to ever come out of your mouth," she responds, folding her arms. "If you just leave people unconscious and defenceless, I'm sure manners aren't in your wheelhouse."

I get angry at that, too. Clearly, the Pixie thinks I just dumped her ass outside of school – or that I'd left her out there in the Gomada Thicket by herself. She passed out. She doesn't remember. I sure as hell do. When I made sure the ghost was gone, I carried her back to campus. I also had to carry my torn-apart shirt, beanie, and shoes. My jeans were shredded and useless. When we were back at school, I had to Shift back so no one would see the Tedla – and I had to avoid the cameras while holding a limp and unconscious Pixie. When she began to wake up, I couldn't let her see me. I was naked from the waist down.

It was a fucking mess!

I'm so angry that she'd think I would do that. Yeah, I'm a douche, but even I have *some* standards. I wouldn't leave someone out there to become ghost bait (apparently, they do eat people) – even if it was the Pixie, Lucy, or Désirée. Do I hate them? Yeah. But I wouldn't just let them die.

Even though I'm mad as fuck that she'd think that about me, I don't say anything to defend myself. I just stand there. Do I believe that she didn't tell anyone? I'm not sure. But the fact that she's so scared of me now might mean that she slips up.

I lean in close to her, causing her arms to unfold and drop limply to her sides. "If you ever even think about telling anyone," I snarl, "I'll make that ghost look like a fucking animated movie."

Her brown eyes are wide with fear. She's crying. I'd usually feel pretty good about inflicting this kind of pain on someone – especially a Nymph – but maybe I'm too riled up from this morning to feel much happiness.

She glares up at me now. Thunder suddenly rumbles in the background. The window to my right flashes with lightning. When I look back at her, the Pixie is eyeing me evenly – or, as evenly as she can, being a Nymph.

"I'll electrocute you next time," she snaps – telling me she remembers everything up 'til she passed out – turning on her heel and getting back to her table.

For a Pixie, her threat is actually a pretty interesting one.

Now that she can use her electricity, she'll be a bigger threat than just tossing air and wind around. Maybe I should–

No way! Even if she *did* try to electrocute me, there's no way she'd be strong enough for it to kill me. And she's probably too nice to try. Maybe she'd make a show of collecting the electricity from the air, but I don't think she'd have the guts to use it to hurt anyone. Useless.

I'm still pissed as hell as I stomp out of the library and head back to Feara. I guess being wet, cold, and hungry aren't helping, either. So when someone calls my name, I turn around, already on the defense.

Ryker is looking at me like I've sprouted two heads. "Hudson?" he says. "What're you doing without–"

"I had business to take care of," I tell him quickly, not wanting to stay and chit-chat. I usually don't mind Ryker that much, but he's been especially annoying this weekend.

He frowns at me. He has a black rain jacket on, and his bookbag looks heavy. Probably studying at the library. Diego and I know that Ryker likes to do his homework there – mostly because he wants his alone time. People like Lukas have soured him about hanging out in the Gleera dorm. Can't say I blame him for that.

"Alright. Well, I'll be quick about it, then," Ryker begins.

"I'll talk to Jasper about Crabtree today," I assert, hoping this is what he's after and he'll shove off ASAP.

But based on the look on his face, there's something else Ryker wants to say. Fantastic. A chatty Enchanter makes for a bad day – and after the morning I've had? It'll make my day even worse.

"It's about Arya," he corrects me.

Just the sound of her name makes me want to hurl. Why the fuck is he bringing her up to me, of all people? I have no use for her – why is he wasting his time talking to me about a Pixie?

"What about her?" I ask impatiently. The last thing I need is Ryker pulling the same shit on me that Diego tried to on Friday. I guess I deserved it from Diego, but I sure as hell don't deserve it from Ryker, who barely knows me.

Ryker folds his arms, but he looks casual. Maybe he won't say what I think he'll say. "She told me you've been giving her a bit of a hard time," he explains.

I roll my eyes. Sheets of rain hit my face when I look up at the black sky. Of course she'd whine to her crush about me messing with her. What a baby! And Ryker's playing right into it, like a knight in shining armour. What an idiot! Maybe he likes her too, and this is his way of trying to get in good with her.

I know I don't care – but at the same time, I don't want to be dragged into this shit, either.

"And?" I finally huff, when Ryker doesn't say anything else. "Why is that your problem?"

Ryker puts his hands up, as if he doesn't want to start anything. Well, if he didn't want to start anything, maybe he shouldn't have made my business his business. "I don't want to pick a fight with you, Hudson. We're good," he tells me. "I'm just telling you to back off."

I glare at him, wondering what his end game is in all of this. Enchanters don't usually care about what Shifters do. Why is Ryker so interested in the Pixie?

Whatever. Maybe I should lay off Arya a little bit, just in

case. Not because I care about her delicate feelings, but because she knows something about me no one else does. Plus, she's already pissed at me because she thinks I dumped her body out into the woods without a second thought. No need to make things worse by actually lighting her hair on fire next week.

"No skin off my back," I finally dismiss, so this pointless conversation can be over.

Ryker nods. "Thanks. Hudson. See you at the campfire next Friday."

I frown, which Ryker finds funny. "Did you forget?" he asks.

Every year, the Academy has a campfire hosted by the Shifters. I think the Nymphs have some dinner at the end of the month (like I care) and share their food with us, and the Enchanters go to a play or something and invite other races to join them. I don't get why the Shifters have to do this damned campfire thing – but at least there's drinking, and since teachers never attend, I can usually smoke, too.

"Yeah," I agree. "Check you later."

I walk away from Ryker before he can even answer me, wanting to prove my point of being done with the conversation. It really burns me that he's getting involved in something that's none of his business. But that's what Enchanters do. They *make* things about them. I didn't peg Ryker for being like that – but I guess I was wrong.

It's Friday during Field Practice class. Professor Xhao is doing her usual afternoon walkaround, looking at the Nymph pairings 'who should be showing a great deal of progress by now'. I know this should be true. We've had ten days of in-class practice, and Professor Xhao wants us to complete weekly logs of 'outside of class' practice. Nora and I practiced last weekend, and we'll practice again tomorrow morning.

And so, after all this time, I get that she would assume we'd be improving. But I'm not.

I'm worried that the electricity I produced last weekend was only because I was terrified – not because I'm fully able to control my Affinity the way I should be at this age. Even when Nora and I take quick breaks from our 'in-class' training and watch other pairs, I've noticed other Nymphs with Air Affinities being able not only to wield, but aim, their electrical component. Some Nymphs with Darkness Affinities can summon up a great deal of dark power without even breaking a sweat. This makes me nervous.

After two weeks, I think my flight and control of air and wind have improved – but not my electricity, which is one of the main sources of power for a Nymph with an Air Affinity.

I've noticed Professor Xhao watching me during her normal walkarounds and writing in her notebook. Whenever she does this, I don't feel good about it. Part of me wants to know what she's writing – and the other part never wants to know.

Nora is getting really good at controlling her Earth Affinity and its different components. Her knack for quickly growing and controlling vines and weeds is much better than at the beginning of the school year. Now, she's working on mud.

Just as I'm wielding a gust of wind to my palms to see if I can control a specific gust of wind better than I could before, a sudden, "Watch out!" rings through the air.

Nora's head whips to the right and mine to the left. It's impossible to see who called out to us because of what is coming toward us now. A wall of fire is closing in on us! Worse than that, the wind that I'm currently trying to master flies against the fire – no, with the fire – and brings it even closer than before!

I see a quick movement in my peripheral vision, and a spray of mud immediately envelopes the large orange-and-red wall. The fire that used to be so full of life crumbles to the grassy floor in a pile of ashes and smoke. The Freshman Nymph, who must have been trying to stop the fire from spreading, is to my left. Nora and I know her from our Nymph Studies class. Her name is Makayleigh Laverdière. We're paired up with her for a group project.

Nora and I stare at one another, horrified. That was the first time someone's Affinity had gotten so out of control that someone had to step in to stop it. This further proves that everyone in this race is more proficient at controlling their

Affinities than I am. It's become harder and harder to ignore, and I'm wondering when Professor Xhao will talk to me about it.

Speaking of which, Professor Xhao was watching this whole thing from a few feet away. Maybe she wanted us to take care of this ourselves – or, she was waiting for things to get worse before she stepped in. Either way, she's scrutinizing us with her hazel eyes. Her harsh eyes and vibrant purple blazer make her impossible to miss.

"I'm so sorry!" Makayleigh gushes, approaching Nora and I now. The wind tosses her black bob as she runs to us. "I don't know what happened. It's like it suddenly got a life of its own."

I open my mouth to tell her that it was no big deal – not wanting Makayleigh to feel even worse about what happened, especially since I was using wind at the wrong time – when Professor Xhao's flowing voice suddenly interrupts,

"That's because your fire had assistance from Miss Willow."

My stomach sinks through the grass as Professor Xhao is now in front of us. It's not like I didn't know I had a part to play in this accident – but by the way the professor is speaking now, it sounds like she blames me for all of it.

"It was a freak accident, Professor Xhao," Nora surprises me by saying to our teacher. "None of it was done on purpose."

Makayleigh and Nora look at me when Professor Xhao says nothing in response to Nora's assertion. I'm so thankful she tried to defend me, but I don't think it'll be enough to save me now. I don't know where to look next, so I just stare at my leather boots.

"Miss Willow. A word, please."

I glance up quickly at Professor Xhao. She's looking at me expectantly, as if I should have been watching her the entire time. This makes me even more nervous. I will my legs to work and finally follow her off to the side, along the fenceline. Snickers and giggles from behind us cause me to turn. Much to my horror, I see Désirée and Lucy watching the end of the Nymph pairings. Arms folded, their eyes are on me and the professor.

"Pay attention, Miss Willow."

The two girls bite down on a laugh, almost at the same time, and slowly saunter away from us when Professor Xhao gives them a hard look.

"This is a serious affair, Miss Willow. You could have set the entire Nymph's Field on fire. You could have severely injured your classmates. You are clearly not taking your position at Gomada Academy very seriously."

Tears well up in my eyes. I know that isn't true, but there's no way I can go up against a professor like Lilith Xhao, so I don't say anything. I'm sure I'd get into further trouble if I tried to defend myself.

"Your Air Affinity is on par with the level of a grade school child. You are months, if not years, of work behind your peers."

A grade school child.

This is the lecture I've feared the most – one that I always knew would come, but since it hadn't yet, I'd always thought I could somehow put it off. But I was wrong.

Tears fall down my cheeks as I try to stop my throat from falling apart. My face is flushed. I'm so embarrassed I can't think straight. Now I can't speak, even if I tried. Even if I wanted to talk in the first place.

"What is the reason for this remedial aptitude of yours, Miss Willow?"

I know I can't lie or sugarcoat this. I can't deny the truth, even if I wanted to. I'm not ashamed of who I am – but I am ashamed that my teacher berated me in front of other Nymphs and Enchantresses. I could even tell her I activated my electrical component just a short while ago, because a ghost and a monster were coming at me – but I doubt she'd believe me. Besides, getting my electricity to only work *once* is not the same as summoning it easily every time I try.

There's no way out of this.

Hugging my chest, I finally murmur, "I'm half-human."

I look up just in time to see a flicker of judgement spark in Professor Xhao's hazel eyes. "I see," she responds.

I swallow, but my saliva gets lost somewhere in my strained and hoarse throat.

"Well, that means you will certainly be leagues behind your peers. I suggest you spend more time working and less time with your friends."

All one of them?

"In the interest of everyone's safety and your own level of learning, I suggest you sit out the rest of practice. I will work with Miss Leith in your stead."

My God! Can things get any more humiliating than this? I want to die!

"Yes, ma'am," I finally sniffle.

She turns on her heel and walks away from me. I take advantage of this by wiping my eyes and praying that nobody was behind us to overhear what I said. I couldn't chance turning around again. When I finally force myself to look, no one is there. That's the only good thing about this horrible afternoon, then.

Watching everyone else practice – and practice well – makes me feel like an even bigger failure than before. I try hard not to cry again, because if I cry again, I'll be hysterical – and there's no coming back from that once I start.

Maybe Professor Xhao is right. Maybe I am a remedial student who spends too much time with other things than I do with my Affinity. Even though I've been practicing, it's true that I've been spending more time wanting to be with Nora and daydreaming about Ryker than wanting to perfect my Affinity. Even my resolve to get tougher to keep myself safe from bullies waned when I hadn't been tormented for a while. I guess I've been letting myself down – and it almost cost Nora her life. I wouldn't be able to live with myself if anything happened to her because of me.

Practice is over now. Students go to where I stand at the edge of the Field to get their bags and coats. Nora is suddenly in front of me, and I didn't hear her approach me. More proof that I'm a loser.

"Arya?" she asks, when I look up at her but don't say anything. "What happened? What did she say to you?"

I shake my head 'no' in dismissal, too embarrassed to explain.

Makayleigh is on Nora's heels. She moves to Nora's left and looks at me earnestly with her brown eyes. "Professor Xhao was wrong," she tells me. "My fire got out of control, too. It wasn't just you. Nobody blames you."

Too late to stop. Tears are falling down my face.

"Arya," Nora prompts when I stay quiet. She takes my arm. "What happened?"

"She wants me to work harder," is all I muster out, through my almost-hyperventilations.

Makayleigh frowns as her black hair blows in the breeze. "Okay. But we all have to work harder," she says softly, causing Nora to nod as she lets go of me. "We're all Freshmen."

"Hey! Lavy!"

"Oh, God," Makayleigh groans, rolling her eyes in what seems to be an affectionate way at the call from her new boyfriend, Alan Freight. He's in our Nymph Studies class, too. He's a funny guy with a good heart, from the looks of things. I guess that's one explanation for him having a Light Affinity.

"Excuse me," Makayleigh adds, beginning to walk away – but not without taking my arm first. "It'll be okay," she assures me. "Don't let her get to you. She's mean to everyone."

As Makayleigh walks away, I try to take in a shaky breath. She's right: I *have* seen Professor Xhao being rough on other students. But she's never once made one of those unlucky students sit out of a Field Practice class before.

Nora gives me a knowing look with her blue eyes. I know she wants me to tell her more than I already have. "What happened, Arya?" she repeats again, but more firmly this time.

It's hard to deny Nora, that's for sure. Nora rolls with the punches and doesn't beat around the bush for someone shy and quiet.

I take a nervous breath, shocked that I'm going to be confessing my biggest secret once again, so soon after the first time.

"I'm half-human," I confess, my voice small and waiting for judgement.

Nora's blue eyes don't change. She folds her arms over her chest. "Okay. So?" she asks, as if she doesn't understand the connection. "I'm sure a lot of students here are half-human. What does that have to do with anything?"

"She says I need extra help. The way she looked at me–" I can't finish my sentence because I'm crying harder now.

Nora grabs my arm. "What?" she snarls, her tone totally

different now. "For a school that's supposed to be so inclusive and tolerant, Professor Xhao is being a complete bitch. This is so hypocritical. We need to talk to the Headmistress."

I shake my head 'no'. "I don't want anyone else knowing," I sob.

Nora frowns at me. "But she can't get away with this, Arya. It's discrimination," she persists. "I get that it's upsetting, but if you let it go, she'll just keep putting you down."

I hesitate. I know Nora has a point. Professor Xhao is just another bully, like Désirée, Lucy, and Cole. But if I go up against her – or, at least, try to – she may take it out on me by failing me. And if I have to deal with her for five years, that'll be a fate worse than death. There's no way I can say anything.

"I'll think about it," I finally assert, knowing that even if my mind is made up, it won't hurt to at least consider going to the Headmistress if things get worse. I like having backup plans or fallback options.

"Uh-huh," Nora huffs, which surprises me. She seems to know me so well, even though we've only spent two weeks together. And in those two weeks, we learned some pretty personal things about each other.

Even though it's awful that I had to tell Professor Xhao my secret, at least I can trust Nora with it. The fact that we can trust each other with our most personal secrets makes the day a little bit better.

Nora turns to look at me. "Well?" she prompts, gesturing to her new outfit. "What do you think? Does this look better than the last one?"

It's hard to pick favourite outfits when it comes to Nora. She has a great fashion sense. Her last outfit was a black leather jacket, a sequin black tank top underneath, and black leggings and high boots. She thought it was 'too dark' for a campfire. Her second outfit is brighter: a white lace dress with the same jacket and boots. She even tied a black sash around the dress to complete the look. With her long black hair tied up into a high ponytail and her sharp blue eyes, Nora looks like she's about to hit the runway.

Tonight is really important to Nora, because she's going to approach Anja Berina and ask her out. On the bus ride back to Nora's house from the mall two weekends ago, Nora told me that she and Anja happened to join the same LGBTQ+ club the first week of classes. That was how they met – at the sign-up table on campus.

I want to say something to comfort Nora, but I don't know much about 'making a move' on people. Besides, with Nora's style, beauty, and way with words, I doubt she'll have any problems going out on a date with Anja.

"I love it," I tell her, hoping I'm supportive enough. "But aren't you going to be cold?"

Nora frowns at me. "A sacrifice, grasshopper," she purrs, causing me to roll my eyes. "You should consider changing, too – no offense,"she tacks on quickly, as if she thinks I'll burst into tears all over again.

I feel just as delicate, but I'm not offended by what she's saying. If it's coming from Nora, it's not an insult. There's a reason for what she's saying – and Nora tells me just that after turning around to add her earrings. She's looking in our vanity mirror on top of our dresser drawer.

"If you want to get Ryker's attention, maybe add some flair, girl," she continues. "I say, go for it. Turn this bad day around and ask him out."

My saliva gets stuck in my throat at her suggestion. I've never once asked a boy out before. I was always too scared. Part of me doesn't dare think about it now because of what Professor Xhao said to me earlier. But am I allowed to think about things outside of school if I've made a new resolution to *really* hunker down on my training? Besides, attending the campfire is mandatory. Each race puts on different events during the term, and the other two have to come. Kind of ironic, considering most of the student body can't stand the other two classes.

Maybe Nora has a point (again). She's being wise and to the point today – another reason why Anja will agree to go out with her (if she knows what's good for her, anyway). Maybe if I want to take charge of my life, I have to do more than just *daydream* about it. I've never been a 'take charge straight away' kind of person. I'd always hesitate and make a 'pro-con' list before doing anything.

When I video chatted with Mom and Dad earlier, to tell them about what happened, Mom did tell me to be brave; to try to rise above the challenges in front of me. Maybe I need to do more than just hope for the best.

"Aright," I sigh. "I'll get changed and figure out what to say."

"Just say what I'm going to say," Nora calls out to me, as I rummage through the pile of clothes on my made bed, trying to find something new that screams 'I'm not a complete mess – it's okay to date me'. "Ask him, 'do you want to hang out some-time?' and see what happens."

That sounds so simple, it just might work. But since it's me, and I have a knack for screwing things up, maybe it won't. But Nora sounds so confident (though she told me she was nervous about tonight), so I try to adopt some of her mandate of 'turning this bad day around'. After all, what could be worse than Professor Xhao humiliating me? Nothing that I can think of, that's for sure. I need to try and turn things around, for real – starting with tonight.

"You look good," Nora assures me, as I smooth out my dress for about the tenth time. It's a party dress I bought for the Winter Formal last year at school – black, knee-length, a bit low-cut, with a slit up the back. Not my style at all, but Mom told me it would look amazing on me, and she bought it for me, telling me 'you never know when this will come in handy'.

I guess mothers always know best.

"Thanks," I murmur, now tugging on the black jean jacket Nora let me borrow from her wardrobe. It's distressed in places, which contrasts nicely with the dress. With my high black heeled boots, it dresses down the outfit enough to make it passable for a campfire – but still 'stand-out-ish (to quote Nora)' enough to make an impression.

I just hope I didn't go to all this trouble for nothing. I'm terrified Ryker won't even notice me. How pathetic is that? But I guess that's what everyone feels when they like someone.

The campfire is out in the Shifter's Field, which means I get that same creepy feeling I got the first day of school as we get closer to Feara. It's made easier because the entire student body seems to be going in the same direction. I feel less worried, knowing that I'm one of hundreds – just a number.

Nora plays with one of her hoop earrings. She has two piercings on each lobe, with a cartilage piercing on her left ear. She looks nervous, but I don't want to point it out by comforting her. That may make her feel worse.

"When's the next club meeting?" I ask instead, trying to direct Nora's attention to something less intimidating.

Sure enough, Nora brightens a bit. "Next Tuesday," she reports. "Apparently, we're going to a black-and-white movie theatre next weekend. We're discussing the particulars at the next meeting."

"Cool," I approve. I love black-and-white movies.

"You should come," Nora tells me, looking at me earnestly. "I may need a buffer, if Anja turns me down."

Well, that plan of mine backfired.

I quickly take her arm. "She's not going to do that, Nora," I assure her. "You're going to make a really awesome impression. Why don't you grow flowers for her?"

Nora throws her head back and laughs at my joke – which was also a suggestion, sort of. "Hmm. Maybe I would, if I knew what her favourite flower was," she responds. "That loosened me up. Thanks, Arya." She grins at me, showing me that she truly does feel more light-hearted.

Despite the darkness, tell-tale signs of a campfire greet us: smoke, muffled laughter, and the smell of barbecue. I kind of forgot about dinner tonight, so I'm especially thankful that there will be food here.

One of the things that worries me about this party – besides asking Ryker out, anyway – is the fact that there will be drinking and probably drugs here, too. I'm sure the student body will keep those things secret – but that doesn't mean they won't happen. It reminds me of the 'don't use your Affinity or Shifting power against other students' mandate: we're told not to do it, but it happens, anyway.

I'm snapped out of my reverie when we finally get close to the entrance to the Shifter's Field. *Mobs* of people seem to be passing through to the other side. When Nora and I finally get close enough to see what the Field looks like now, we see that it's not just one campfire here, but lots of campfires. I'm surprised – wouldn't all this fire be dangerous? I'm met with a suffocating sadness when I realize how dangerous said *fires* could be, especially when I'm around. Maybe these fires are being controlled by Enchanters or Nymphs in an attempt to foster inclusivity between the three races.

Nora looks around at the party. Other than the campfires, laughing, and the occasional *popping* of beer bottles, it's hard to believe that this could be a 'party'. So many people are around that it's hard to see much of anything.

"Well, I'm starved," she announces, causing me to realize that she was looking for the barbecue station.

"Me, too," I agree, relieved that we can go get food together instead of me going off by myself. How pathetic – again!

When more partygoers disperse around us, clearing a path of sorts, Nora's blue eyes suddenly light up. "Holy crap! There's Anja!" she breathes. I'm surprised I can hear her over the commotion of laughing, talking, and mingling.

I try to follow Nora's gaze. I see a lot of girls standing near a large tree. I'm not sure which one is Anja. But I know Nora's nervous and probably ready to make her move, so I don't want to stall her.

"Go for it," I nudge her. "I'll wait here."

Nora whips her head around to look at me. "Are you sure?" she all but whispers. I can read her lips and see the confusion on her face.

I nod enthusiastically, even though being alone in a sea full of people makes me want to pee myself. "Sure," I tell her.

Nora touches my arm in thanks and quickly makes her way through the grassy area, now approaching the group of five girls. Maybe they're all Nymph Sophomores, or all members of the LGBTQ+ club. I do recognize a few of them from our Field Practice class.

Just as I'm preparing myself to turn around, to give Nora privacy, I hear someone state loudly from behind me,

"I'm surprised you're showing your face here – especially around so much fire."

I whirl around. I'm face-to-face with Désirée Chapin and her cousin, Lucy. Désirée is literally sparkling in a red sequin dress with an open cream-coloured trenchcoat. Lucy is quiet beside her, but equally *loud* in a short black dress with high heels.

But their outfits and Désirée's smug face do nothing to distract me from what was just said.

Désirée and Lucy know about the incident with the fire. I know she and Lucy were watching the show between Professor Xhao and I – but I thought the professor had ordered them away. Had they stayed and listened to our private conversation? That must mean that they overheard–

"Your kind doesn't belong anywhere near professional magic," Désirée states coolly, as if she's talking down to a little kid or a novice. According to Professor Xhao, my Affinity is on that level, anyway, so I guess it works.

My kind?

"That was a private conversation," I begin to accuse, causing the corners of Désirée's red lips to turn up into a cruel smile.

"Oh, no, *was* it?" she asks, her tone even more condescending than before. "Oops. I guess I shouldn't have told a few people about it, then."

I gape at her words.

"Well, it was actually a few *dozen* – whoever would listen – but I digress," Désirée continues as if what she did was meaningless; like she wasn't actively trying to ruin me and my family by doing what she did.

I'm so devastated and angry that I feel the wind kicking up around me. Désirée gives me a smug smile and her eyes *go red*.

"Don't even think about using your Affinity, Halfling – if you can call it that," she warns me sourly. "You'll set the *entire field on fire*," she finishes, to quote Professor Xhao.

I'm paralyzed by fear. I want to run away, but I can't. I also know if I try to use my Affinity, I could severely injure everyone here – the entire student body, from the looks of things. Even if, by some miracle, I got my electrical component to work, I know that, too, could be unpredictable. More people could die. I'm furious that Désirée is right. I'm furious that I'm powerless.

Coming to Gomada Academy was a mistake. People want to see me fail at every turn. Even my professors want me to leave!

Maybe I'm overreacting, but it doesn't really matter. It certainly feels like many people are rooting for me to crash and burn. Can I prove them all wrong? Or am I only proving them right by standing here, shaking and scared?

"Let's go, Dé," Lucy shocks me by asserting to her cousin.

I haven't heard much from Lucy over the past two weeks. Whenever she and her cousin *glide by*, it's usually Désirée who speaks. I used to think it was just blind loyalty on Lucy's part – but the look Désirée gives Lucy in return tells me that it may be more about control than anything else.

"Why? I'm having so much fun. Aren't you, Luce?" she responds lightly, her tone not matching the fiery look she gave her relative.

Lucy shrugs, her blue eyes looking dismissive now. "Not really," she responds, turning on her heel and walking away. I'm stunned by this. I've seen and heard that Lucy is just as big a bully as her cousin.

Désirée watches Lucy leave, but it's only a brief pause before looking down at me again, as if she's prepping herself to torment me further.

"Well, you've bored my cousin. That's evident enough. So, why don't you do us all a favour and just go back to where you came from, Nymph-Lite? What's the politically correct term for someone like you, anyway?" she adds, folding her arms as I wipe my face. "Do you even know it?"

"Witching hour already, Chapin?"

Désirée and I both flinch at the sound, but Désirée's more courageous than I am because her green eyes shoot above me, looking for the source of the voice. I know I need to find out for my own safety, so I finally turn around, wondering if this will turn into a bloodied group beating.

Désirée doesn't look intimidated anymore when she locks eyes with Cole. "I suppose it's natural for the riff-raff to be here, since it is your low-key affair we're attending," she scoffs, causing Cole to roll his eyes sourly, unaffected by her taunt.

I've never been impressed by anything Cole does, but right now, I wish I could have his 'couldn't care less' mantra about bullies and insults. Of course, I'd never tell him that.

What is he doing here, anyway? Is he coming to join in on the fun? It's not like Cole has ever held back from ridiculing me.

Wait. It's been maybe a week since Cole has tried to harass me. At first, I didn't really think anything of it – maybe it's just a coincidence – but now, I'm wondering if Ryker did have that talk with him about leaving me alone. Maybe asking Ryker out will go better for me than I thought, if he's trying to make my life easier for me. But I don't want to get my hopes up too high. Besides, I have to survive this altercation first.

"You can always leave," Cole states, sucking in a drag of his disgusting cigarette. I don't know how he has any friends or acquaintances with that disturbing habit of his.

Désirée narrows her eyes up at Cole. "Do you know what's curious, Cole?" she asks of him, but I can tell it's rhetorical. "Why you've never shown anyone your so-called *alter ego*. Is it truly hideous and disturbing, just like you?"

Instead of being gutted by her, Cole gives Désirée a frightening grin after blowing out the smoke from his cigarette. "You have no idea," he tells her, his tone eerie. Even the smoke following his words looks creepy. It makes what he said terrifying – especially since I've seen first-hand what his alter ego looks like.

I never thought I'd see the day that Désirée Chapin would move away from and even turn her back on someone, but she does so with Cole. Of course, she gives him one last evil look before doing it.

As soon as no one else can overhear, I glance up at Cole warily. "Why did you do that?" I ask.

He looks down at me. "Do what?" he answers, sounding robotic, like he doesn't want to talk to me. That makes two of us.

I frown. "Get her off my back," I finally try to say. Maybe he wasn't doing it for me, though. There could be dozens of other reasons why Cole did what he did – and I'm sure that they have nothing to do with–

"Don't flatter yourself, Arya," he tells me flatly. "You only have time for one bully."

Talk about 'flattering yourself', I think dryly, but refuse to say it out loud, because I have no more courage left. But since I have some paranoia left over, I ask, "Did you hear what we–"

"You're half-and-half? Figured as much," Cole interrupts, causing fire to rip through my chest. I want to electrocute him all over again.

"How kind of you," I snap.

He gives me a frown. "I couldn't care less, actually." He glances behind him suddenly, then looks back at me. "Little tip: the small white pills getting passed around will kill you," he states sourly. "They're not Halloween candy."

I glower up at him as he sucks on his cigarette like a helpless addict. How stupid does he think I am that I don't know what drugs look like?

When he smiles at me, I get even angrier. "Go bother somebody else," I almost spit out, through clenched teeth.

Cole rolls his eyes, the smile still plastered to his stupid face as he blows smoke out of his mouth. I'm surprised it doesn't hit me, but maybe the wind shifted at the last minute. I'm usually more attuned to air and wind patterns, but I guess I'm too rattled to focus right now.

"It won't be as fun. But fine," he responds, his green eyes staring down at me in a weird way as he passes me. It's like he's trying to figure out how best to mess with me next time. It sends a shiver down my spine.

*I **hate** him!*

Fourteen

COLE AND RYKER'S DISCOVERY

I hate these damned campfires.

Shifters have to do the same stupid thing every year for everyone else on-campus. I don't know why we have to do this for people who spit on us daily. It's annoying as fuck. I don't go to the Nymphs' dinner or whatever sophisticated shit the Enchanters and Enchantresses put on. It's all a waste of my time.

I *was* feeling pretty good until just now. I got to cut down one of the Chapin creatures, and freak out the Pixie, to boot. Of course, with Ryker being within range of the entire thing, I couldn't mess with Arya the way I really wanted to.

On the other hand, though, maybe that has run its course. Sure, I think she's a waste of space, but I have more important things to worry about – like the fact that a fucking ghost is closing in on campus. Little boarding school games don't mean much when you stack them up against ghost hunting. And right now, it's ghost-2, Cole-0. I hate being outsmarted by people – even ghosts.

Walking over to the edge of the party, I reach the fringe of dark trees outlining the Shifter's Field. I begin to smoke again. Out here, no one will bother me, and I'll be able to think clearly.

I'm surprised that Headmistress Frow – or even Professor Qadir – is leaving me alone right now. Even though I tried to avoid those security cameras last weekend, I'm sure I wasn't a hundred percent successful. And I was naked from the waist-down, carrying a girl. You'd think I'd be kicked out for that. Nobody would believe the ghost story thing – except for Frow. If Qadir heard about this, he'd kick my ass from here to Vyquean.

I guess I could've had a golden horseshoe up my ass, and all that was recorded on-camera were shadows and shit, but my luck is normally never that good. Factor in the Pixie, and my luck is even worse. She does something to me. I get so mad I can't function. Even now, when I was just *helping her* (sort of), she had to get all bitchy on me. Ungrateful little–

I almost choke on my own cigarette smoke when none other than Arya herself is walking a few yards ahead of me, with Ryker. It looks like they're talking. I yank my black hood up over my head and grunt in frustration. Apparently, Ryker thinks he's above centuries of mistrust between the Nymphs and Enchanters. Having the same Affinity but on two completely different levels is enough to usually get most of them going at it. But not Ryker. Annoying.

It's not like I'm trying to listen in on them. With the wind carrying their words and my super-senses, I'm kind of annoyed that I *can* hear them. I wish I had brought my Bluetooth head-phones, so I wouldn't have to be tortured like this. The way Arya is trying to be all cute and interesting is enough to make me puke. And here I was, thinking Ryker would be more concerned about getting Diego and I to one-up Crabtree tonight. We'd sent him a group message earlier, but he hasn't responded yet. Probably too busy thinking about getting in the Nymph's pants.

I put my head down and try hard not to laugh – because with my luck, someone would hear me – when I hear the Pixie stammer,

"So, um, I was wondering if you'd like to hang out sometime. With me, I mean."

It's so pathetic that I'm actually in pain trying not to laugh. I'd figured they were past this shit by now, but I don't care. I take a drag of my cigarette to try and distract myself from cackling.

"Uh, sure," Ryker responds. With my head still down, I can't make out his face, but something about his answer is weird.

"But, you know, maybe as friends," Ryker shocks me by admitting, causing me to look up at the two of them.

Wow. I had him pegged wrong. Here I was, thinking he was all into Arya because he legit found me at school and told me to keep away from her. I thought he was trying to be a *hero*, or whatever. Turns out he was just being, well, *Ryker*. Yeah, he's an Enchanter and an annoying guy, but he's nicer than a lot of people here.

I think it has something to do with the fact that Ryker has both Light and Darkness as his Affinities. It's rare to have two 'conflicting' powers like that. He probably feels like everyone's watching him. Diego and I get that. We even respect it. Hell, he's the only Enchanter I'd ever speak to willingly.

I snap back to reality when Arya clears her throat and gives Ryker a small smile. "Oh. Sure. Okay," she agrees. I'm surprised at how quickly and easily she got that out to him. I would've thought she would've been a goner by now.

"Great. Maybe coffee or something," Ryker goes on, folding his arms and stepping back from her. It's obvious he's trying to move away from the whole thing. "Enjoy the party," he tells her, giving her one last smile before passing her.

"You, too," she responds just before he passes her.

Well, I was going to laugh before, but now isn't the time anymore. I got too distracted with my smoking and thinking about Ryker's Affinities. Plus, it's hard to laugh at someone when they look so crushed. Usually, I'd have no problem doing that, but–

Arya reaches into her jacket pocket and pulls out her phone. Probably going to message one of her friends about her crash-and-burn. Again, I should be laughing, but I'm not. It must be a cold day in Hell, because I actually feel sorry for her. Thank God no one will ever know about that.

Loudness is heard from the other end of the Shifter's Field – probably drunken shit by Crabtree and his goons – which makes the Pixie turn around to look.

I roll my eyes at how scared she always is – but at the same time, she's not bad to look at from this angle. She may be a crybaby and annoying as fuck, but she has a great ass. That tight black dress made me notice her for the first time. Her top half isn't so bad, either.

If a bag could be thrown over her head, or if she could be shut up with a muzzle or something, I wouldn't mind–

Damn!

I can't believe I'm thinking about sleeping with a *Nymph*! Fuck my life! I want to ignore it, but it's hard to do that when she's standing right in front of me. With the wind picking up her long brown hair and stupid sad face, I feel a *pull* to go over there.

What the fuck is wrong with me? She's a waste of space. She's a halfling. She's weak and useless. She's a *Nymph*! She's the worst partner in crime for ghost hunting. I should want nothing to do with her.

And I know I feel that way. She's just, well, hot. And I feel sorry for her, like I said before. But that's it. It probably won't even last that long, anyway.

Thank God for my phone vibrating in my jeans pocket. I pull it out, seeing an entirely different kind of red when I read a text from Diego.

> Crabtree's dead. He's messing with Taylor again.

I want to smash my phone against the tree trunk behind me, but instead, I hold in my anger and just reply,

> I'm on my way.

And begin to ease my way back toward the party. I know Taylor's scent – I'll be able to find her without Diego giving me her location. He's got similar senses, so I bet he's doing fine, too.

Lukas is Taylor's Mentor. I shouldn't be surprised that an Enchanter like Crabtree is messing with a Shifter like Taylor. If anything, I'm doing pretty much the same to Arya. The difference is – Taylor doesn't deserve it. And Shifters take care of their own.

As I pass Arya, she's still so wrapped up in her stupid rejection from Ryker that she doesn't even notice me. She's so brainless! It's hard not to mess with her all over again, but I have bigger fish to fry.

I weave in and out of partygoers, who all look the same to me now. Drunk, high, or just plain partying – they're all annoying. I hate stupid things like this. I'd rather party on my own, or with Diego. And now, Lukas is fucking things up even more by bothering Taylor. I'm angry that he thinks he can do this without suffering any kind of whiplash.

That reminds me.

I pull out my phone again and message the group chat between Diego, Ryker, and I.

> Johnson, Crabtree's shitting on Hayden.
> We're going to put a stop to it.

> Lead the way, Hudson.

> Taylor's safe. I'm staying with her for now.
> Crabtree's heading toward the thicket. I'll
> meet you guys there in five.

I'm surprised. Lukas acts like a rebel but secretly hates doing anything on the edge. Diego saw him going to the Gomada Thicket. It just doesn't make sense.

> I'm closer to the front of the school. I'll
> get him.

> On my way

I write, just so Ryker knows he's got backup. Lukas can fight dirty, from what I've seen.

Getting back to the thicket, it's definitely not safe for even someone as useless as Lukas Crabtree to be heading there now. With that ghost lurking around–

At least I'll be making good on my 'deal' with Ryker, and Diego and I can finally kick Crabtree's ass after a year of being on the cusp of it. Perfect.

When I pass the professors' dorms and can now see the front of campus, I'm surprised that no one else is out here. It's like a ghost town – bad choice of words. Everyone's at the party – but it's weird that no one is out here, not even teachers.

It's quiet. Too quiet.

And it's cold out here, too. Maybe because no one's out here – but still. The wind seems thicker, somehow. Creepier.

Fuck.

If I thought I was thrown off before, I'm stunned to see Ryker standing right in front of the gates to campus. He's looking stiff, freaked, even from behind. And it doesn't take me very long to figure out why.

Fog is suddenly spreading out all over campus. It wasn't there just a second ago. It's almost like Ryker skidded to a stop as soon as he saw it.

"Johnson!" I yell, even though part of me is too scared to make noise or call attention to myself now.

Ryker turns, but it seems hard for him to do it. Is he scared, too, or in pain? It's hard to tell.

"Get over here! Get away from it!" I order.

"I can't – I can't move!" he protests.

What a coward! I begin to think – but hearing the fear in his voice makes me realize something.

Maybe he can't move because he *can't move*. When I first saw that ghost, I felt frozen, too. I wasn't sure if it was just me being freaked, or if the ghost had anything to do with it. But if it's happening to someone else–

I finally sprint over to him. Why the hell am I risking my life for an *Enchanter*? But I know why. Most days, I don't mind Ryker. And I figure he'd do the same for Diego and I. And he was even willing to stick his nose out for Taylor. I won't forget that. Annoying or not, Ryker's got a code of loyalty he lives by.

It's weird. I'm skidding to a stop beside Ryker, but I can still shake his arm and turn my body to look at the Gomada Thicket. He may be frozen, but I'm not.

"Where's Crabtree?" I ask.

Ryker can't even turn his head to look at me now. He's

sweating. He looks horrified. His brown eyes are wide and nervous.

"He saw me tailing him. He began to run. Then he became like a– like a *zombie*," Ryker breathes, his voice shaking now.

"Like the TV show?" I frown.

It looks like Ryker's trying to move – shrug, or shake his head – but he can't. "Sort of. He just became slower and less calculated. Almost like he was being hypnotized."

Hypnotized?

Just as Ryker finishes that last word, more fog surrounds us and the higher hills at the fringe of the thicket. It's dark and creepy. A damp feeling splashes over my back, making me shiver. I try to force the Tedla to come out, but he actually pushes back. He's not coming!

What the hell?!

"I can't even use an Affinity!" Ryker gasps. It's like he's also trying to fight back but can't. "My Light won't break through, and even the fucking Darkness doesn't want to!"

I don't know much about Light and Dark Affinities, but I do know they draw power from Heaven and Hell. If those two places aren't going to help–

I'm almost blinded when a strong light flickers on top of one of the hills. It's so bright that Ryker and I squint. It's not from the moon, making the fog look like claws trying to choke something.

We suddenly see an outline of a person against the light. A tall person, with blonde hair–

"Holy shit, it's Crabtree!" Ryker exclaims.

"Crabtree! Get out of there!" I scream. Lukas may be a dick, and I hate his guts, but I don't want him to die or get eaten by a ghost. There's no other explanation for what's out there.

"Crabtree!" Ryker screams. "Move it! Get outta there!"

The fog is now wrapping around him, like those creepy claws I thought they were. Someone hollers against the howling wind – and then the light goes out.

Ryker throws his head down and sucks in a deep breath. "My God. I can move," he exhales, grabbing his hair with his hand. "What the fuck was that, Hudson?" he asks, looking at me wide-eyed now.

"That's the ghost," I say simply as if it's common sense.

His jaw drops as he stares at me. "Say what?" he asks.

"Arya and I have seen it," I tell him. "It's been coming near campus over the past couple of weeks."

"You and Arya?" he asks, as if he can't understand what I'm saying. "Who else knows about this?"

"Diego – sort of," I explain. Might as well tell him everything now. "And Frow. She tracked it the other night. Don't know what else happened."

And it's true. I don't. I saw her at school last Monday, so I know she's still alive – but I don't know what happened to her that night.

Ryker shakes his head, like he's still struggling with the idea that a ghost can be around here.

"Ryker!" I shout at him, pointing toward the thicket with my right hand. "We fucking saw what it can do! Get your shit together!"

He sucks in another breath. "Fine!" he snaps. "Just give me a second, Hudson! This is some crazy shit!"

Ryker turns his head, and I follow in case he sees something else now. But all we see are the dark hills, trees, and bushes. No more fog. No more weird light.

It was the ghost, for sure.

Thunder ripples above us, causing us to look up at the sky. Churning black clouds are swarming overhead.

"Where the fuck did Crabtree go?" Ryker asks me.

"The ghost got him," I respond quietly, but simply again.

"Ghosts can't just materialize and *get people*!" Ryker tells me, like I'm the stupid one. "We gotta go up there!"

Part of me thinks that us going off-campus to look for Lukas is a waste of time. There's no way he's still up there. He screamed. He's either captured, eaten, or dead. The Lukas we knew isn't up there.

But at the same time, I know Ryker's right. We can't just leave him if he's up there. And asshole or not, we need to do what we can for him.

We get to the locked-up gates. Ryker throws his hand out and a blast of darkness hits the wrought-iron locks. They clank open, unbroken and ready to be locked up when we get back.

"Thank God I can still use these," he sighs, as if he wasn't fully *himself* without his Affinities. I understand. When the Tedla couldn't, or *wouldn't*, come out, I felt less myself, too.

I know the cameras probably see us. But this is a new game, entirely. Maybe we'll be able to talk our way out of this one. Maybe not. Either way, we're going.

It's almost like I'm not running fast enough as I throw myself in the direction of the hills, where we last saw the back of Crabtree's head. Ryker's right. We need to see if we can find him. He may be hurt, dead, or worse.

Ryker is shorter than me, but he somehow bounds ahead of me and leaps up the last few feet of the hill. Right on Ryker's heels, I finally skid to a stop beside him.

Nothing.

"Holy shit," Ryker breathes.

"Maybe he was dragged off," I suggest.

"There's no blood trail. No sign of him even being moved," Ryker responds as we walk a bit.

I'm annoyed that he's right again, but it's true. Now that I'm less panicked and my senses are working better, I can't follow any kind of trail. It's like Lukas' scent just stops here. The wind doesn't give away any clues, either.

"So, he was taken," Ryker thinks out loud, stopping and rubbing his forehead. "Fuck. This isn't good."

"Things aren't looking very good for you two, either, gentlemen."

Ryker and I spin around, freaked by the third voice because we know who it belongs to – and that's not good, either.

Headmistress Frow is standing right behind us, with Greyson at her side. He doesn't scare me, but the way Frow is looking at me now sure as shit does. Even her red-tailed hawk Familiar is circling, eyeing us.

Diego sinks onto his bed and holds his head. "Good God, I leave you two morons alone for five minutes," he sighs as Ryker stares down at him angrily.

Our window is only open a crack, and we still hear the drunken shouts and laughs of partiers out at the Shifter's Field. Morons who don't have a clue while the three of us are in here, shitting ourselves – and even worse, Crabtree is ghost chow.

"Shut up, Jasper," he snaps, surprising me. Maybe Ryker's still riding his adrenaline high, and his usual 'nice guy' self is on hold. "We saw Crabtree get fucking murdered by an evil spirit!"

"He screamed. And he wasn't up there when we went after him," I tried to explain.

Diego looks up at us now. "So, let me guess. Frow is expelling both of you?"

Ryker wipes his eyes. He's tired and clearly pissed off that Diego's a step behind on everything. Not really Diego's fault because he wasn't there, but I can get why Ryker's frustrated. I was the same when he asked me about the ghost in the first place.

"No," Ryker responds.

"He sweet-talked her," I smirk, causing Ryker to glare at me. "He said we saw Crabtree go off-campus and got worried, so we followed him. Then, we heard him screaming and went to check it out," I add, to get Ryker off my back.

"And she bought that?" Diego asks, looking surprised.

"It wasn't Hudson selling it," Ryker states immediately, causing me to frown at him.

"True," Diego nods. "You don't do shit like that, ever. Lucky you were there, Johnson."

Ryker sighs. "Not really, man. I can't believe we were en route to kick Crabtree's ass when an evil spirit did it instead. Now I feel bad."

"Don't feel bad," Diego and I say, almost at the same time.

"You didn't cause it to happen," I tack on, because I actually feel bad for Crabtree, too. I even feel bad for wanting to kick his ass in the first place. I definitely need to be drunk for the rest of this conversation.

"Crabtree has been fucking with people for a long time," Diego agrees. "Who knows why he went up there in the first place."

"That's the thing," Ryker pushes, his brown eyes wild with confusion. "I have no clue why he went up there. As soon as he got to the fenceline, it was like he became somebody else."

"Like a zombie?" I press, causing Ryker to nod without looking at me.

"So, you think the ghost did it?" Diego guesses.

Ryker and I stare at each other. We were both thinking that, but didn't have the guts to say it.

I frown at Diego. "Thanks for finally believing me, dipshit," I grunt.

Diego gives me a smirk now. "Sorry, Hudson. I guess I listen to Johnson more than you."

I roll my eyes and huff at that, causing Ryker to snort in annoyance. "Are you two done squabbling, or should I leave you alone?" he sighs impatiently.

"We're done," I respond.

"So, what're we gonna do about this?" Diego asks us. "Crabtree is missing – or worse. People are going to notice."

"We heard – or Hudson heard – Greyson and the Headmistress talking when we left her office," Ryker informs Diego. "Sounds like they think he was taken, too. The school's gonna get an email or something about this soon. Or a meeting. We're not sure."

"We didn't want to stick around outside. Too risky," I add. "If we hung around and got nabbed for it, Ryker's 'innocent' cover would've been blown."

Diego stands up now. "Well, alright. I guess we lay low until then. Don't want the Headmistress or security to think we know about the ghost."

"All we told them was that we saw a bright light, fog, and heard screaming," Ryker affirms. "No need to let them know what we know."

"Not like they'd do the same for us," I grunt.

"Until this gets sorted, no one should go near the thicket," Diego states, folding his arms and suddenly looking at me.

"Why the fuck are you looking at me, now?" I demand.

"Because you've been there, three times," Diego snaps back.

"Four times," Ryker corrects, causing Diego to gape at me.

"No," I order Ryker, who ignores me and says to Diego,

"He went with Arya last weekend."

"Arya?" Diego repeats, looking at me in a weird way now. "The Nymph you hate?"

"She saw the ghost, too, remember?" I shoot back at Diego – even though I actually can't remember if I ever told him that.

"Uh-huh," Diego sighs.

"Can it," I order.

Ryker looks from Diego to me. "Well, I'm tired, and Zola needs to be fed and walked, so I'll leave you two to bicker."

Diego and I both make an answering face at Ryker as he walks to our dorm room door. "Best to keep this under your hats, boys," he tells us.

Diego nods once. "Yeah. Don't want to get anyone panicked."

"The meeting or email will do that, anyway," I agree, but as Ryker unlocks and opens the door to leave, I think twice about that.

When Diego gets a phone call and steps out – making me believe that Lucy is the caller, and I don't want to waste any more time on it – I decide I need to do some errands of my own. It's still thundering outside, so I grab my beanie and yank my hood up over my head as I leave our dorm room.

Making my way back to the Shifter's Field, I wonder how stupid I'm being for doing this. Maybe I'm just freaked from what happened. Or maybe I have no idea what I'm doing anymore – and just don't care how brainless it is. Truth is, if that ghost can control people, we're all goners.

What can Frow and Greyson do about that? It's a fucking ghost! It's not a criminal or a serial killer. It's not someone you can throw in prison or slap cuffs over and make them useless. There's no way to stop it. It's on a fucking rampage, and we're all going to pay the price for some unknown reason.

Maybe Frow knows more than she's letting on – or maybe someone at school is messing with dark stuff. Anything is possible, I guess.

But if that was true, why target Crabtree? He's a jerk, but he's not stupid enough to mess with things that don't concern him. Besides, his Affinities are – or were – Poison and Earth. Don't think he was capable of messing with dark magic. People with a Darkness Affinity, like Lucy and Ryker, are the only ones who can dabble in that shit.

I'm distracted by that when I walk by the Dark Witch herself. She's standing across from her cousin. It's weird to see this, but they're both yelling at each other. Désirée, who would have been able to see me walk by – isn't even paying attention, because she's screaming something at Lucy.

These two bitches never fight. If anything, I figure they didn't know how. Weird that they're fighting tonight, of all nights. Maybe I'd use that to my advantage if I wasn't in such a freaked-out mood. But not right now.

It's late, and the sky is heavy with rain on the way when I finally find Arya. She's sitting with Nora and some other girl I don't know. All I know for sure is that she's another Nymph.

It looks like they're deep in some girly talk, but as soon as they notice me, they clam up fast. I don't care.

Nora stares me down – which is interesting, because she's sitting down and much smaller than I am. I gotta say, for a Nymph, this one is pretty surprising.

"We're having fun – don't bother us," she tells me sourly. The girl to her left snickers at that, while Arya doesn't do anything except smile.

What a bunch of idiots! People are dying, and they're still playing preschool games!

Ignoring Nora completely, even though she just pissed me off and sent me through the roof, I look down at Arya.

"Come on," I order.

She frowns. "What?"

"Just get over here," I snap, slower and hopefully with some hidden meaning telling her this is serious business.

"Don't tell her what to do," I hear Nora telling me. Her friend even says, "You can't talk to people like that," but I ignore both.

Maybe Arya realizes that this is about the ghost, because I'm pretty sure she wouldn't get up and follow me normally – because she stands up and folds her arms.

"I'm not your trained animal," she tells me angrily.

I cock my head to the side. "You got up, though," I smirk.

She glares up at me now, causing me to smile. Well, I feel a bit better now.

I hold my hand out, and she stomps past me. I hear Nora muttering something with 'jackass' in it as I follow Arya. She stops at a quiet spot away from the fires and the drunken laughter of Freshman idiots. I can tell they're Freshmen, because they're stoked by the idea that they suddenly have a bit more freedom than before. It's annoying, especially when you think about the fact that Crabtree doesn't have any more freedom left. Asshole or not, he didn't deserve to go out like that. It makes me mad.

"What is this about?" Arya asks me, arms folded again and looking at me like she's trying to figure out what scheme I'm planning against her.

"Don't go back to the thicket – ever," I tell her, not wasting any time with her games. "And don't leave the school. Make sure your friends don't, either."

Her dark brown eyes widen. "Why? What happened?" she asks.

Fuck. I should've known she'd ask. "Your boyfriend and I saw the ghost nab an Enchanter," I tell her.

She glares up at me like she wants to see my head chopped off with a chainsaw. But her jaw drops when she realizes the seriousness of what I just said.

"The ghost took someone?" she exclaims.

"Shut up!" I hiss, looking around quickly, just in case. Maybe if anyone heard that, they'd be too drunk to understand it, anyway.

She hits my arm, causing me to look down at her again. "Who is he? Is he dead?" she asks quietly.

I shrug. "You don't know him. Don't know for sure," I add, even though I'm pretty sure Crabtree is a goner.

Even though I don't really want to tell her everything, I feel like I may have to, so she's not added to the ghost's kill count.

"We think he was hypnotized or something," I tell her. "He left campus and walked right into the woods. We followed him."

I spare her the creepy fog fingers and the screaming.

"My God," Arya breathes. "Wait," she stops. "Did you get in trouble?"

I shrug again. "Of course not," I respond, even though I'm still shocked by the fact that Ryker and I escaped Frow like that. He really does have a way with people.

She scoffs at that. "Figures," she mumbles.

I smile at her. "If you broke the rules more often, you'd be better at not getting caught, or punished."

She rolls her eyes. "Fantastic life advice, Cole."

Folding my arms now, I frown down at her. "Don't be a hero and try to find him, or figure it out," I tell her firmly. "You'll wind up ghost chow."

She looks up at me as if she's trying to challenge me. "Since when do you care?"

I roll my eyes this time, a smile on my face. "I don't. Just figure you should know, since you saw it, too."

We look at each other. Arya looks freaked. I guess if I gave a shit, I'd think about the fact that she had a rough night. Found out by Désirée, screwed over by Ryker, and now stressed over ghost shit.

I feel bad for her. Feeling bad for Crabtree must be making me soft. Now, I feel bad for everyone? Who the hell am I?

"Well, thanks – I guess," she sighs, as if she didn't really want the warning. She'd rather end up dead than worry about some paranormal crap. She's like everybody else here.

It's hard for me to swallow. "Whatever. Happy to ruin your life again," I respond.

Arya scowls at me when a few girls stumble over to us. One drunken girl slams into Arya from behind, laughing as she goes. Arya screams and tumbles forward – uncoordinated and stupid, as usual. I grab her so she doesn't knock me over, too. Her hands grab my chest, as if she just wanted to grab something, anything, so she wouldn't fall over.

"Watch it!" I snap at the three of them, who just chortle at us as they trip to the next campfire.

I look down at Arya, who's now staring up at me. She looks like she's a mixture of embarrassed and scared – like she thinks I'll shove her face into the dirt for bumping into me by accident. And maybe I would have. But not tonight.

Looking at her now, with my hands on her waist, it's hard for me to swallow again. My heart is thumping in my ears. Her big brown eyes kind of swallow mine up.

"Sorry," Arya tells me, still looking like I'm going to eat her alive, or something.

With her this close to me, it's kind of hard to think. I try to remember all the reasons why I hate her; why she's useless and a waste of my time. But with her eyes on me and her hair blowing against my fingertips, it's hard to focus on how annoying she is to me.

I let go of her. "Whatever. Just do what I say, for once," I tell her sternly.

Arya rolls her eyes and hugs her chest as she steps back from me. She does it as soon as I let go. "Yes, master," she shoots back at me, causing me to grin down at her.

She turns around and walks away. My eyes trail from her flowing brown hair to her perfect bubble butt as she all but scampers off. I fold my arms, still feeling her waist on my fingertips as sweat clings to the back of my neck.

This entire night is fucked up. With a good night's sleep, I'll probably feel better tomorrow.

Fifteen

ARYA'S BROKEN SPIRIT

I tremble as I walk away from Cole – but not because I'm cold from the weather or the frigid rain drizzling down from the heavy clouds. I'm terrified over what has happened – to a student I don't even know.

Someone was taken – or worse! – right from under the nose of the authorities at Gomada Academy. I guess I'd thought that since the ghost hadn't shown up at campus for a while, it was just gone, and nothing would come of it. It was probably really stupid to think that way. I guess I wanted to focus on making friends and crushing on Ryker. And then when Professor Xhao cut me down today, well–

It seemed better and safer to focus on reality, not the supernatural. Or paranormal.

But it's impossible to ignore this now. A ghost out there is now deliberately taking students away from campus. Maybe it's a one-off thing, but I don't know who this Enchanter is, so I have no idea if he was someone who could have been involved in something paranormal.

It's hard to know anything for sure when you know

nothing at all. It's obvious that Cole knows way more than what he told me – and it bothers me that he's not telling me things I deserve to know.

Who was abducted, or killed? What were the circumstances behind it? How did Ryker and Cole not get into trouble, when they went off campus past curfew to discover what happened?

Why is Cole keeping all of this from me? Is it because he hates me, or does he not think I can handle it? Regardless, I deserve to know what I'm up against!

I'm walking in a blind trance, because I abruptly stop in front of the campfire where Nora and Anja are sitting. It looks like the sudden rain hasn't done much to affect their conversation. I watch them before turning around again, deciding not to go back and interrupt. I'm not sure what the circumstances were of Nora asking Anja out – but it looks like she was successful, because we've been hanging out together all evening. I don't want to mess up any potential date for them, though – and I'm getting wet, cold, and scared out of my mind – so I turn around and head back to Meera.

It's hard to get around the groups of students partying without a care in the world. I was once one of them – if you count talking and not engaging in drugs or alcohol 'partying' – but now, I'm irritated by it. Someone is missing; a ghost is haunting campus, and these people are *having fun*?

I eventually gently push through a few people to try and find my way toward the front of the Shifter's Field. On my way out, I spot the black-haired boy Cole is friends with, and Lucy. They seem to be involved in an intense conversation. I'm surprised by this. I thought Shifters didn't make friends with anyone outside of their race. Ryker seems to be the exception.

Ryker.

As soon as I think about him, I'm drowned in mortification and sadness. I can't believe I asked him out, for one thing

– and the fact that he said 'no' really threw me. It was my first-ever rejection, and even though I tried not to get my hopes up, I still thought he'd say 'yes'. I truly thought he liked me.

Keeping me safe from Cole and fixing my Trinket were mere acts of kindness. I don't know much about boys, so maybe I'm not supposed to find anyone. It seems like winning the lottery, and getting struck by lightning, are easier to come by than liking someone who likes you back.

I'm fighting tears when Lucy suddenly makes eye contact with me. She touches the boy's arm, leaves him, and approaches me.

No way. She has to be going somewhere else. There's no way she's going to–

"Arya?" she begins, stepping in front of me now.

Well, crying isn't an option anymore.

I don't respond because I'm afraid my voice will be shaky, and I don't know what to say to her. I can only assume she's here to pick up where Désirée left off.

"I wanted to apologize for before," Lucy shocks me by saying, adjusting her black jean jacket against her short black dress.

I say this out loud before even thinking about the consequences of going up against an Enchantress like Lucy, whose Affinities I don't even know about yet. "I don't believe you."

Lucy doesn't look surprised by my statement. "I'm sure you don't, but... Well, our behaviour was out of line."

I fold my arms, trying to distance myself from her. "If that's all you came to say–" I begin, wanting to get as far away from her, the party, and people as possible.

"It isn't."

Lucy looks from left to right – something people seem to do in Gomada that bothers me because it's so cruel – then back to me.

"I'd like to get to know you and Nora a bit better," she proposes. "I don't really have many other acquaintances other than my cousin, and... I want to branch out a bit."

I'm shocked – again. In my whole life, I've never been asked to be someone's friend like this. I don't believe this, either. Is it some kind of trick? Is Désirée in on the whole thing? This sounds like the perfect kind of 'mean girl game' Lucy and Désirée would play.

"You'll have to talk to Nora about that," I respond – which I hope also spells out 'I'm not interested'.

Lucy seems to get my double message because she quickly runs a hand through her shoulder-length blonde hair, her blue eyes darting away from me.

"Well," she begins. "Have a good rest of your evening." She walks away from me – and for a split second, I feel bad for hurting her feelings. But then I realize that she's probably playing me, and I try to squish the feeling.

It seems like most students at Gomada Academy are schemers, bullies, and rivals. I really wish I could go back home. Normal human bullies and everyday teenage problems seem much better than ghost hauntings and girls with Affinities that could kill you in your sleep.

I finally get to Meera. As soon as I'm on the fourth floor, I feel safer and more relaxed, so thoughts of what happened tonight start to flood back.

How am I supposed to go about everyday life when someone was taken from the school?

What if this is just the beginning? What if the ghost plans on taking even more students away from Gomada Academy? And why is the ghost doing it?

What's going to happen with my training? How can I get better – 'better enough' that Professor Xhao leaves me alone?

How will I face Ryker for the next four years after what

happened? It may not mean much to him, but it's so embarrassing to me that I'm not sure I'll be able to act normally the next time I see him.

What kind of creepy schemes are Désirée and Lucy cooking up against Nora and I? And what about the fact that so many people now know about my family secret? Just thinking about that makes me want to cry all night long. And then there's the fact that I'm totally slacking on the Mentorship Program – but only because Cole is evil.

I'm so tired and scared that I wonder if the two will clash, resulting in a sleepless night. I really hope I can sleep. I'll need all the rest I can get if I must survive in this realm.

As soon as I get to Room 407, I feel my phone vibrate inside my jacket pocket. I pull it out, seeing a message from Nora.

Where did you go? Are you okay?

Just got home. Kind of partied out

I report as I place my key into the lock, hoping Nora won't put two and two together and feel bad that I left her alone with Anja. Nora is the kind of person that would feel upset if she thought she inconvenienced someone.

You didn't have to leave!

She responds when I'm inside and locking the door, proving my point.

It's okay. I'm really tired

I try to assure her. It's not like I'm lying. I could fall asleep standing up if I stayed still long enough. I just hope I'll be able to close my eyes without seeing ghosts.

Looking at my pink duvet and my made bed that's still full of party clothes and dresses meant to make Ryker like me – or like me more – I walk over to my bed and throw all my clothes onto the floor. Tears fall down my cheeks as I toss clothes over my shoulder like they don't mean anything. I never treat my possessions like this, but I'm devastated. This is all too much.

When I finally have an empty bed, I sink onto it and swing my legs on top of it. I hold my head, trying to get my breathing under control.

I don't think I can handle this much stress. Each one of my problems seems impossible – and now, I feel like I have way too many to count.

But at least you're not dead. Or captured by a ghost, I remind myself, taking in a shaky, uneven breath and looking around the room.

Nora's flower pots on top of her desk make me feel better. I'm not sure what kind they are, but their scent and appearance make me calmer. Nora seems to be the only positive thing about my experiences at Gomada Academy so far.

Looking at my phone again, I see a text from Mom that I hadn't noticed until now. I probably would have seen it earlier, but finding out about ghost attacks stopped me from doing anything normal.

> Please give me a call tonight if you can,
> honey. Macey wants to talk to you, too.
> She misses you.

Two tears slide down my cheek at my mother's message. It's way too late now to call or text her. If I do. Mom will think something bad has happened to me (even though it has, I don't want to worry her).

I can't believe I missed this text! And my little sister, whom I thought wanted nothing to do with me, wanted to talk to me, too, and I blew it!

I'm even more devastated than before – and now, I'm angry at myself.

I finally shove myself off my bed and go to the bathroom, getting ready to brush my teeth, wash my face and take off my make-up. I yank at the zipper to the back of my dress. I'm barely able to reach it when I'm alert – and now that I'm tired, annoyed at myself, and brokenhearted, it's even harder.

When I finally pull down the zipper and step out of my dress, I stare at myself in the mirror. I don't know who I see there, staring back at me. She's someone who's always played things safe – but didn't have much to protect at the same time.

I'm not strong. I'm not brave. I'm not pretty, smart, or interesting. I'm not even a good Nymph.

No wonder Professor Xhao treated me the way she did.

No wonder Ryker rejected me.

No wonder everyone here thinks I'm a waste of space.

I wipe at the tears that fall down my cheeks. My weaknesses seem even worse now, with my smudged eyeliner and blood-shot eyes in full view.

When I'm done getting ready for bed, I walk back into the main room, holding my dress in my hand. I blindly toss it on top of the dresser and look for pajamas. I find a tank top and leave it at that – I'm way too drained to look for a pair of pajama shorts or pants – close up the drawer, and go back to my bed, looking at my phone again, just in case Mom messaged me again. Nothing.

I want to talk to Mom now more than ever, but I know I can't call her when it's almost midnight. I need to try and deal with this on my own. And if that means crying myself to sleep,

I guess that's what I'll have to do. It may sound pathetic, but that's me.

It's Monday morning. I spent all Saturday doing homework and Sunday in the Nymph's Field with Nora. We worked hard on the methods taught during Field Practice class. I told Nora she didn't have to come with me, but I appreciate that she did. It made the weekend less lonely.

It's raining as I get my things together for first period. I have a History test this morning, so I got up early today. Nora is out for her usual run, so I'm not as quiet as I would've been as I finish getting my books together. I plan to go to the library to get some last-minute studying done before classes start. I'm one of those people who studies until the last possible minute, no matter how prepared I feel.

Heavy fog above the grass causes my skin to crawl as I make my way to school. But I don't get that same *damp feeling* I'd always get when the ghost would be around, so I'm hoping this is just weather and not the work of a paranormal killer.

Sure enough, my phone tells me just that as I pull up my weather app. I breathe a sigh of relief – and am about to put my phone away when an email from Headmistress Frow, herself, pops up into view.

'Attention Students' the subject line reads. This can't be good. I step to the side, away from passing students, and open up the email, my nerves on fire.

Good morning, students;

I have some regrettable news to share with you. We have cause to believe there is a threat to Gomada Academy residents lurking about campus. This email will be sent to your families, with further information surrounding campus security and specific measures in place to protect all Gomada Academy residents.

We want to keep you informed and secure, so please heed the following:

Curfew has been moved from ten o'clock to eight o'clock. Any student caught violating these rules will be suspended.

Please do not go anywhere alone. Always walk in pairs, or ask a professor to escort you to your dorm.

No one is to leave campus without the permission of a professor or myself. You must report back to a faculty member upon your return.

Freshmen and Sophomore students: it has come to my attention that many of you are not taking your Mentorship Program seriously, despite the fact that it finishes this Friday. As such, I am extending the program until the end of the term. Effective immediately, you are not to go anywhere alone. Your Mentor or Mentee will escort you. Hopefully this forced proximity will foster further camaraderie and training.

If you have any questions or concerns, please seek out myself or our school counsellor, Doctor Ogvert. Her office hours and contact information are below.

We are all in this together. You have my assurance that you are cared for and safe here.

Sincerely;

Leona Frow

Headmistress, Gomada Academy

. . .

My jaw drops to the grass as I read and reread sections of the email. It didn't take very long for Headmistress Frow to announce a 'threat to Gomada Academy residents' – but she didn't mention that an Enchanter was missing or a ghost was behind it.

Is this to cause less of a panic? Why keep such important information from us?

I'm worried that Mom and Dad will be notified about what happened. It's bad enough that they'll get a phone call today about my breaking curfew – and now, they'll be getting an email about threats to my safety. This is enough to make me want to run home as fast as I can – and I have my grandpa's pocket watch with me.

I'm not bothered by the curfew adjustment or the stricter rules about coming and going from school. After what happened last night, there's no way I'm leaving school for a long time. But what really bothers me is that Cole and I are going to be thrown together all over again.

Damn! He's like some kind of foot fungus that keeps coming back. It's true that I haven't taken my Mentorship Program very seriously – but I'd rather not associate with an obnoxious, cruel monster like Cole Hudson. I wish I could ask Headmistress Frow for a different Mentor, but I don't know if that sort of thing is possible.

Then again, it may not even happen that Cole and I will spend more time together. It's not like he takes rules, school, or anything seriously. I'm sure he's about as interested in spending time with me as he is getting operated on while awake. If I'm lucky, he won't ever talk to me about this or even see the email – and I can go on with my deranged life as best I can.

Remembering that I have to cram for my History test, I'm

just putting my phone away when the scraping of wet, slippery grass from behind me makes me scream.

When I spin around, Cole frowns down at me, cigarette in one hand and a to-go cup of what smells like coffee in the other.

Coffee and cigarettes? Gross!

"What's your problem?" he asks, but it's more of a casual question than his usual, blatant and hostile insults.

I narrow my eyes up at him. "Stop doing that!" I snap.

He smiles at me. "Good morning to you, too, Arya."

"What do you want?" I continue, not in the mood to be pushed around or manipulated by another bully.

He squints, as if he's confused. "The email from her highness?" he asks.

I'm stunned that Cole is taking the email seriously. Just when I thought my luck could be turning around! *Damn!*

I fold my arms. "What can you possibly do to protect me?"

He laughs dryly. "Uh, big-ass creepy monster? Ring any bells?"

"You hate rules and authority," I try.

Cole shrugs. "Yeah. But Qadir's riding my ass about this. So I gotta do it."

Cole sighs and rolls his eyes when I must have a blank look of confusion on my face. "Professor Qadir. Shifter," he explains – if you can count three words as being 'explanatory'.

I guess there's no way out of this messed up Mentorship Program for either of us. I hate my life!

"I have to go study," I tell him.

He sighs. "Of course you do." He takes in a drag of his disgusting cigarette. I wait for him to blow it in my face, but instead, he turns to the side and exhales.

"Could you not smoke when you're around me?" I find myself asking him firmly.

He smiles at me. "Why?"

I gape. "Because it's unhealthy and disgusting "

He rolls his eyes, takes another drag, and shocks me by putting out his cigarette with his fingers.

"Didn't that hurt?" I can't help but ask.

He shrugs again. "Let's get this over with," he sighs instead of answering me, showing me that this awful day truly has begun.

I'm frustrated all over again as Cole and I head through the crowded hallway toward my Freshman History class. I can't believe I have to spend more time with this horrible person! I'm just waiting for the cruel, insensitive, and inhumane comments he's going to dish out at me until the end of term. Between this, the ghost, my Affinity problems, and everything else I have going on, I don't think I'll be able to survive.

Even though I feel irritated, Cole seems calm (for once) as we make our way toward my classroom. I don't think the rooms have changed over the years, because Cole seems to know where to go without me saying anything.

I look up at him when we finally get to my History classroom. "You didn't have to walk me to class. I'm not completely helpless," I protest.

He frowns. "Could've fooled me," he responds, causing me to bristle all over again.

"Goodbye," I snap up at him.

Cole rolls his green eyes, a smile on his face. It's weird how even his smiles can look devious and creepy. He doesn't need acting classes: he could star as the villain in any horror or thriller show created, as himself or his alter ego.

"Fine. See you later." He seems to pause, but I don't know why. Then, he reaches into his jeans pocket and hands me a piece of paper.

I unfold it and stare at it, half-expecting to be scared out of my wits. Instead, it's just a set of numbers.

"My number," he tells me. "Don't flatter yourself. Just use it to hit me up if you need help."

I stuff the paper into the side pocket of my black leggings. I know it's probably a good idea to exchange numbers, just in case – even though I'd never use it. If I needed help, I'd rather call up a stranger than him.

Cole scratches his dark hair, then passes by me without another word. I want to get as far away from him as possible, so I dart into the classroom, ready to forget about everything and just write my test. Gomadian history is way more interesting than current life events.

Sixteen

COLE'S DILEMMA

It's not like I pay attention in History class, anyway, so when Professor Shan isn't looking, I pull my phone out and reread that email from Headmistress Frow. The big-ass classroom is full of kids on their phones: I won't be noticed if I do this now. Besides, what's the big deal if I get detention? Crabtree fucking *died* last night! I heard his final screams! And there was nothing Johnson and I could do to stop it. A week's worth of detention is nothing compared to that.

I don't get why she was all *mysterious* with the whole 'threat to Gomada Academy residents' thing. I guess she couldn't go full-out 'ghost serial killer' on our asses, but at the same time, she's not giving us anything to go on. For all the rest of the students know, it's some random guy out in the woods with an axe.

After passing Professor Qadir at the entrance to Feara this morning, I got the feeling he saw the same email and wanted me to do exactly what the Headmistress said – so as soon as I could, I found Arya. It's not like following each other around is my dream come true, either, but if I want to finally get out from under

Qadir's thumb, I have to do it. And with a ghost killer circling the drain, it couldn't hurt for the Nymph to have some kind of protection. God knows she's not entirely capable of doing it on her own.

Walking through the halls, it's impossible not to hear people talking about the email.

"It's probably just a trick to get us to obey curfew."

"How did the Headmistress find out there was a threat, in the first place?"

"It's all a bunch of bullshit. I haven't noticed anything going on."

"This is kind of fun."

Well, since Arya isn't alone, I don't have to worry about her safety...

I wanted to punch the asshole who said that, but he ducked into a Freshman classroom just as I was heading over to him. He wouldn't have been worth my sore knuckles, anyway. He was just an Enchanter.

Like Crabtree...

I got distracted from all the chit-chat about the ghost, so I totally forgot about going to Freshmen History and walking Arya to her next class. I don't know how far this 'Mentor thing' is supposed to go, but I guess I don't want to take any chances. With Professor Qadir keeping an eye on me and this stupid thing being extended to four months (well, almost three, I guess) instead of three weeks, it's going to be a definite pain in the ass. Ryker tells me he's also trying to keep an eye on Nora, so at least it's not just me who's stuck doing this all day.

Lunch finally comes, but I'm not hungry. First time for everything, I guess. But I get a text from Ryker, asking me to meet him in the Dining Hall. I don't know what it's about, but I feel it can't be anything good, not after what happened last night.

As luck would have it, because I'm never lucky at all, and everyone and everything seem to be against me, I see Arya and Nora walking ahead of me through the open wooden doors to the Dining Hall. Well, since she isn't alone, I don't have to worry about her safety – a big relief, because I'm hungrier now than I was five minutes ago – but I still want to have some fun with her before I find Ryker. Something tells me our conversation won't be nearly as fun as the one I'm going to have with her.

I move around a few small groups of students – mostly on their phones, morons – and get right behind her.

"Hey," I say darkly, causing her to yelp and turn around. As soon as she stares up at me and her surprise or fear turns into anger, I laugh. Hard.

"*Stop doing that!*" she exclaims. Of course, she hits me.

"Sorry," I laugh. "It's not my fault you're a scaredy-cat."

Nora turns to glare up at me, too. "Maybe he's the one skulking around and threatening students," she guesses. This actually pisses me off – and from the looks of things, Arya doesn't know what to say, either – so I shrug and say,

"Everyone would know if it was me. I take credit for my shit."

"How honourable of you," Arya sighs.

I'm jonesing for a smoke, and I know I have to meet up with Ryker, who likes things to be on *time*, so I shove my hands into my jeans pockets and look down at Arya. "Meet you back here in an hour?" I check.

Arya scowls up at me.

"I think she'd rather meet up with the so-called threat than hang out with you any more than she has to," Nora counters quickly.

This distracts me enough that I stop dead in my tracks

(wrong choice of words) and stare down at Nora. "You don't think anything's out there?" I ask.

Nora rolls her eyes. "I don't think anything is out there. It's probably some older students playing a prank. And even if something is out there, the faculty will—"

"What? Save us?" I challenge her.

Nora gets really mad, but it looks like Arya is in the middle. I think she's feeling the same way I am (God forbid): that the faculty may be useless against a paranormal threat. Even though Nora doesn't have all the pieces to the puzzle, it's still insane that she thinks a group of teachers can protect us from an evil spirit. Nothing would save us if Frow couldn't get rid of it that weekend.

"What makes you think they can't?" she fires back, her blue eyes trying to burn a hole in my skull. Creepy. "Some of the most powerful of all three races teach here. It's narrow-minded to think they can't be helpful if there actually is a threat out there."

I lean back slightly, laughing at how mad Nora is right now. Her black hair moves when she shakes her head at my laughing.

"Talking to you is pointless," Nora sighs (like I haven't heard that before), looking back to Arya. This Nymph is making me feel like I'm wasting her time.

Arya gives Nora a small smile, like she agrees with her. That pisses me off, too, for some weird reason.

Both of them walk away from me, so I decide that the damage is done and find Ryker. As per usual, he's sitting at a corner table by himself – mainly because his big-ass black panther sits at his feet, grooming herself. Probably just swallowed a moose from the thicket.

Ryker looks up at me when I get closer. Of course, his Familiar noticed me first. Her freaky green eyes follow my every move as I get closer to her master.

"Why'd you bring the– Zola?" I finally ask. I don't dare mess with this Familiar. It's not like Whitney or something, where the worst I can get is a little scratch. Speaking of which, those damned claw marks from Ebony hurt like a mother. At least now, they're practically gone.

Ryker smiles up at me, probably catching on that I don't want to insult his beast of a Familiar. "What better protection can I possibly have?" he points out, looking down at the panther with love or something in his eyes.

I've only known Ryker for a little over a year, but something tells me he wouldn't let anything happen to Zola.

I take the seat across from him. Ryker rolls one of the two apples in front of him across the table. Impressed by how he notices the little things about people (not that I'd tell him), I nod at him in thanks and catch it in my right palm.

"I did some research in-between classes," he tells me, leaning forward a bit.

I frown at him, waiting for him to tell me the truth.

He sighs. "Okay. I did it during History class."

I think Ryker and I are actually in the same History class. We just haven't seen each other in it for three weeks (ish), because the class is in an auditorium.

I smirk at him. "I was rereading the email," I admit.

Ryker runs a hand through his cornrows. He has huge hands and feet – something Diego and I would tease him about every now and then. But he makes fun of Diego's ponytail and my smoking, so I guess we're all even.

"I guess it's hard to concentrate when we know what really happened," he whispers, sliding his phone across the table. It stops in front of me. The screen's already unlocked. Looks like it's open to a website or something.

I pick up his phone, curious about what sites he's been to today. Ryker is different - he's smarter than me, and probably even Diego. I think he looks at things differently – so if he's found out something, I want to know what it is.

It looks like Ryker's been visiting paranormal and ghost websites. I don't know much about spirits. Apparently, people in the Overworld don't always believe in spirits – but in Gomada, Chimara, Houssan, and Valis, everyone believes in them. They're not very common – but you don't want to mess with them. I guess I made that mistake, and now a few of us have.

On the plus side, because there are so many people in the realms who do believe in spirits – good and bad – there's gotta be a ton of research on them.

I begin to read the website Ryker's been looking at – and I gotta say, it doesn't make me feel much better.

Despite having immense power and the ability to move through concrete boundaries and realms, malevolent and benevolent spirits cannot possess a physical stronghold on our reality.

I don't get most of this, but the gist doesn't sound great. "What the hell does this mean, Johnson?" I finally ask, feeling dumb.

"Ghosts can't touch us or mess with our reality physically," Ryker explains. The fact that he's saying all this without any 'you're stupid' insults makes me feel even dumber. "So I don't know how it could have killed, or taken, Crabtree if it couldn't have laid a hand on him."

I guess Lukas could've just run off – but then again, we couldn't find his trail anywhere. But I guess we didn't have much time to double-check with Frow on our asses five seconds later. But I can't doubt my senses. My sense of smell is *good* – and Crabtree's weird aftershave crap, and his general *scent*, were nowhere to be found. It was like they had disappeared.

"Keep going," Ryker says, jutting his chin out to the phone. I put my head down and keep reading.

Ghosts have a firm grip on what we see as metaphysics. It is easy for them to tamper with our perceptions of reality. They can manipulate weather or cause hallucinations.

Hallucinations? What does that mean? Did we just *imagine* Crabtree going off-campus? But how could Diego, Ryker, and I all see the same thing? Are ghosts that powerful? What about Ryker and I hearing Lukas screaming? Can people hallucinate sound?

Paranormal entities are mostly benevolent, and do not cause mischief. If a spirit has unfinished business, it could turn malevolent and wreak havoc on those it deems responsible for its displeasure.

What could Lukas have done to have pissed off a spirit? He's just your typical annoying kid who cares more about his phone and getting girls to notice him than he is about messing with darkness.

So if Lukas didn't do anything to piss off the ghost, why kill him? And how could a ghost kill people if it can't touch them?

"So, what're we taking from this? It's not a ghost?" I ask Ryker. "No offense, but I saw it, Johnson. I know it's a ghost."

He shakes his head, as if I didn't piss him off by challenging his theory. "I know. I'm just showing you what's out there. What I saw up there... It wasn't normal. I don't know what could have caused it. A ghost seems like the only logical explanation." Ryker laughs a bit when he says 'logical', as if he doesn't think logic and ghosts can go together. After seeing the ghost more than once, I'm having fewer issues with that.

I don't want to ask him this question – this shit creeps me out, and I Shift into a monster that creeps out other people – but I know I won't be able to stop thinking about it if I don't. I don't think I would've thought of this if it wasn't for Ryker's Affinities.

"Do you think Darkness has anything to do with it?" I ask Ryker.

He looks at me, surprise in his brown eyes. "That's kind of what I was thinking," he admits – so now, it's my turn to be surprised. "But I don't think an Enchanter or Enchantress can channel enough darkness into creating a ghost or turning into one. We can't alter our physical bodies like that. No way."

Well, there goes that theory. I should've known that even if an Enchanter or Enchantress with a Darkness Affinity is super-powerful, they're not strong enough to create a ghost, or become one. That brings us back to the ghost theory. So far, only Lukas, Arya, and I have seen the ghost. And one of us isn't alive to talk about it. It's hard to talk about it with people who haven't seen it yet, but kind of know it exists.

I frown suddenly. Thinking about the ghost and who's seen it made me realize–

"Where's Diego?" I ask Ryker. "I would've figured he'd be here."

Ryker shrugs, his black dress shirt catching the light. A few girls pass by him and stare at him – or maybe they're staring at the big-ass panther at his feet. Either way, Ryker's the stud around here.

"Couldn't get a hold of him," Ryker says, then takes a bite out of his apple.

Figures. He's probably hanging out with Chapin, I think, but don't bother saying that to Ryker. Being an Enchanter himself, I don't think Ryker will find Diego's relationship as annoying as I do. Besides, I'm trying to let it go (which is harder than I thought), so I shrug it off.

"Alright," I respond, taking a bite out of my own apple.

I slide Ryker's phone back to him. He catches it without looking, his brown eyes scanning the cafeteria. I wonder who – or what – he's looking for.

"Well, I gotta go," he tells me. "I need to run a few errands before I walk Nora back to class."

"How's it going, Mentoring a Nymph?" I ask him, hoping he'll tell me it sucks, that he wants out, that he's bored and pissed out of his mind.

Instead, Ryker pushes out his chair and gives me a knowing smile. "It's fine, Hudson. But I'm not the tolerant, non-confrontational guy that you are."

I frown up at him as he grins at me. "Hilarious," I grumble as Zola stands to her feet and stretches. She's so huge that she's even bigger than the height of the table. She swings her large head to her left and looks over at me as Ryker walks over to where I'm sitting. I stand up, and he clasps my shoulder.

"We'll figure it out, man," he tells me. "In the meantime, just watch yourself. And no more field trips."

I roll my eyes at that, but nod down at Ryker. "Yeah. No worries," I agree – knowing that being almost-nice to Ryker now is kind of a life-or-death sort of thing, with his Familiar eyeing me.

As Ryker and his tank of a Familiar walk away from me, I wonder about what he said. 'No more field trips'? Who does he think he's talking to? I've been breaking the rules since I was old enough to walk. Some ghost won't stop me. I'm going to get to the bottom of this shit.

I'm not waiting for very long at the doors to the Dining Hall when Arya finally decides to show up. Still, I'm pissed that I had to wait at all. I clearly said 'one hour', and she took her sweet time getting back here.

Maybe she can sense that I'm ticked off because she moves faster when she sees me waiting here.

"Took you long enough," I grumble.

"Are you always this obnoxious?" she asks me.

I shrug. "Come on," I order. "The sooner we get to whatever class you have next, the sooner we can be done with this shit."

It doesn't look like she disagrees with what I said, because she adjusts her pink bookbag (figures) and gives me an even look. "Wonderful," she grunts, as we head out of the Dining Hall.

Part of me wants to share what Ryker and I found out about the ghost, but the other part of me wonders if she'd be able to handle it. Not only that but does she really want to *hear about* Ryker right now? After what happened on Friday, I kind of doubt that. And I don't really want to bring him up, anyway.

Arya pulls her phone out of her leggings pocket. Maybe it went off or something. When she's on it for a while, I roll my eyes and demand, "What?"

She looks up at me, surprised. "Oh, did you actually want to talk?" she asks me, as if she thinks that's not true.

I roll my eyes. "More than anything," I state sourly.

Shoving her phone away, Arya mentions, as we turn the corner and head for the side stairwell at the end of this hallway, "My little sister just got her first cell phone."

Arya is a big sister? That surprises me. Older siblings are supposed to be – protective? Smart? Whatever. Not my business. I'm an only child, so I don't know much about having a brother or sister.

"How old is she?" I finally ask.

She looks uncomfortable that I'm asking her a direct question. Come to think of it, I'm a little weirded out by it, too. But if it gets us to her Lit class quicker, I guess I'm all for it.

"Seven," she responds, hugging her chest.

"A little young for a phone," I comment.

She frowns up at me. "Thank you for your useless opinion, Cole," she barks up at me.

I laugh. "Fine. Forget I said anything."

I open the door to the side stairwell. Going up and down these stairs at night is pretty fun, with all the lights off and less chance of the cameras catching us. Diego and I broke in here once and scared the shit out of Greyson. He tried to catch us, but he couldn't get to us, and didn't know who we were.

I smile at that memory. I guess now that Diego is busy with Lucy, those nights spent with him are long gone. And it doesn't look like Ryker's much for breaking rules or playing pranks on people.

Arya stands there, looking at me. I don't know why she's still here. I finally hold my hand out.

"Go on," I order.

She frowns up at me. I guess she thinks that I'm always this huge asshole with no manners or common sense. I guess that's usually true. But today, I'm holding the door for her. Maybe tomorrow, I'll threaten to push her down the stairs. But for now, I'm trying to be nice. Sort of.

Something changes when she realizes I'm trying to be nice. Her big brown eyes dart to the floor and then look up at me. "Um, thanks," she tells me, walking through the open door and jumping up the stairs.

I follow her, wondering why I'm actually wasting time by being sort-of-nice to her. I don't like thinking this way, but I know something changed that night I Shifted into the Tedla when Arya and I were in deep shit. I told myself I Shifted to freak out the ghost, to fight, to save my friends – but deep down, I knew there was another reason. For some fucked up reason, I also Shifted to protect her.

Carrying her back to campus also made something snap inside of me. I don't know what. Maybe because she wasn't yammering on and on, I didn't find her as annoying as I usually do. Sure, she was unconscious, but still.

Then, seeing her on Friday night at the campfire, and figuring out more about her than I ever wanted to in the first place... Well, I guess I realized there was more to her than being just an annoying and useless Nymph.

I don't know what all of this means – but I know it can't be anything good.

I need a cigarette.

When we get to the top, Arya opens the door, leaving it open with her back. As I walk past her, I can practically feel her flinch when I get close to her. I'm used to this sort of thing by now. But when she does it, it kind of sucks. I don't know why.

Now that we're walking down this super-crowded hallway, I figure we better hurry up if I want to make it to my own Lit class on time. I normally don't give a shit about things like this, but with Qadir on my ass like this, I don't really have a choice. I guess I'm picking up the pace a bit, because I hear Arya struggling to keep up.

I stop at the Freshman Lit class doorway when I see Ryker and Nora across the way, walking toward us. Arya immediately tenses up beside me, beginning to play with her hair. I don't know shit about girls, but I'm guessing this is a nervous habit.

"Just go in there," I tell her quietly, so they don't hear me.

Arya looks up at me, confused by what I said. You always have to be nice in her world, even to guys who stomp all over you. Too bad she doesn't use that same logic on me. But I guess Ryker never tried to set her hair on fire.

"Go on," I order when she doesn't make a move to say or do anything. Maybe if I piss her off enough, she'll leave and won't make herself look like an idiot in front of Johnson.

I don't know why I'm helping her. Maybe I'm trying to get this stupid 'Mentor' thing over ASAP. That's what I'm going with, anyway.

Arya glares up at me and walks into class. Nora frowns at me, confused, and heads in behind her friend.

Ryker stops in front of me. "Fancy seeing you here," he smirks at me, causing me to roll my eyes.

"Hilarious," I breathe, my smile leaving my face (since when was I smiling?) as we both turn around to head to our own Sophomore Lit class.

"So, you don't look like you hate your Mentorship Program as much as you say you do," Ryker says as we walk.

"What the fuck does that mean?" I demand, causing Ryker to throw his head back and laugh at me. I'm pissed that he's finding this funny. I want to slam his head into the brick wall to our left.

"Well, you're not being as merciless as you were before," Ryker smirks. "I damn near say you were hitting on her."

My jaw drops. "Have you lost your mind, Johnson?" I snap.

Ryker shrugs. "Fine. I was wrong, then. But I don't see you smiling very often – especially at a girl."

"I'm gonna smile when I slam your head through a wall," I grumble, as we step into the large auditorium.

"Do that, and I'll send you straight to Hell, Hudson," Ryker jokes – but I figure he has that power, so I shut up quickly.

Besides, I was so mad about his accusations that I completely forgot that Zola was at Ryker's side this entire time. She looks like she wants to have me for dessert now. Fuck my life. Like I don't have enough problems.

Seventeen

ARYA'S DETENTION

The rest of the day was great because Cole was nowhere to be found after third and fourth period. Even fourth period went better today. Professor Xhao was too busy berating a poor Freshman Nymph to bother with me. Even though she quickly walked by us and gave me a pointed look as she went, I think spending all of Sunday practicing made me feel better about being back at the Nymph's Field.

Was I good enough – or passable enough – that Professor Xhao left me alone today? Or is she just pencilling in another lecture for later?

I don't really have time to think about that, though, because I have to go to Headmistress Frow's office now. She sent me another email today, around lunchtime, reminding me I'm only finished with my first week of detention. No one mentioned my community service again (probably because of the ghost), so I got detention for two weeks for breaking curfew. Mom and Dad were disappointed in me, but they didn't give me a hard time about it when I told them it would never happen again.

Headmistress Frow was very specific in her email last week: if I break curfew again, I will be suspended from school for a week and my GPA will suffer. I have detention from three o'clock until five o'clock, Monday through Friday. I can't do homework or be on my phone. I'm supposed to spend the time thinking about what I've done – which shouldn't be hard to do because I've felt guilty about breaking curfew since it happened.

I stumble in my pace to the Academy when I realize I should probably text Cole so he doesn't think the ghost ate me if I'm unreachable for a few hours. It wasn't an issue last week because things with the ghost hadn't escalated.

I'm hoping that if he knows where I am, he won't bother me by showing up or waiting for me at the Headmistress' office. Cole has a problem with authority, so I'm banking on that saving me from suffering another 'walk' with him.

I pull out the piece of paper from my leggings' pocket and enter his phone number into my Contacts app. I wonder if my phone will explode as a result. Finally, I pull up a new messaging conversation and type in his name.

> I have detention for two weeks. I'll be in the Headmistress' office from 3-5.

> Detention? Since when?

I'm surprised he's messaged me back – and right away, too. I've never seen Cole on his phone before. He doesn't seem like the kind of guy to use one – or use it because he has a ton of friends to keep track of.

> Since we broke curfew

That is all I can say, mad that I got caught and he somehow didn't. How unfair is that? Plus, I'm pretty sure I've already mentioned this to him. Of course, since it wasn't about him, he never remembered.

Have fun with Frow

He says, which causes me to roll my eyes and turn my phone off. If it even vibrates while I'm in her office, I'm sure the Headmistress will tack on another week to my sentence. At least while I'm in her office, I'm as safe as can be from the ghost and from any other bully I've met at school.

I knock on the door to the Headmistress' office. It's on the same floor as the Reception Hall, so I knew where to find it last week.

"Come in, Miss Willow," Headmistress Frow calls from inside. A chill spins down my spine at the fact that she knew it was me at the door. Am I the only student at the Academy with detention this week? Is that possible? How embarrassing!

When I open the door, the Headmistress is busy pulling on a black, fancy-looking trenchcoat. Is she going out? I'm surprised by this. Usually, when I would have detention, the Headmistress would always be seated at her desk, working. I guess she does this to keep an eye on the students who should be remorseful of breaking the school rules. So why is she leaving now?

"I have an important errand to run, Miss Willow," Headmistress Frow tells me, stepping forward. I move out of the way of her closed office door and go to my usual spot: at one of the smaller tables near the other end of the Headmistress' library-like office.

Headmistress Frow's large red hawk is perched on her neatly tidied desk, looking at me in a curious way. Her Familiar scared me the first few times I had detention here, but now, I'm used to him. His name is Leopold.

"Come, Leopold," she calls. I jump a mile when the bird takes off from her desk and lands on her shoulder. I wonder if a bird of that size is really heavy for someone, but it doesn't look like the Headmistress is struggling.

"I hope you remain here and resume your last week of detention without issue," she continues.

I feel bad that the Headmistress seems to have gotten the wrong impression about me. I've never broken the rules before – and now, at the beginning of the term, she must think I'm all about rebellion.

"You won't have any trouble from me, Headmistress," is all I can think of to say. My voice is quiet, guilty.

She nods. "Very well. You may retire from my office at five o'clock."

She closes the door behind her, leaving me alone in her office. I'm still shocked that she's stepping out to do 'an important errand' and leaving me here alone. It doesn't seem like something she would do.

Then, I get an idea.

It's probably a bad idea – but I just can't get over the fact that the Headmistress is doing an errand on a Monday afternoon instead of supervising detention. It doesn't add up. Even someone like me can see that.

I turn on my phone. Even if I had Ryker's phone number (I never did have the guts to ask Nora for it), I know I'd never have the courage to message him about anything now – let alone this.

> The Headmistress just left her office to run
> an errand she said was important

Great. Go through her stuff and see if you
can find out anything about the ghost

Cole answers me, less than a minute later.

I frown. I never once thought of that as an option! There's no way I'm getting into more trouble by snooping through Headmistress Frow's personal files. My spy skills are the same as my breaking-curfew skills.

No way! I was hoping you could follow her

I'll follow her if you'll go through her shit.

Somehow, I feel like Cole would know if I lied here, so I huff out an aggravated breath and answer.

Fine

I'll hit you up when she heads back

I don't bother answering him. Instead, I put my phone back in my pocket after setting it to Vibrate. I'll need to be able to hear my phone go off if the Headmistress is on her way back to campus – if she's even leaving campus, to begin with.

I look around Leona Frow's massive office. Books, shelving units, filing cabinets, and an antique cabinet greet – or intimidate – me. I'm not good at sleuthing. I wouldn't even know what to look for. And what makes Cole think that Headmistress Frow knows more about the ghost than she's letting on?

Then again, her tailing the ghost by herself and her sending out those vague emails – telling the students enough to keep them careful, but not enough to terrify them – *does* seem suspicious.

I hate that he's right.

I start at the most obvious place: her desk. Even though no one else is in here right now, and I'm sure there are no surveillance cameras in a private office, I'm still scared out of my wits to approach her desk. Finally, I will my feet over to the ornately carved wooden desk and step close to her office chair.

Her desk is open in the middle with two sets of drawers sticking out on either side, allowing her chair to push in all the way. When I look closer, I notice that there is a centre drawer in the middle of her desk. With her chair being right against it, I almost didn't think to look for anything there. What's really weird about this middle drawer is that it's locked. There's a silver keyhole embedded in the wood.

What could she be keeping in this normal-sized desk drawer? And what are the odds that this is the first thing I look at that may be useful?

I don't waste time by fidgeting around or thinking too much. I slowly pull out her chair, half-expecting alarm bells to go off now that I've touched something that doesn't belong to me. When nothing happens, I hesitantly tug on the drawer. It's locked. There's no way I can open it without having the key, and I'm betting the Headmistress has it with her right now.

This could also be nothing, I tell myself. *It could just be important stuff for her laptop – USB sticks or essential equipment. It may have nothing to do with the ghost.*

What if all this is a waste of time?

I quickly push the chair back to where it was before, feeling stupid for thinking I could help and because I got sucked into another rule-breaking scheme.

Still, why would the Headmistress have this drawer locked? Her office is already locked from the outside. What could she have in this drawer that needs to have another lock and key associated with it?

This could still be nothing! I warn myself as I pull my phone out of my leggings' pocket again.

One of her desk drawers is locked.

Okay. Pick it. I'm kind of busy, Arya.

I fume at that. I'm the one risking everything trying to poke through the Headmistress' stuff, and he's just out and about on campus, before curfew, following her around? I'm in way over my head!

I'm not picking her lock. I have nothing to pick it WITH!

Fine. Just keeping looking around. I'll be there soon.

Damn! I didn't want him to show up here, but I guess that means I won't be the one doing the actual lock-picking. But if I'm helping – or, at least, reporting news – I'm sure that's plenty to feel guilty about later.

In ten minutes, the door to the Headmistress' office opens. I slam myself onto the chair in front of the table – thank God I was at the bookshelf close to my usual spot when the door opened – jamming my knee against one of the table's legs.

I'm caught! This is it! I'll be suspended, for sure!

What are Mom and Dad going to say?

Even though this school is full of monsters – both inside the walls and out – I'll miss Nora, going to class, and pizza night on Fridays at the Dining Hall.

It's hard to breathe. I can't think straight. And it's even harder to concentrate when Cole closes the door to Leona

Frow's office, looking around in a confused way. He scowls when he sees me from across the room, and his shoulders slump.

"Have you been there the whole time?" he grunts. When he talks, something jiggles in his hand as he approaches the Headmistress' desk.

*Are those **keys**?*

Ignoring his usual hostility, I jump over to the desk and step to his right as he's pushing the office chair behind him. "How did you get the key?" I gasp, as Cole begins jamming different smaller keys into the middle desk drawer.

He shrugs as he cycles through the endless supply of keys on the large silver keyring he's holding. "Greyson always gets take-out for dinner. He leaves his office unlocked for an hour because he's a dipshit."

"Who's Greyson?" I all but whisper.

Cole looks down at me. "Head of security. Not that he ever does anything that matches the job." He looks back to his work and jams another golden key into the drawer. When it doesn't open, Cole curses under his breath.

"What about the Headmistress? Where is she?" I ask.

Cole frowns at me. "Can you give me a second?" he demands, causing me to clamp my mouth shut as he gets back to the keyhole. His green eyes are intent as he sticks another silver key into the lock.

When Cole tugs on the drawer and it slides open easily, he sighs. "Finally," he grumbles.

"What's in there?" I ask, trying to lean in closer, so I can have a better look. So far, he's hogging everything.

Cole surprises me by stepping a bit to the side, so I can move in closer. "Just typical shit," he muses, rummaging through papers and little boxes with his hands.

"Don't mess everything up!" I hiss, causing him to scoff in an irritated way. "She'll know someone was in here!"

Even though I know he heard me, Cole ignores me and picks something up from deep into the drawer. "What the fuck is this?" he asks, holding up a black-and-white photograph. It looks like it was taken with one of those old polaroid cameras.

I lean in over his arm, so I can see. "That looks like Leona, when she was our age," I murmur.

The caption underneath the photo reads *Leona Frow and Izaak Johnson, September, 1990*. It looks like the photo was taken from a dress-up dance or something. Balloons and streamers are in the background. Izaak has his arm around Leona. It looks like they're together – or they were together at the time.

Cole clears his throat. "Why'd she keep this with all her important shit?" he asks – but I don't think he's asking me that question.

I pull my phone out of my pocket.

"Now's not the time to be texting your little friends," Cole snaps, as if I'm clueless enough to waste time while we're doing even *more* rule-breaking.

"I'm not!" I protest. "I want to take a picture of this." I quickly snap a photo of the two teenagers before Cole can say anything else.

Cole puts the photo back. "Well, this whole thing was a waste of–" he begins, then yanks out something else buried in the drawer.

An old newspaper clipping, with the heading '**Izaak Johnson expelled from Gomada Academy for feats of dark magic**' in big block letters at the top of the cut-out.

"He got into some pretty nasty shit," Cole grumbles, his green eyes scanning the article.

"I want to read it, too," I all but whine, just as a loud sound from outside causes me to jump a mile.

"Fuck!" Cole spits. "Take a picture of this!" he calls.

I quickly take the picture and shove my phone back into my pocket. Cole shoves the clipping back into the drawer and quickly rearranges everything, so it is in almost exactly the same place as it was before. He closes the drawer and locks it hastily.

I don't know how he went about putting everything away in such a deliberate way. To me, Cole is a careless delinquent, not someone who pays attention to little details like where things go in a drawer.

"Greyson's in the hall. Fuck my life," Cole grumbles, shoving the large set of keys into the pocket of his jeans.

Before I can even say anything – or ask him how he knows that – Cole shoves himself under the desk and yanks the chair so it's practically on top of him. I guess that means that Greyson, the head of security, is coming into the Headmistress' office!

I scamper over to the small table where I left my bookbag and cram myself into the chair just as the door opens.

A shorter man with blonde hair and brown eyes enters the room. He looks at the space in a scrutinizing way, then looks over at me. He seems surprised to see me sitting here at the table.

Is this Greyson?

"You, there," he grunts. "What's your name? Why are you in the Headmistress' office?"

"Arya Willow," I squeak. This man is nothing like Cole described! "I have detention, sir," I stammer.

His frown slowly disappears. "Oh," he remarks. "Well, have you heard any roughhousing or weird stuff happening out in the halls?"

"Um, no," I respond. Thankfully, this isn't a lie, so I don't feel as horrible about this conversation as I do about searching through the Headmistress' personal belongings.

"Well, my keys seem to have gone missing. D'you know anything about that?" he asks, leaning against the width of the desk.

I can't believe I'm thinking this way, but I'm actually scared that this Greyson man will catch Cole under the Headmistress' desk. I never thought I'd be scared for Cole's safety, ever. Even when we were in the Gomada Thicket with the ghost, Cole didn't seem very scared. I don't think much gets to him – probably because he's a bully with no empathy, or feelings.

"No, sir," I tremble. All I need to have happen next is to be accused of taking Greyson's keys!

Greyson leans off the desk, straightening out his jacket. "Well, if that's the case, I'll–" he begins, then frowns and turns around.

"Hey! There they are!" he laughs, stooping down to pick up the large keyring full of keys that must have been behind him. "I guess I forgot to look in one of my pockets. Phew," he sighs.

Did Cole just–

"Sorry about that," Greyson tells me. "Anyway, be good." He turns on his heel and heads to the closed office door, opening it and leaving me alone after shutting it behind him.

It's quiet for less than twenty seconds, then the office chair is pushed back and Cole unfolds himself from under the Headmistress' desk.

"What a dipshit," Cole sighs, stepping to the side and pushing in Headmistress Frow's office chair.

When I think it's safe to move, I get up and walk over to the desk. "Did you make it look like he dropped his keys?" I ask.

Cole smiles at me. "Told you he was useless."

I frown. "He's head of security, and you stole his keys," I remind him.

Cole shrugs. "And I returned them without him even realizing I took them."

"That's something to be proud of," I scoff.

Cole frowns down at me. "Is this the thanks I get for helping you?" he asks.

I gape. "Helping *me*?" I gasp. "What we found may not even be worth anything!"

Cole rolls his eyes, like I'm talking nonsense. "Send me those photos. I'll decide whether or not they're worth anything."

I fume up at him. "What is that supposed to mean?"

He smiles down at me. "I'm the brains of the operation. You're just... There," he finishes.

My jaw drops again, causing Cole to laugh. I smack his chest. "Shut up!" I order.

He folds his arms. "Well, I'm bouncing. Have fun in detention." He shoves his hand into the middle pocket of his hoodie, pulling a chocolate bar out of it.

*Is he going to choose **now** to eat? Wouldn't he want to smoke instead, since that's all I ever see him do?* I think, wondering how weird that is.

Cole surprises me by holding out the chocolate bar to me. "Here," he grunts.

I frown. "What did you do to it?" I ask firmly.

Cole sighs. "Just take it. I was gonna give you this to keep you quiet while I used Greyson's keys."

How rude! I want to shove this chocolate bar down his throat! How does he have any friends at all?

The only thing is, being stuck in detention with nothing to do makes me very bored, and very hungry. I'm suddenly craving that chocolate bar and hoping Cole didn't tamper with it.

I finally reach out and take the chocolate bar from him. It's Caramel Way, one of my favourite kinds – not that I'd ever mention that to him.

I'm kind of freaked out by this. Why would he give me a chocolate bar? Or, was he planning to eat it and just pawned it off on me at the last second? I'm so confused.

I still think it's laced with something, but the wrapper looks like it hasn't been opened.

"Um," I begin. "Thank you."

Cole glances at the door. "Send me those pictures," he seems to remind me – as if I'll forget, after he asked me to do it not even thirty seconds ago.

I roll my eyes. "I will," I grumble.

Cole opens and closes the door. I look down at the chocolate bar. Now that I'm alone, I turn it over in my hands. It still looks like nothing sinister or creepy was done to it. Maybe it's safe to eat. I am getting kind of hungry...

I unwrap the chocolate bar – but not before returning to my table and sitting down. That was a very eventful and horrifying chunk of my detention. One hour and forty minutes to go.

Eighteen

COLE AND LUCY

Thank God this insane week is almost over. Between a Lit test I'd forgotten about on Monday, to this stupid Field Practice fitness test Professor Qadir wanted to run (surprise! Not) on Friday, I was pretty much ready to call it quits. Making matters worse, no one seemed to notice that Crabtree was missing – save for Taylor. Diego and I let her in on the campfire shitshow on Sunday.

Even though Lukas had just finished tormenting her and hadn't been the best Mentor, Taylor still felt bad about what had happened to him. But, weirdly, nobody else seems to be talking about him. He had friends, didn't he? And I'm pretty sure he was on some stupid sports team over here – baseball or something. I don't pay attention to that crap.

Finally, on Friday afternoon, I check out Lukas' social media pages. I guess this is who I am now: someone who breaks into things, snoops around, and spies on people. Whatever. This is for the greater good.

Sure enough, Lukas has – or, *had*, poor bastard – over one thousand friends on social media. Scrolling through the list of 'people I may know', I see that lots of them are from Gomada Academy. So how come no one's noticed his absence? Could these friends be just non-friends, people he met once and never spoke to again? Enchanters stick to their own. He may have friends on here who are Shifters and Nymphs, but I doubt they're missing him now.

Suddenly, I lay eyes on someone who is friends with Lukas – someone who's part of his race; someone I know, too.

Lucy Chapin.

I look again. Her poisonous cousin, Désirée, is not on Lukas' friends list. Well, the dead guy had *some* class, at least.

I leave the Shifter's Field and go looking for Lucy. I didn't really have the energy to get up and leave once classes were over. Sure, I'm hungry and need a cigarette and a nap, but all that would actually involve getting up – easier to do in my head than in real life.

I don't use my phone much. I find it annoying, especially when it's all other people seem to think about here. Face-to-face, or not at all, is so much better. But for a split second here, I wish I had Lucy's number so I didn't have to track her down for hours. Even with my super senses, if Lucy took the long way home or went to get coffee or some other shit with her cousin, I'll be going in circles until I do find her.

That reminds me.

Friday night, Lucy and Désirée sure as hell weren't sipping coffee or beer by the fire. When I saw them, they were in some kind of weird cousin cat-fight. I don't get why they're fighting – mostly because they never do. But that gives me an idea. Maybe I should check out the Enchanter's Field to see if they're still at it. Nymphs and Enchanters split that field in half, and since classes only ended a half hour ago or whatever, chances are good they could still be there. With Désirée's need to be perfect at everything and Lucy always at her heels, I bet I'll pick up their scents closer to the Enchanter's Field.

I put away my phone and change course. I was originally heading toward the Academy, but now, I'm going to the Enchanter's Field. That should've been my first thought.

Bingo.

Ugh. Don't think I've ever used that word before. But whatever. I picked up both their scents after walking for the Enchanter's Field.

On the other hand, just because I picked up their scents now, doesn't mean they're still there. Maybe they were there for class – brown-nosers that they are – but they could've left right after that. Either way, I know I'll be able to trail them from there, no problem.

When I close in on the Field, ignoring the security guard who gave me some kind of 'watch yourself' look as I walked right through the open gates of the school, I hear raised voices. Since the Nymph's Field comes up on you first, I begin to walk around it. Some Nymphs are still out here, practicing. I don't know any of them – and it's not like I go out of my way to know Nymphs. I keep going.

"You ungrateful little whore!" I hear. Even though it's clearly not directed at me, I can't help but notice the poison or evilness in the yell. That's Désirée's voice. She has to be talking to her cousin. Lucy and Désirée's scents are way too strong now. I'm not just following them – they're stationary, up front.

"I can't believe you're choosing to spend time with that smelly dog over me!"

I frown at that. Désirée has her wires crossed because Diego's alter ego is a Phoenix. But it's not like I'm going to correct them. They've never seen our true forms.

When I get closer to the Field, I get a direct line of sight to the two girls. They're squaring off at about five yards. Désirée has her arms folded and is yelling. Lucy is on the other side, quiet and mad. I've never really seen Lucy mad like this before – and it's not like I try to see Lucy doing *anything*.

They're fighting over Diego. Maybe Désirée's mad that Lucy's spending more time with Diego than with her. I never thought I'd think this way, but I kind of relate.

But at the same time, Diego is happy. I mean, I don't get it, and I probably never will, but there it is. He's even reading more – something I've never seen him do before – and he actually seems less stressed about other things in his life. The Phoenix thing, the rumours, the pressure – they don't get to him as much as they used to. I hate to say it, but maybe Diego dating Lucy is a *good thing*. I gotta get my head examined for thinking that – but it's staring right at me. I know it's true.

Just like me and my 'judgemental douche' self, Désirée has to get over it.

"You're just mad that you can't control me anymore!" Lucy shouts back. Even Whitney, who's usually draped across Lucy's shoulder and looking happy and stupid, is now on all fours, snarling and growling at Ebony, who's hissing and spitting across the way. Like master, like Familiar.

Désirée doesn't look happy to hear that. "You're a pathetic little mouse!" she throws at Lucy. "You're nothing without me!"

Lucy looks upset by that but doesn't say anything. Whitney's growling is all that's heard from Lucy's side of the field.

"You don't even know what your second Affinity is, Mouse!" Désirée taunts Lucy, whose blue eyes shift. Even I can see that, and I'm nowhere near her. "You need me, and you're choosing some Shifter flea instead!"

"I *don't* need you!" Lucy hollers, and her eyes suddenly go white.

I take a step back. This isn't some Air Affinity crap. This is way bigger than that. Part of me thinks I should leave, but the other part wants to see what happens next. It's kind of the same thing as a trainwreck.

Intense light blasts onto the Enchanter's Field. Désirée screams. I shut my eyes and grab at them with my hands. Holy shit!

Well, Lucy is way more powerful and capable than I thought. She doesn't just have a Darkness Affinity. Just like Ryker, she has both Darkness and Light Affinities. That's a rare combo to have – meaning that Lucy will be sought after by profs and the Headmistress so she can get better control of her powers. This makes her stronger, better, than Désirée. And I'm sure Désirée knows that. That's probably why, when I force my eyes to open and see red splotches, I can sort of see her raging from far away.

But being an Enchantress who doesn't want to get dirty, Désirée grabs Ebony and runs off. Even though she's leaving from her end of the Field, she finally catches sight of me. I don't know if she can see this from where she is, but I grin a happy 'you're finished' smile at her. You can't be Queen of the Castle when your cousin has the crown.

The ground under my feet starts to shake. I look across the way, seeing cracks jutting out from around Lucy. Her powers are growing out of control. I know what's happening, because of what happened (still does) when I try to control the Tedla. If Lucy loses control, this whole place will be screwed. Even Whitney is yelping and running around in a frenzy.

"Lucy!" I yell, over the roar of cracking ground and the blinding light that almost seems to be ringing in my ears now.

Lucy whips her head to the left and sees me, her eyes widening when she realizes there was a witness to her fight with her cousin. Of course that's what she's thinking about now –

not the fact that she's going to rip apart the entire Enchanter's Field.

"Get yourself under control!" I scream, trying to run around the cracks before they open up and swallow me whole.

Even though Lucy was never my favourite person – I don't think I really have one – she's Diego's girl. Diego's my best friend. I gotta do what I can to help her – even if it's weird.

"I can't!" she cries as Whitney jumps onto her shoulder and nibbles at her ear. Even her Familiar's trying to help her. Well, Whitney and Zola seem to be the only useful ones around here.

Getting back to Lucy, she sounds helpless. I can sense it, too, as I run up beside her.

I step in front of her and grab her shoulders. When nothing happens except for more ground cracking around us, I shake her as gently as possible but hard enough to try to get her to sober up.

"You gotta snap out of it!" I order. "You're gonna wreck this whole place!"

"I don't know how!" she exclaims. She's crying. It's weird, seeing tears pour out of pure-white eyes with no eyeballs.

It's only a hunch here, but I bet her anger brought out her Affinity (how weird is that, since it's a Light Affinity?).

"Stop being mad!" I scream in her face. I kinda feel bad doing that, but between her crying, the splitting of the earth around us, and my ears about to crack off the sides of my head, I feel like I need to pump up the volume.

"Think about Diego!" I try. Lucy has a thing for Diego and chooses to be with him over spending all her time with her cousin. Because of this, I'm betting he'll trigger more positive vibes from Lucy. It may–

Suddenly, her blue eyeballs roll to the front of her head, and she stumbles. I grab her before she passes right out in front of me. The ground stops shaking. The painful ringing in my ears stops – sort of. My red splotches are slowly starting to go away.

This crazy bitch almost killed me!

But this crazy bitch stood up to the craziest bitch here, all for my best friend. I owe her. And I'm more than a little impressed. I never thought I'd think this way, but...

She's okay with me.

"I can't believe I almost caused an earthquake," Lucy breathes, as we make our way off the Field.

"Almost doesn't mean you did," I remind her, causing her to give me a pretend eye-roll or whatever.

"I suppose so." She folds her arms and steps in front of me. "So, why help me, Cole?" she asks, as Whitney nibbles at her blonde hair. "I'm quite certain you despise me."

I shrug. "If Jasper's good with you–" I start, cut myself off, and finally sigh, finishing, "I guess I am, too."

Lucy looks shocked by what I just said – but instead of making fun of me, like I kind of thought she'd do, she gives me a small smile. "Well, I appreciate you showing up when you did – even though eavesdropping is rude," she adds, but it's not in a mean way.

I shrug again. "It's me. You get what you get."

Lucy smiles at me. "How can I repay you?" she asks. Her blue eyes get a little freaked for a minute – and I know why.

"I won't tell anyone," I assure her. "Besides – who'd believe me?"

She gives me a small laugh in response. She looks drained from everything that happened out in the Enchanter's Field.

"But there is something you could help me with," I finally admit.

Lucy looks interested in that – and a little surprised, too. "Oh?" she asks. "I never thought you'd ask for my help. But how can I say 'no' after what you did for me?"

I take a quick breath. This one Enchantress could've brought down the entire school if she hadn't snapped out of it. Since I usually steer clear of these people, I've never really seen one in action – outside of watching a random Field Practice class with Diego every now and then. When we did that, I thought it was to make fun of them. Clearly, Diego had other plans.

I fold my arms, trying to look tough, even though I still feel like I'm gonna puke from the ground shaking under my feet for what felt like three hours. It's super-quiet now, making it creepy that there was so much noise before. All of that was her.

"You know Lukas Crabtree," I say, not asking it or looking for a 'yes' or a 'no'.

Lucy looks confused now. "Yes, I do," she responds, tucking her hair behind her ear. "He was in all of my classes last year – unfortunately. We got paired up in group projects."

"But you're buddies on social media," I point out, not falling for her 'I hate him' story just yet.

Lucy frowns at me. "You've been looking at my pages?" she asks, suspicious now. Great. That's all I need: an Enchantress with a new Light Affinity kicking my ass. I'd be dead before I could finish my Shift.

"No," I answer. "I was looking at his."

Now, Lucy looks even more confused than before. "Why?" she asks.

"He's missing," I report – finally deciding to tell her at least part of the truth. Besides, how long until Diego fills her in on a bunch of it, anyway?

Lucy raises her blonde eyebrows at me. "Pardon?" she gasps.

"Missing. AWOL. Nowhere to be found," I explain dryly.

Lucy huffs and rolls her eyes. A typical response to me, I

guess. "I understand the concept, Cole. I just don't understand how he's missing and how you know about it."

Well, shit.

"Can't say. But I had nothing to do with it," I add fast, when her blue eyes look even more suspicious now than they did before.

This is why I don't talk to girls.

"Does this have something to do with the 'threat' Headmistress Frow mentioned in her email?" Lucy asks me.

When I stay quiet, Lucy looks around. She looks upset when she sees all the damage to the Enchanter's Field. As if she can read her master's mind, Whitney licks Lucy's ear. Can't say I'd want to have an animal doing that to me. I guess it's enough that I turn into one.

"Don't worry about it," I find myself telling her. "They'll get someone with an Earth Affinity to fix it."

Lucy gives me a small smile. "Well, I can't say I've noticed Lukas' absence. But I can ask around – see if anyone knows anything. And I'll be discreet about it," she tacks on at the end, as if she can read my mind. Creepy.

"Thanks," I tell her. I wonder if I should add this, but I finally say, "And don't go into the thicket."

Lucy looks like she's trying to figure me out – something Professor Qadir and Lukas wanted to do since the beginning of the school year. It weirds me out.

"I won't," she finally answers, as I turn around and walk away.

Nineteen

ARYA'S ANXIETY

It's the second week of October, and I'm exhausted. Midterms are this week and next week, and even though I've been studying non-stop, I still don't feel prepared. I'm most nervous about my Field Practice test. It's a hands-on exam conducted by Professor Xhao – and that's all we know. She wouldn't give us anything more to go on.

I've been practicing when I haven't been studying – and even though my air control has improved, I still can't get my electrical component to work. Last week, I *did* get a few sparks to come out of both hands – but then they evaporated before I could even think of what to do with them.

Nora and I had our History midterm a few hours ago. It was hard, but I'm hoping I at least passed with a grade in the seventies. I'd love a higher one, but the test was harder than I expected, even though I spent hours prepping for it. After that horrific test, I spent a few hours in the library, studying for my midterm tomorrow.

At least when it's 'Midterm Season', as the professors like to call it, classes aren't in session. All your time can be put toward studying and working on your Affinity. I've really appreciated the extra time. And now that my detention sentence has been over for a while, it's been easier to study and get focused.

I slowly make my way up the stairs to the fourth floor. I could have taken the elevator, but I need the exercise. I feel like I've been cooped up in the library all day – or every day for the past three days. Today is Wednesday – though it feels like I'm in another dimension (again).

When my phone vibrates inside my jacket pocket, I pull it out, realizing I'm getting a phone call. I brighten when I find out that Mom is calling me.

"Hi, Mom," I huff as I open the door to the fourth floor. I'm out of breath, and ready for a nap. I don't usually nap during the day, but–

"Hi, sweetie. You sound out of breath," Mom greets me, sounding concerned.

Even though I just spoke to her two days ago, I realize how much I miss her when I hear her voice. I try not to cry as I march down the hall.

"I just finished going up four flights of stairs," I admit.

She laughs. "Too much library time?" she teases, causing me to bite down on a smile.

"Yeah," I agree. "How are you?"

"I'm doing fine. Your father is already thinking about Thanksgiving, and Macey's soccer team is going to the regional semi-finals."

I feel a pain in my chest at the thought of missing out on my little sister's soccer games. Macey loves sports and loves it when her family watches her even more. But with the strict rules of no one being allowed to leave campus – coupled with the fact that two more students have gone missing – I don't think I'd be permitted to even use a Trinket to leave the realm.

"That's great," I breathe, realizing too late that I passed my dorm room, turning around to go back.

"Are you keeping safe, honey? We got the email about there being two more abductions."

I can feel the blood draining from my body when Mom asks me that question. I don't know whether these students – one Nymph and one Shifter – are alive, let alone missing. They could be dead. If the ghost is behind all this, and their fate is the same that met Lukas–

"Yes," I tell her sincerely, so she doesn't worry about me more than she already has. "I go home right after school, or stay at the library. And I'm always back at my dorm before dark."

There's a brief pause. Then, Mom lets out a sigh of relief. "Well, that's good news," she responds. "To be honest, Arya, your father and I were thinking of pulling you from school. But we know you need this kind of education."

I don't know what to say as I approach my dorm room. Part of me wouldn't mind being free of this place. Between Désirée and her evil minions making fun of me for being a *halfling* (something I didn't tell my parents in case it hurt Dad's feelings), the ghost picking off students one by one, and Professor Xhao scaring the pants off me, I wouldn't mind giving normal high school another try.

But at the same time, I don't want to leave. I really like Nora. I've gotten closer with Makayleigh and Anja, too. And I really want to get my Affinity under control.

"Arya? What do you think about that?" Mom asks, probably concerned that I haven't answered her yet.

"I... I'd like to stay. I want to get better control of my Affinity," I reiterate to her. "But I promise I'll let you know if that changes."

After a pause, I add, "And if you change your mind, too–"

"We want it to be your decision," Mom surprises me by admitting. "We'd love to just swoop in there and bring you back to San Francisco, but... You're living on your own. You're growing up. We want you to be able to make your own choices."

It sounds like this is a painful thing for Mom to say. I don't know much about being a parent, but I guess it would be hard for Mom and Dad to let me do what I want when they want to make sure I'm safe.

"I promise I'll talk to you if I change my mind," I assert.

"Great. Thanks, honey. Well, I won't keep you. You sound tired. But please give me a call or a quick text before you go to bed."

"I will," I murmur, my throat uneasy. "I love you, Mom. Please hug Macey for me–"

"If I can," Mom laughs, causing me to let out a tight laugh, too. Macey doesn't really like physical affection from her family – not anymore. When she was younger, she loved being hugged, kissed, and cuddled.

"And please tell Dad I love him," I add.

"I will, sweetie. He said he wants to plan a video chat with you."

"That'd be great," I respond.

"Take care, honey."

"Bye, Mom," I bade her, ending the call and looking at the closed door in front of me. More than anything, I want to turn off my mind and sleep – but I know that's not possible. I still have a long way to go before I'm ready for Thursday morning.

And this is only the beginning. This is only my second midterm out of four. Then, I'll have final exams, next term, and Sophomore Year to worry about – if I survive until the end of the school year. With a ghost kidnapping students and probably killing them – and telling me it likes to eat Nymphs – I'm pretty sure my chances of survival are pretty low.

It's hard to think about midterms when I'm thinking about the ghost, and it's hard to focus on the ghost when I'm trying to study for midterms. I don't know how this sort of thing can happen – but it's probably another reason I want to sleep right now.

As I unlock the door, I'm hit with another tidal wave of guilt for not telling Nora everything I know about the ghost. And now that Anja and Makayleigh are hanging out with us more often, I feel even guiltier about keeping quiet. I guess part of me doubts they'll believe me, while the other is frightened they'll panic if they find out it's a ghost and not just some random person behind all this. And since we're all Nymphs, I feel I have a bigger responsibility to protect them. What if the ghost zeroes in on one of them – or all of us, one day? We still don't know how the ghost captured those other two students. Did it get closer to campus? Did it manage to get on *campus*? It can't be that every single student here is breaking the rules. Ghosts, from what I know about them (and it isn't much) don't need to open doors or hop over fences to get to private property. There are no limits, no rules, with paranormal creatures.

When I open the door and step inside, Nora turns around in her chair to give me a bright smile.

"Hey!" she greets me, her blue eyes excited. I love how Nora's almost always in a good mood. It matches her Affinity, too: she helps plants and people blossom. "How did you think our–" she stops mid-sentence, pulling earbuds out of her ears. "Sorry," she adds. "How did you think our midterm went?"

I sigh as I begin to take off my jacket. "It went okay. I guess I'm too busy crapping myself about our Field Practice midterm to concentrate on anything else."

I walk over to the small rubber boot mat we bought at a little store on campus about a week ago to remove my Fall boots. Now that it's even colder, people say that Gomada may get snow earlier than expected. I can't say I'm looking forward to that. San Francisco has never gotten any kind of snow – and whenever we did, it was a record. I've been cold since late September, and it will only get worse. On the other hand, Nora is excited about tobogganing and sleigh rides.

"Maybe it'll go better than we expect. Ryker said his first Field Practice midterm wasn't too terrible," Nora calls just as I put my jacket away in our shared closet. I may have to break down and actually buy a Winter coat sooner than expected, because my Fall stuff isn't cutting it now.

My chest twists at the mention of Ryker. I've been avoiding him ever since he turned me down at the campfire party. I still can't believe I was dumb enough to think he actually liked me. There's no way he's changed his mind about me. For someone like Ryker, who has his pick of girls, why would I even come up on his radar?

I try not to let Nora know about my sadness because I've been trying to tell her—and myself—that I'm over what happened with him. "Hopefully that's what happens," I try to agree, closing the closet door and walking over to my bed.

Our Nymph Studies midterm is tomorrow, so I plan to get as much done tonight as possible. The only break Nora and I allow ourselves is dinner with Anja and Makayleigh at six o'clock. As much as I worry about taking longer breaks (what if I forget everything I've just studied?), I know I'll need it, especially come dinnertime. I'm already hungry, and it's only five o'clock now.

Nora and I weave in and out of crowds of students as we make our way to the Dining Hall. Now that everyone is writing midterms, there's no set time when areas of the school are vacant. Plus, with students vanishing into thin air, no one really wants to go anywhere by themselves.

As we're reaching the opened double doors to the Dining Hall, Nora nudges me and says, "Maybe we should find a table first, then head into the kitchen to get our food."

That may be a good idea. Finding a table now may mean we won't have to eat standing up.

"I can go find one while you get food," I suggest as we're making our way through the Dining Hall toward the entrance to the kitchen.

"No way!" Nora laughs, tossing her black hair over her shoulder as we walk. "I heard your stomach with my earbuds jammed into my ears."

I roll my eyes at that – but Nora's probably right. When I'm hungry, everyone knows about it. It's embarrassing.

"Well, look who's waiting in line," I tease, pointing up ahead. When Nora follows with her eyes, she gives me a pretend scowl. Anja is waiting in line to get her dinner.

Over the past few weeks, Nora and Anja have gotten closer. They're now officially dating. Nora still tells me that 'she can't believe this happened to her' – but I don't believe that for a minute. With Nora's kindness, beauty, and knack for witty comebacks, it doesn't surprise me that Anja took notice of her.

"Fine," Nora sighs, nudging me now. "But tomorrow, I'm saving the table."

"Okay," I agree, watching Nora walk off to see her girl-friend. It's like Anja has some sixth sense that Nora is in the room because their eyes meet almost instantly. When Anja's face brightens, I turn away, not wanting to share in this should-be-special moment of theirs.

I hate to say it, but as I'm looking for a table for four, I feel jealous of Nora and her newfound relationship. I hate negative feelings, but I can't help it. I wish I could have that kind of relationship with someone who likes me for me and isn't afraid to show it. I'm happy for Nora and Anja – but I wish I could have some of that same happiness they seem to have.

Does that make me a bad person? Probably.

I finally find a small table that could probably fit four chairs, but it only has three. I turn around to start searching for a fourth one when I almost bump into Cole.

I haven't seen Cole for a while. As soon as midterms started this week, we more or less stopped with the 'Mentor' garbage we have to endure until the end of term. That's the only good thing about Winter: I'm one step closer to being free of him.

Tonight, though, Cole doesn't have his usual cruel look about him. He just looks tired. Maybe annoyed. Not much better than his 'cruel look', if you ask me. Tired just means he'll get ticked off more easily.

"What are you doing?" I ask, surprised I didn't get that damp feeling I'd normally get around Shifters. Then again, I'm tired, too, and Cole kind of snuck up on me. And I guess it's been hard to conjure up enough fear to be afraid of Professor Xhao, Désirée, a ghost, and Cole, all at the same time.

Cole frowns at me, as if I've asked a stupid question. "Signing up for welding lessons," he reports dryly, causing me to roll my eyes.

I go to step around him, but he suddenly walks in the same direction, blocking my exit. Before I can tell him to screw off (unlike me, but I guess I have a shorter fuse when I'm tired), he pulls his phone out of his pocket.

"Check this out," he tells me, suddenly holding out his phone to me.

I'm surprised he's showing me anything personal or private. I'm also surprised to see that I'm looking at that picture of Leona Frow and Izaak Johnson. I don't know why

Cole is showing me this. I know what the picture looks like. I sent it to him in the first place!

"Notice anything?" he asks.

I frown at him after racking my brain for a response. I'm sure he'll berate me for not knowing this supposedly easy-to-come-by answer. "No," I respond.

Cole sighs, as if he knew this was coming. "Johnson," he tells me, as if I have hay for brains. "Ryker's last name," he adds, his green eyes shifting slightly when he says it. I don't know why.

Hearing Ryker's name again makes me flinch – literally. I hate that Cole probably saw that, so I cover it up by asserting, "Johnson is a super-common last name, Cole. Anyone can have–"

"He told me it's his uncle," Cole interrupts me, which shocks me to my core. "A long-lost, disowned uncle, or whatever. Can't remember the details."

That doesn't surprise me, I think dryly – then clamp up when Cole narrows his green eyes at me.

Crap! I must have said that out loud!

"Hardy har," he comments sourly.

"So what if it's his uncle?" I ask him.

Cole rolls his eyes now. "Good God," he groans as if I'm asking a stupid question again. "Why would Frow have a picture of her and some random guy under lock and key?" He adds, causing me to remember the connection in a whole new way, "And Izaak was expelled for experimenting with dark magic. This is the guy. Ryker's uncle."

Ryker's long-lost, disowned uncle was the one who was expelled from Gomada Academy for experimenting with dark magic? Still, what does that all mean? Leona dated this boy? So what?

I hate to say it, but Cole *does* have a point about the weirdness of the Headmistress keeping these things under lock and key. Why would she do that? I don't think she'd do it if it wasn't important.

Cole sighs again and puts his phone away. It's pretty obvious that he doesn't like it when people challenge him or disagree with him. He's so immature!

"I'm going to ask Ryker more about dark magic – unless you want to," he tacks on at the end.

I would've gotten mad at him again, but he doesn't say all this in a mean or condescending way. It's *different* – but I don't know how to describe it other than that. Could it be because Cole knows Ryker rejected me? But since when does Cole spare me my feelings?

"You can ask him," I blurt out quickly, wanting to get this conversation over and done with as fast as possible.

For one thing, I'm still not really sure if this has anything to do with the ghost that's been haunting Gomada Academy. Maybe Izaak Johnson is important for another reason – a reason we don't know about just yet.

For another, I really want to stop talking about Ryker – especially with Cole. But I guess so long as Cole is my Mentor and we're wrapped up in this paranormal mystery, Ryker is going to be a part of it. But I don't want to be involved with him past that.

"Alright," Cole responds, again sounding *off*, not himself, shoving his hands into his jeans pockets.

Silence crushes us. I don't know why he's still standing there. Usually, we can't get away from each other fast enough.

"Arya! Your turn!"

I whirl around, surprised that Nora and Anja are already back from getting their dinner. It was Anja who called out to me. Nora looks from Cole to me, her blue eyes staring him down as only Nora can. Looking at their plates, I guess eggplant parmesan is on the menu. It's not my favourite, but I'll eat it if I have to.

I turn to look back at Cole. Even though I hate his guts, it's not really nice to just walk off without saying something. Much as I hate to admit it, Cole *did* save my life that night – before leaving me stranded on campus, which still bothers me – so I guess I owe him *something*.

"Bye," I finally decide to say. Saying something like 'see you later' or 'talk to you later' implies I want to do either of those things – which I don't. 'Goodbye' sounds way more final.

Cole looks surprised that I said anything at all. He nods his head in response. I turn around and rush for the kitchen. I can't stop thinking about the weirdness of that conversation. The only light at the end of this tunnel is that as soon as that ghost is apprehended and the term is up, I'll never have to speak to Cole again.

I take a seat across from Anja. I'm at the end of the table, with Makayleigh on my right. Makayleigh gives me a big smile in greeting. Makayleigh is almost always in a good mood – just like Nora – but she's way more of a joker than Nora and I put together.

"Where's Alan?" I ask Makayleigh after giving her a smile in return.

Makayleigh rolls her eyes, but there's a smile on her face, so I know she's kidding around. "Studying," she responds simply. "Or playing foosball with his roommate at the Student Life Centre. One or the other."

Nora bites down on a chuckle. "That'll get him an 'A'," she teases.

Makayleigh laughs at Nora's comment. "I guess gamer guys get me hot," she admits, causing Anja to all but choke on her eggplant parmesan.

"TMI," she protests, as I scrunch my face up into a grimace.

"Yeah," I agree.

"Babies," Makayleigh teases again.

I'm surprised when Makayleigh puts down her glass of soda and looks at me in a curious way. "So, who's the guy you were just talking to? I didn't know you were seeing anyone," she adds, which causes me to practically puke my pasta with cheese and butter all over the table.

"Absolutely not!" I gasp. Maybe that's not really an answer to her question or assertion, but it's the only thing I can get out besides potential vomit.

"Cole Hudson," Nora explains sourly, as if to jog Makayleigh's memory.

"No wonder she forgot who he is," Anja grumbles.

Makayleigh frowns at all three of us. Our responses were almost simultaneous. "Right. Cole," she recalls. She folds her arms and looks down at me. "He comes around a lot," she says, almost like she's reminding me of my troubles.

"That's because he's her Mentor," Nora persists.

"Am I talking to you?" Makayleigh frowns at Nora, who puts her hands up in defeat and continues to eat her meal.

"Are you sure that's all it is?" she persists, causing me to put my fork down and yearn for the fetal position. "It didn't look like you were talking about Mentor-Mentee stuff before."

Makayleigh must not know the extent of my so-called 'relationship' with Cole. If she did, she never would have asked me that question. Plus, we also have the ghost mystery to deal with – and since I can't tell the girls about that, I have to come up with another explanation as to why Cole was talking to me.

"I'd rather die by a thousand cuts than go out with him," I grumble, deciding to just continue pleading my case. I still can't believe that Makayleigh actually thinks Cole likes me.

Since when does constant beratement equate to a declaration of love? But if Makayleigh doesn't really know Cole (lucky her), I shouldn't blame her for thinking this way about us.

Gross! Like there'd ever be an 'us', in any of the five realms of this seemingly-endless world we live in! Maybe if I had a death wish, I'd consider it. But with a ghost closing in on the school, that's kind of already arranged.

Makayleigh raises her eyebrows in surprise at my dramatic response as Nora chuckles darkly from across the table.

"O-kay then," Makayleigh responds, returning to eating her pasta.

COLE'S DARK SECRET

Maybe it's not so much of a change from the usual, but I'm in a bad mood today. I have my Shifter Studies midterm this morning. Thanks to a creepy glare from Professor Qadir at the Dining Hall last night, I figured I'd better buckle up and start studying.

So now I'm sleep-deprived and pissed off about it. My midterm is in an hour, and I'm still trying to memorize stupid dates and names of Shifters who 'set everything in motion for my race'. I hate learning about the past. The past can't help you with the shit you're going through today. How are dates and names supposed to keep me alive from a ghost who's taken three students from Gomada Academy?

I finally snap my books shut. I'm done with this shit. If I don't know it all by now, I never will.

Even if I'm up early, I don't worry about making noise. Diego was up and showered a long time ago. I think he's getting breakfast with Lucy before their midterms. After what happened the other day at the Enchanter's Field, Diego was really – I don't know, *thankful* – that I helped Lucy. I guess it's better if the three of us get along – or, at least, don't want to kill each other.

And it's not like Ryker and I have made any progress on the ghost, so I don't really have anyone else to hang with other than Diego. All Ryker and I know for sure is that his uncle (who's still alive – he thinks) is definitely in that photo in Frow's desk. Ryker also doesn't get why she'd have that locked up tight. 'It makes no sense', he said.

Damn. I'm getting a headache from this whole thing. Between studying, lack of sleep *because of studying*, and this ghost thing, I can feel my temples flaring. I haven't smoked since last night, so that could be it, too.

I push out my chair, grab my jacket, and shove it on as quickly as possible. I can grab a quick smoke, get a coffee, and maybe study a bit more – *maybe* – before my midterm at nine AM.

As I'm pushing in my chair – Diego's been complaining about tripping over or bumping into my crap – I spot my phone on my desk.

I guess there's another reason why I'm pissed off.

I haven't been able to think about it much. Over the past couple of weeks, I realized I didn't hate Arya as much as I thought. Spending so much time with her, being forced by Ryker to quit hassling her... When all those things happened, I realized there was more to her than I saw before. And God help me, I like what I'm seeing.

Something *had* changed the night we found the ghost. I tried to ignore it and spin it in a way that made me feel better, but it didn't work after a while. I even got annoyed with Ryker. If he suddenly changed his mind and went after her, I'd be screwed. And when I stopped to think about that, I knew I couldn't *spin it differently*, either.

I have a thing for a *Nymph*!

This is the first time I've admitted it to myself – and it feels like I'm sticking a fork into my face.

This can't be possible! It's like I'm somehow being punished for being a 'judgemental douche'. This is the biggest shitstorm I've ever been in, and the crappy thing is I did it all to myself.

All I know for sure is that I need to keep this problem to myself. If I told anyone, I'd be the laughingstock of Feara. Even if people like Diego and Ryker, who seem more accepting of other races, ever found out about my secret, I'm sure they'd be quick to point the finger at me.

You're a hypocrite!

*You rode my ass about Lucy for weeks, and now you have a thing for a **Nymph**?*

I can just hear the jokes, the arguments, the non-stop ribbing. I don't want to put myself in that position. There's no way I can let anyone find out. Then again, it's not like I'm a big blabbermouth, so I guess it won't be hard for me to keep my trap shut about it.

I'm outside, pulling up my hood so the falling snowflakes don't get to me. Even with my jacket on, it's still cold out here. Damned Winter. Looks like it's coming early this year.

I *was* going to walk behind Feara and smoke, but since it's like the Houssan Mountains right now, I'm going to the Academy's coffee shop thing and getting a hot drink. Then, I'll have my smoke.

Looks like I'm not the only one with this idea when I head into the Academy, turn right, and head to the small shop. The line-up is huge. This makes me antsy. I may not have as much time for my smoke as I thought.

This place is run by students. I know a few people who work here – some Sophomore Shifters and even an Enchanter or two. It's not like I talk to them, but I know who they are. I don't mess with them, and they don't mess with me.

I begin to pull my phone out of my pocket to text Diego. My plan for today is to write my midterm, sleep, and then hang with Diego – as long as he's not chilling with Lucy. You'd think having breakfast with a girl would be more than enough – but even if I'm trying to be cool with Lucy, I still get the vibe that she likes being in the driver's seat.

Anyway, if Diego's busy (which seems to happen a lot), maybe I'll go to Gleera and see if Ryker will say anything else about his uncle. He seems embarrassed of the guy, or even afraid of him. It's hard to tell. I don't know Ryker well – and maybe now, I'm regretting it, because it'll be harder for me to figure out this ghost shit without us levelling with each other.

I'm distracted when a sudden scent blows along with a stray Winter breeze. The doors must be opening and closing a lot, and sending the wind with it. Without turning around, I know Arya is behind me. I'm not about to look for her but based on the strength of her scent, she's either right behind me in line or a couple of people back.

I check my phone. No messages. Big surprise. I quickly text Diego about meeting up after our midterm. He actually answers me back quickly – so he can't be playing tonsil hockey with Chapin right now.

Sorry, bro. Can't hang today. Tomorrow?

Does the fact that there's a fucking ghost zooming around killing people not freak out anyone else? Why am I alone in this? But there's nothing I can do about Diego being busy.

No worries.

I send the text, moving up in line without looking. This is taking forever! I'm bored already, and I've only been in line for maybe five minutes.

Finally, I turn around to see how far back in line she is. If the long wait for coffee won't kill me, talking to a girl who hates my guts probably will. It's really pathetic how I've suddenly started to like someone who wants nothing to do with me.

I wish I could've just left her alone that first day of school. Requested a transfer Mentee. Didn't hassle her all the time. Didn't approach her about the ghost when I found out she saw it, too. Done something, anything, other than putting myself around her.

But there's no way out of this, either. I can't just wish it away, or ignore it. I've already tried both over the past few weeks. No dice.

Of course, Arya's looking at a notebook and not paying attention. If she knew I was in front of her–

I hear the girl's footsteps in front of me, so I back up in line and am about to turn around myself when Arya doesn't move with the rest of us.

The guy behind her looks pissed off, so I flick the front of her notebook using my thumb and index finger. Arya jumps a mile. As soon as she realizes it was me, she closes up her notebook and slaps me with it.

I can't help but laugh hysterically as she follows me in line, giving me the evil eye as she goes.

"What's your problem?" she demands.

"You're holding up the line," I say.

She rolls her eyes and shoves her notebook into her bookbag. She does look over her shoulder and says a small 'sorry' to the guy behind her.

I turn around, folding my arms. At least laughing at her like that loosened me up a bit, and the line moved without me thinking too much about it. I'm finally at the counter, asking for an extra large, dark roast black coffee. I pay for my order, and step to the side, waiting for the girl at the machines to make my coffee. I really need to get out of here so I can smoke and get in the zone before my midterm. If I don't get Qadir off my ass–

I glance to the right when Arya is rummaging through the crap in her bookbag. It's a frantic thing she's doing. I can practically sense the anxiety from the other end of the counter. She's forgotten her wallet. Now, the guy behind her is really pissed.

I guess this won't paint me as the usual evil asshole she thinks I am, but maybe it'll help me out a little bit. I don't really know what I want to happen with her – because me not telling anyone about her means I'm not telling her, either – but I do know I get mad thinking about Ryker changing his mind and going after her.

I don't get jealous. Not like this. Not about girls.

I approach the cash after getting my coffee from the girl who I think is a Nymph. Since I just put my change from my own order into my left pocket, I pull it out and flick them onto the counter. The guy at the register just takes it without asking Arya if it's okay. He probably wants to get this long-ass line over with just as much as the guy behind her.

Arya stares at me like she's in some kind of weird, other reality. "Um–" she begins as the guy closes the cash register and points for Arya to go to the other end of the counter to get her drink.

"Thanks," she finally manages to say as we walk over to the dip in the counter, where the same Nymph from before is making her coffee.

I shrug. "Whatever," I dismiss – even though, for once, that's not how I feel on the inside.

"I'll pay you back," Arya surprises me by telling me, just as she gets her coffee from the girl. She smiles at her – I guess as a 'thank you' – and then looks at me seriously.

I open my mouth to object, but Arya beats me to the punch by saying,

"I don't like owing people money. I can go home and get my wallet after my midterm, and–"

"It's not a big deal," I try to dismiss again.

Arya frowns at me like she's trying to figure me out. Good God, am I really that complicated?

It suddenly weirds me out that she's staring up at me like this. I probably look like a pile of shit. With no sleep and no energy, I'm always a–

*Holy shit, am I actually worrying about what I **look like** right now?*

"Just forget about it," I respond again, hoping she'll finally get the hint. It looks like she does, because she moves her ponytail away from her shoulder and shifts in place, like she doesn't like what's happening, but is accepting it, anyway.

"Okay. Thank you," she murmurs.

It's hard to concentrate when she's this close to me, the smell of vanilla and her high brown ponytail shining under the light of the school. Suddenly, I don't care if she always hits me with her notebook or yells at me. I just want her to be doing something, paying some kind of attention, to me.

How fucked up is that?

No way am I telling anyone about this.

Arya stares down at her coffee like she's trying to find a way out of this situation. It kind of hurts, but I guess I'm in the same boat.

"Well, I have to cram for my midterm, so…" she trails off,

looking up at me like she's afraid I won't let her go without dumping my coffee all over her first.

"Same," I nod. "Later."

I decide to walk away from her first. Maybe If I get out of her way, not the other way around, it'll show her I'm not up to anything. Besides, this morning just got crazier, and I don't really have the time to hang out here any more than I already have.

Twenty-One

ARYA'S WORST FEAR

I don't know how, but I survived my Nymph Studies midterm. Between worrying about the ghost, my caffeine buzz making me jittery, and stressing over what fresh Hell Professor Xhao will put me through next week (Makayleigh's words, not mine – though I totally agree with her on that), I'm surprised I even finished the test, to begin with.

I'm in a stupor as I walk out of our usual classroom. This is a Freshman class for first-year Nymphs only, so it's smaller than my History and Literature classes, which house all enrolled Freshmen of each race.

Getting back to time and place, I realize I'm starving – probably because I skipped breakfast in favour of more cramming – so I wander over to the Dining Hall to see if they have any snacks available. Lunchtime isn't for a couple of hours.

When I grab a bagel and a small packet of jam, I practically wet myself when I see Ryker Johson and a few friends sitting at a table. It looks like they just have to-go coffee cups and are telling jokes or something, but it still makes me nervous to be around him. I leave my jam packet behind and rush out of the Dining Hall. I don't care how stupid or cowardly it is. All I want to do is get out of here.

When will I finally feel able to face Ryker again? It's not like he did anything wrong. He doesn't like me the way I like him – that's not his fault. It still hurts, though. I hope I can get over it sooner rather than later because until then, Ryker seems to be popping up everywhere. And it doesn't help that he also knows about the ghost, which means we may have to talk at some point. Thankfully, Cole seems to be taking point on that. I feel weird thinking that, because I never thought I'd be thankful to Cole for anything.

As I rush through the open double doors to the Dining Hall, a new terror grips me besides the probably-not-going-to-happen possibility that Ryker may notice me: the ghost.

Just like always, it takes over.

I don't know what to do. The other two emails from Head-mistress Frow and Mr. Greyson, head of security, tell us 'not to worry, not to panic'. But those same emails tell us that other students have been taken. They remind us there will be 'steep repercussions' if we break curfew. They assure us that they'll 'remedy the situation'.

But it's been almost a month, and there have been three students 'taken' – their words. I know the truth. The ghost killed them. Why else would they not come back to campus? They're obviously dead, and the school either knows this and is keeping it from us, or they don't know this and aren't considering it. Either way, they're wrong – even if I hate to think that way. I've always put my trust in authority, in following the rules, in trusting my superiors. But people are still going missing. No – they're dying. So whatever Gomada Academy is doing, it's clearly not enough to get the ghost to stop.

When will things get better? When enough of us go

missing that the King and Queen of Gomada (who apparently live within the continent of Vyquean, thanks to my professors) notice and send over the Gomadian Army? Or when wealthy parents of a missing student sue the school, shut it down?

And what happens if someone like Nora, Anja, Makayleigh, or Ryker is next? What if it's me, and our superiors still don't take action – not how it's needed, anyway?

I'm uncomfortable thinking this way, but I'm filled with despair and a lack of faith in everything as I make my way to the library. Even if I feel like garbage, life still goes on: I still need to study; I still need to pass my midterms; I still need to graduate. I don't think a thorough understanding of Nymph culture and history will help me if I ever run into the ghost again – but this still has to be a priority of mine.

I'm drowning in a never-ending fear that pricks my skin to the point of numbness. I'm thankful for the blast of quiet that engulfs me as I walk into the two-storey room. Maybe this will force me to concentrate on my notes, not my horrific thoughts. But I never have that kind of luck.

A few Nymphs move out of the way for me as I go inside. I don't know them, and I'm sure they don't know me. It's been a month and a half, and I haven't really made that many friends. I guess after seeing the ghost one too many times (and once is *too many*), I've been more concerned about surviving than being social.

When I glance up at the large wrought-iron-looking clock at the far wall of the library's second floor, I'm stunned to see that it's already past seven thirty at night. Dinner is over, and I'm dangerously close to missing curfew! Even though I doubt the leaders of this school, I still don't want to get suspended – or worse. I'm pretty sure the consequences for rule-breaking are now expulsion.

I quickly pack up my books, all but throwing them into my

bookbag. I'm surprised the staff who work here haven't done their usual walkaround, to tell lingering students that it's almost time to pack up for the night. Everything on campus shuts down right before eight o'clock at night, to keep in line with the new-ish curfew mandate.

It's cold and dreary as I walk briskly for Meera. It's misting now, but the air is heavy and uncomfortable, as if it will soon turn into heavy rain. I need to get back to my dorm before this happens. Now, I'm in an even bigger rush than before. The atmosphere is so dark and creepy that I feel like someone is breathing down my neck, following me in the shadows. But whenever I turn around, no one is there.

I finally rip open the door to Meera, feeling only slightly safer than before. I take the elevator to the fourth floor, too afraid to bound up dark stairs by myself.

I unlock and open the door to Nora's and my room as quickly as possible, as if my life depends on it. As soon as I'm inside, though, I'm met with a very unsettled feeling that's impossible to shake.

The room is empty. The bathroom door is open, revealing a dark space. Nora isn't here.

Her desk is a mess. That's not like her. And her chair is pushed out, like she left the dorm in a hurry. I glance around the room for anything else that could be sinister or suspicious. I don't see anything.

Could Nora just be down the hall, hanging out with Makayleigh? Or in Anja's dorm until curfew starts? But Nora is a rule-follower. She'd for sure be back in her room by now. I even check the time using my phone. It's 7:49. There's no way Nora would be cutting things super close like this. She told me last night that her greatest fear is getting suspended or expelled from Gomada Academy. She'd never risk it all by hanging out with Anja or friends right up until curfew.

And this *feeling* I have now…

Oh, my God. It's damp, cold, horrible. The very same way I felt when I saw the ghost for the very first time. I half expect fog to be seeping up through the floorboards.

The ghost was here. Or, it was near here.

What if it has Nora?

I never thought I'd do this, but I yank my phone out of my bookbag, which drops books and pens to the floor, and frantically search for Cole's number. I'm already crying.

What if Nora's dead? What if the ghost already has her? What other explanation could there be for this damp feeling in the room? It can't be the furnace, or an open window. I may be exhausted, but I'm not imagining things. I hate to say this, but Cole's the only one who will be able to understand.

One ring.

Two rings.

I can't wait for him to pick up! I panic, spinning out of the room without even locking the door. I'm surprised I even thought to close it on my way out.

Third ring.

"Who the hell is this?" he grumbles. It sounds like he's half-asleep.

"Cole!" I can't help but weep.

He pauses – or it seems that way. I'm now running downstairs, so I can't hear well. "Arya?" he groans.

"I need you!" I exclaim, just as I'm getting to the first floor landing, yanking open the door to the lobby. I don't care how desperate and pathetic I sound. I need all hands on deck to even have a prayer of saving Nora.

"What's wrong?" he asks. He sounds more awake now.

"I think the ghost has Nora!" I sob, sprinting for the exit to the dorm. No one is in the lobby now, even though it had a few stragglers just a few minutes earlier. No one wants to get expelled by being out past or around curfew.

"What makes you say that?" he asks.

"I need your help! Now!" I urge, not in the mood to explain the intricacies and clues I found in my dorm room. We can split hairs and he can mock me later once I know Nora is alive.

"Calm down. I'll meet you at Meera."

"Hurry up!" I gasp, trying to suck in shallow breaths, but it hurts to breathe.

I'm already outside. It's blacker than before. It's raining. It's creepier now – maybe because I'm afraid Nora has been taken, manipulated by the ghost somehow, or because of the weather. Either way, I'm terrified.

"I am. Wait for me before you look for her." He hangs up, which makes me remember that I'm holding my phone in my right hand. I don't know how it got there. I can't even remember dialling his number.

I glance left and right, trying to see through the darkness. I can't see anything. It's like someone has a blindfold over my eyes.

All I can think about is Nora, alone with a killer ghost. There's no way I can wait for Cole. He's taking way too long. By this point, Nora could already be dead.

I launch forward to look for Nora, even if I can't see well, when someone yanks my jacket from behind. I'd scream, but I'm so out of breath that it comes out as a yelp instead.

When I turn around, Cole lets go of my coat. I can tell it's him because of the overpowering smell of cigarette smoke, and because he's standing right under a lamplight. But his hood is up, so I doubt the Meera security cameras will catch him. Me, on the other hand–

But I don't care. All that matters is saving Nora.

Instead of berating me for trying to go off by myself, Cole points behind us – maybe to Meera, or around it, but I'm not sure. "I smell her," he tells me. "Just come with me. We'll track her."

His words don't make sense. All I can understand is 'come with me'. He seems to speak in such a way that he can find her, so I don't question it and just run after him. His legs are much longer than mine, so I have to sprint to try and keep up with him. But I don't care about that, either. If he's faster, he'll be able to get to Nora before me.

The rain is coming down in ominous slants, hitting us at weird angles, as we rush through the wet grass. We pass a building, but I forget what it's called. I slip on a rock, crashing to the slippery grass with a thud, tasting blood. I scamper to my feet and chase after Cole, who's now farther ahead of me because of my stupid fall.

It's darker as I follow him. For a split second, I wonder if he's helping Nora and I, or just being a jerk and playing us. But I don't think he'd do that – not when the ghost could kill someone else.

Cole skids to a stop in front of a fenceline. I almost slam into him, because I'm not expecting it. Some sanity returns, because I realize we're in front of the Shifter's Field. The gates are locked – but that's not what worries me.

Oh, no!

Even with the fence and gates clouding our vision, we can still see the thick and menacing fingers of fog seeping around the Field's entirety and even the fence's outer rims.

I leap forward, about to yell out Nora's name – she has to be here, if Cole led us here – when Cole grabs me and drags me away from the fenceline.

"Don't get too close!" he hisses, but I don't listen, because I hear Nora screaming.

Cole clamps a hand over my mouth just as I scream Nora's name. It comes out like a strangled muffle.

Cole surprises me by suddenly tossing me to the ground and taking a running leap for the gigantic gates that house the Shifter's Field. It's a bit easier to see in the dark – but not by much, because of the heavy rain – but I can still grasp that Cole is running faster than usual. I wonder if the monster inside of him is causing this to happen.

Cole lets out this guttural, terrible roar. Suddenly, splitting and ripping sounds are heard. The fog fingers curling around the wrought-iron fenceline flicker. I back up, now struck with fear, when the person sailing over the gates is no longer Cole but the creature.

More screaming happens. *That's Nora!*

I try to get up, and when I do, I'm suddenly met with the realization that there's nothing I can do to save her. I'm useless against a serial killer ghost. There's no point in my being here.

No.

This isn't about me. It's about Nora.

She can't die. She can't be the fourth victim.

A bright light suddenly slams into the Shifter's Field, almost blinding me. It takes me a moment to figure out that the bright light was lightning. Was it from the storm?

But the light also seems closer. When I look down, I see circuits of churning electricity flying out of my hands.

I'm temporarily paralyzed with fear and panic. I can't control this massive amount of electricity! I've never been able to get this far before! Who knows what kind of damage I can cause with this?

The ground shakes around me as more roaring and snarling sounds are heard from deep into the Shifter's Field. The electricity from my hands makes my entire body shake with pressure and with – power?

I remember my dad once saying to use electricity like you're a pitcher in a baseball game. I used to think that analogy was funny, because it's more of a trick Macey would remember and even use, but not me. But now, I wind my arm back and chuck what now looks like a flashing, spiralling ball of electricity. It explodes into the field.

A second light – unnatural, cold, and just as blinding as the lightning – suddenly rocks the field, and then everything is black. No more light. No more fog.

"Nora!" I scream,

I grit my teeth, now activating my wings to fly over the fence to find her, when a dark shadow flies over the fence.

I see my wings disappear in my peripheral vision when an enormous wolf on two legs is now in front of the Shifter's Field, with a trembling Nora in its arms. Nora runs for me as soon as it places her onto the grass.

"Arya!" she weeps.

Even though I'm hugging her, I still can't believe that my closest friend is alive, standing in front of me.

She didn't die.

I clutch her black hair, crying relieved and horrified tears. Nora is sobbing hysterically. She's shaking so badly that it's hard for me to prop her up.

"It's – gone," she breathes.

I place my hands on either side of her face. "Are you okay?" I gasp. "Did it hurt you?"

Nora shakes her head at me, her blue eyes and sapphire pendant shining in the moon that's trying to break free of the rain and clouds.

"No. It didn't have time to hurt me," she musters out in a huff. She's out of breath and almost hunched over. "That... That thing attacked it."

When Nora and I turn around, the wolf is now darting for

the gates to the Field again. It flies over them with barely any space for a jump.

I don't know why, but something stops me from telling Nora that Cole is the person inside that monster. And now that it's gone, I know there's no chance of me being able to thank him for saving Nora's life.

Friday morning is dark and damp – but the blackness outside and the wet chill to the air have nothing on what happened last night.

I get up early – at six o'clock in the morning, even if I don't have a midterm today – and get dressed as quickly as possible, not even bothering to brush my hair. Nora is still in bed, so I want to be quiet and considerate as I move. A close call with a ghost makes you want to sleep and dream your terrors away. Watching Nora rest, safe and sound in bed, is such a relief to me that my throat becomes heavy and uneven as I unlock and leave our shared dorm room. I lock it this time, feeling like I still need to tread carefully to make sure I don't wake her or anyone else who's still sleeping.

The morning air is cold and unforgiving – as if it's known that I broke curfew and was a part of a paranormal showdown at the Shifter's Field – as I head in the direction of the Professors' Dorms. I'm scared to get close to the building, and even more afraid to pass it and keep going, but I'm too set in my decision to turn back.

I don't have a plan for what to do as I close in on Feara. I owe Cole more than just a 'thank you'. Over the past few weeks, he's been less obnoxious. Even more than that, saving

Nora's life by risking his own in the process has shown me that maybe redemption is possible for someone like him.

I'm surprised to see Cole standing close to Feara, wearing his beanie and a black hoodie. He has a lighter in his left hand, its flame making an orange and red glow around the misty air, and a cigarette in his right. This disgusts me, but it shouldn't surprise me. And right now, I'm so thankful that I don't see the need to lecture him about it.

He looks up, maybe because he hears me coming. I now understand what he meant last night. Because of the creature he can turn into, he could pick up Nora's scent. He can probably see, hear, and smell better than other people. It's a little creepy – but still, now is not the time to judge him.

His green eyes look surprised and even confused to see me here. I guess it's early, for one thing – and for another, it's not like Cole and I make great strides to hang out. He probably thinks I've lost my mind.

"Hey," he says, closing the lighter and tossing it into the wide pocket of his hoodie.

I thought the chances of this would be less than the odds of finding a four-leaf clover, but I wrap my arms around him and shove my face into his chest. I heave in a breath, and tears pour down my face.

"Thank you so much," I sob, ignoring that he will mock me for this now or later. There's no way I can let this situation go without showing him how grateful I am – even if it may cost me later.

But instead of making fun of me, shoving me away, or making me feel stupid, Cole places his arms around me and pushes me against him.

"No worries," he responds.

The way he's talking causes me to look up at him,

surprised. His voice sounds different, like the encounter with the ghost last night changed him.

So many questions flood my mind as we stare at each other. Nora said he injured the ghost – but how did he do it? If Cole was able to attack a ghost, does that mean it's not really a spirit? Is the ghost still alive, or did Cole kill it? And where did Cole go after Nora and I reunited? Did he try to track the ghost, or did he go somewhere else?

I don't realize I'm holding my breath until I'm dizzy. Maybe it's because of a lack of oxygen, or I've never noticed, but Cole's eyes are really green. When he's not so obnoxious or atrocious, his green eyes light up his entire face.

I shut my eyes and tilt my head up, suddenly feeling Cole's lips against mine. A strange fire burns up inside of me as my own lips press against his at the same time. His hand takes a fistful of my knotted brown hair, his opposite hand pushing me closer. This shared moment is so jarring and exhilarating that it's all I can think about. And I don't want it to stop.

Acknowledgments

It takes a village. This saying is true of many things – and writing a book is no exception. Many tender-hearted and encouraging individuals enabled me to write, polish, and tend to *Gomada Academy* and for that, I am forever grateful.

To my husband, Nathan, who encouraged me to follow my writing dreams, wherever they may take me and him by extension (sometimes to scary, emotional, exciting, and uncharted paths). Thank you for listening to my endless rambling about magic, Shifters, and ghosts. Your patience is as long as my run-on sentences! Love you forever, Hubbage.

To my son, William: I was four months pregnant with you when I began to write this book. I like to think that you were a part of the writing process. Now that you are born, I hope we can go on many magical adventures together. I love you, Mr. Goo Goos.

To my mother and brother, thank you for being so steadfast and loving. You encouraged me to pursue my dreams of writing and publication. You are the first to jump on the 'supporting Cynthia' bandwagon. To my mother-in-law and my aunts-in-law, who cheered me on and offered support and encouragement – I appreciate you.

To my editor, Rachel, who is just as magical as the beings portrayed in this book: thank you for turning a messy and cluttered first draft into something I was proud to showcase. To my Midnight Tide Publishing family: your insight, friendship and constant support throughout this process has been invaluable. It still feels surreal to be a part of such a wonderful group of storytellers. I am honoured that *Gomada Academy* stands amongst such splendid works.

To those who are reading this book, I hope you find adventure, enjoyment, and a little magic sprinkled within these pages. The world is a messy place, as is the fantastical realm portrayed here. If you are struggling with feeling "less than," I hope that the characters in this book inspire you to stay true to yourself and remind you that you are worth so much more than you think.

Happy reading!
Cynthia Brubaker

The Official Playlist

1. Throne – *Bring Me the Horizon*
2. I Hate Everything About You – *Three Days Grace*
3. You Give Love A Bad Name – *Bon Jovi*
4. Unstoppable – *Sia*
5. Fly on the Wall (Live Version) – *Miley Cyrus*
6. Fight Song – *Rachel Platten*
7. Natural – *Imagine Dragons*
8. Wonderland – *Neoni*
9. Animals – *Maroon 5*
10. The Heart Wants What It Wants – *Selena Gomez*
11. Robot – *Miley Cyrus*
12. Relax, Take It Easy – *Mika*
13. Animal City – *Shakira*
14. Toxic – *Britney Spears*
15. Me Too – *Meghan Trainor*
16. Look What You Made Me Do – *Taylor Swift*
17. Still Missing You – *COMET*
18. Popular Monster – *Falling In Reverse*
19. The One That Got Away – *Katy Perry*
20. Survivor – *All Good Things*
21. Crazy – *Gnarls Barkley*
22. Birds – *Imagine Dragons*
23. Darkside – *Neoni*
24. DONTTRUSTME – *3OH!3*

About Cynthia

Cynthia Brubaker lives in two worlds. One is populated with loved ones, her cat, and coffee. The other is a realm made authentic by the words she uses to create vivid characters and unique adventures.

Cynthia has been writing since childhood but became serious about her craft in the Spring of 2020. Since then, fantasy (urban, dark), romantic suspense, and contemporary romance works have been her passion. Her début romance novel, Masquerade, was published in June of 2022. Her true sanctuary is writing fantasy- and supernatural-themed novels.

In a word, Cynthia can be described as "quirky." She can usually be found sipping coffee, cuddling her cat, hugging her husband, and/or attempting to navigate the wondrous waters of being a first-time mom.

More from Cynthia

Masquerade

More Books You'll Love

If you enjoyed this story, please consider leaving a review!

Then check out more books from Midnight Tide Publishing!

Siren's Song by Heather Kindt

The shadowy folds of Mo capture both souls and secrets.

Catron's father intended to scare her with his words. After all, her mother traveled far from home, losing herself to both the shadows and her wayward spirit. But instead of heeding his warning, Catron longs for more than her life as a glass blower's apprentice. When Dawkin, a member of the King of Mo's illustrious guard, offers her a place at the Vradian Academy, she willingly accepts.

Fivlon would rather gouge both of his eyes out with an iron stick than attend the Vradian Academy. Messing around with his friends is a lot more fun than attending school with a bunch of stuck-up future leaders. Following in his father's footsteps as the head of Ferox isn't a priority. Until one of his friends disappears.

Now at school, Catron and Fivlon face a much larger task than their ethics homework. As students and staff disappear from the academy, they must figure out who is behind it before they become the next victims.

Available Now

Secrets of Galathea by Elle Beaumont

Journey to the depths in this fast-paced collection of four short stories, based in the same kingdom, spanning from centuries to weeks apart.

A merman and his brother are tasked with protecting what belongs to their people and failure is not an option. When two seventeen-year-olds witness their Prince threaten an infamous sea-witch, they have no idea how soon all of their lives will be intertwined, and what secrets lay in the depths. A prince must decide what is most important: the people or his relationship with his brother. And a soon-to-be-king must do what is right, even if it costs him everything.

Each story highlights a specific character and their current struggle in the kingdom of Selith, but one thing is always the same-the strength of the characters and the magic that lives within them.

Available Now

www.ingramcontent.com/pod-product-compliance
Lightning Source LLC
Chambersburg PA
CBHW050804190726
48285CB00005B/1791